A Time to Search

Joyce T. Strand

McCloughan and Schmeltz Publishing

This book is a work of fiction, although it is set in the city of Santa Rosa, California and was inspired and includes actual events that occurred in World War II in the area. In addition to Santa Rosa, the cities of Tulelake, Redding, Klamath, and Eureka, CA and Grants Pass, OR mentioned were all in existence at the time covered and have been represented as historically accurate as possible. However, the town of Herfordton, CA is fictional.

The Tule Lake Segregation Center (now a national monument) was real, and all effort was made to report it accurately. And the Klamath Radar Station (Radar Station B-71) now a national park was also real as is Jack London's home, now a state park near Glen Ellen, CA.

All characters are fictional, except for mention of historical figures, and are the product of the author's imagination or are used fictitiously, and any resemblance to actual persons, living or dead, is entirely coincidental.

However, for the purposes of the plot I mention some actual restaurants, theaters, and other sites, and events, such as the Victory Lunch diner in Santa Rosa and Rogues Theater in Grants Pass, OR. Also, Alfred Hitchcock's movie, *A Shadow of Doubt,* was filmed in Santa Rosa and there was a midnight premier of it for the citizens of Santa Rosa that Hitchcock's daughter attended. The murder trial described that the reporters covered is based on an actual murder of a youthful friend of Jack London named Helmuth Seefeldt; Roy Cornett was convicted of his murder.

ISBN-13: 9798378724147

Printed in the United States of America.
McCloughan and Schmeltz Publishing, LLC
3773 Howard Hughes Parkway
South Tower, Suite 500
Las Vegas, NV 89169-6014
Cover design by: Natasha Brown

For information about the author and her books and to sign up to receive her newsletter: http://joycestrand.com

Acknowledgements

Inspired by Actual Events

I was inspired to write *A Time to Search* by my visit several years ago to the Klamath Radar Station (Radar Station B-71) near Klamath, CA. During World War II, the U.S. protected the Pacific Coast from additional Japanese bombings following the bombing of Pearl Harbor, either from air or submarine, with several secret radar stations—among other means. When studying the war, the main historical event that over-shadows events in the U.S. is the invasion of Pearl Harbor. But later Japanese threats to attack the Pacific Coast areas were real. Among others, a submarine managed to shell an oil field north of Santa Barbara in February 1942; and the Japanese made advances in the Aleutian Islands. This intrigued me to explore.

My original concept for *A Time to Search* was to base the mystery on an actual living author in the 1940s. However, after reading daily newspaper articles from the Santa Rosa *Press Democrat* from 1940 to 1943, I was driven toward creating a picture of war-time California rather than that of the life of an author. Therefore, Clara Bow Wilson is entirely fictional, created originally in a previous novel, *The Judge's Story*.

The actual puzzle that is the mystery is entirely fictional, but the surrounding restrictions of war time, such as the "dimout," (a less severe restriction than the "blackout"), the severe rationing of gas, rubber, butter, etc., the internment of Japanese Americans, the shortage of labor due to the high conscription of eligible men all were heavily described in the news media— with the exception of details about the internment camps— resulting in my coverage of them. Few details were included in daily media coverage of the time about the internment camps, and when writing this book I wondered how the everyday citizen, beyond the areas where they were located, would learn details about them.

Support from Many

First, a special thanks to friends Bonnie and Cecil Hornbeck for their tour of the radar station, and the towns of Klamath, Eureka and other parts of northern California with its redwood forests. You inspired this book.

Second, thanks to the Sonoma Public Library (and, yes, I have a library card) for help with research and for the online availability of the Santa Rosa *Press Democrat* newspaper archives. What a treasure-chest of first-hand history. I thank the reporters and publisher of the newspaper—possibly posthumously—for their daily coverage of war-time and local events.

So many people have helped me produce my stories. A huge thank you to Pat Becker, David Strand, Laura Strand, and Gail Troutman for their ongoing plot suggestions, marketing, sales, and research support.

Finally, to Bev Katz Rosenbaum and Laurie Gibson, editors extraordinaire, thank you for making the story as polished and better-told as possible.

Nonetheless, despite all the incredible assistance from so many, I take the blame for any errors, typos, or inconsistencies—because sometimes I can be stubborn and not listen to advice!

In Memory of my husband, Bob Strand.
Remembering him still inspires me (and sometimes
makes me laugh!)

Chapter 1

Clara braked suddenly to avoid hitting the truck parked in front of The White House department store on Santa Rosa's main street. Her ten-year-old hand-me-down Schwinn bicycle shuddered, but obeyed. She quickly dismounted and landed on a rock, twisting her ankle. "Damn!"

Little light was available due to the 1943 "dimout" required to hide the town from any lurking Japanese submarines that might want to bomb the area as a follow-up to Pearl Harbor.

She was returning home after viewing the midnight premier of Alfred Hitchcock's movie *Shadow of a Doubt*, which had been filmed in town and was being shown especially for the citizens of Santa Rosa ahead of its full release.

Despite the pain from her ankle, she started to get back on her bicycle to head home. "Hurry it up!" she heard someone yell.

If only she could see better. Suddenly a figure carrying what looked like a radio passed near the back of the truck. "Hey, who are you?"

Clara's stomach reeled. The figure came toward her. Another came from the store window. A flash of light showed glass scattered on the sidewalk and road.

Oh my god! They're robbing the store.

The second figure ran out and threw a bag into the truck. The first figure ran toward her. He was taller than her and heavier—making him threatening.

Clara mounted her bike and tried to move the pedals with all the strength her twenty-year-old legs could muster, given her throbbing ankle. The man at the truck was gaining on her with just a few feet between them as she managed to pull away.

She heard some cussing and pedaled faster. It was close to 2:00 a.m. Although many people had thronged outside the theater and nearby streets, she was now many blocks away so it was deserted. Should she go to a police station in the hopes someone would be there? Or should she go home where she would be safe with her parents, and they could call the police?

Home was closer.

She did not let up, even though her ankle was screaming at her. She did not hear anyone behind her, so she kept going, hoping that the few lights allowed in the dimout would enable her to see well enough to ride fast.

It seemed to take forever to reach her parents' porch, less than ten minutes away by bike. She painfully dragged her bike up to the front door, which her parents had left unlocked for her.

She checked her bag to be sure she hadn't lost her notes with all the information she'd gathered, part of her job fact-checking for the local newspaper. The door opened with her father standing between her and safety.

Catching her breath, she panted, "Got to call police. Men robbing White House store. Saw me. Chasing me."

Her father didn't question or hesitate. Dressed in a bathrobe, he somehow managed to hurry to the phone appearing distinguished and controlled. He asked the operator for the number and repeated what Clara had told him to the police. He turned to her and said, "He wants to talk to you."

Clara limped to the phone, and said, "Yes, this is Clara Wilson. There were two of them. They must have broken the window. One of them started to chase me. Oh, I was on my bicycle. It was about ten or twenty minutes ago." She gave her address and phone number, then allowed her father to help her sit on the nearest chair to her.

"What happened to your leg?"

"I twisted my ankle on a rock when I got off my bike to keep from hitting their truck."

Clara's mother entered the room, also in her bathrobe. "We waited up for you. I wish you'd let your father pick you up instead of riding your bicycle."

Her mother held up her hand to stop Clara from speaking. "I know. You're an adult. But riding a bicycle at two in the morning is not a great idea, despite the manageable distance over major roads." She smiled and shook her head, with her tied-up dark hair streaked with grey. Clara wondered, not for the first time, why she hadn't inherited the good looks of her parents.

Her father pulled off her shoe and grimaced. "It's swollen. For now, get some ice and let's wrap it in a bandage."

Her mother said, "I'll get it."

The phone rang, and her father answered and handed the receiver to Clara who responded, "Yes? It was a truck, but it was hard to see exactly what kind. And I only saw the one guy somewhat clearly. He was kind of big—at least taller than me. I couldn't say how old—he wasn't a kid, maybe in his twenties or thirties, but I'm not sure. He didn't look that old. Dirty slacks, suspenders, and I don't recall his shoes. As I said, I only saw the other one from farther away. Were you able to get there in time to stop them?"

"No ma'am. We were too late. There are officers on-site investigating now to determine what they got."

"Oh, sorry. I was on my bicycle so I couldn't get away very fast to find a phone to call you." She hung up and said,

"They got there too late. Bunch of stuff is missing, but they'll know more after they investigate."

Her mother re-entered the room. "Well, you did your best. By the way, how was the movie?"

"Hitchcock knows how to make a thriller. And the scenes of Santa Rosa were fun. Hitchcock's daughter was there, but he wasn't."

"Well, we'll catch it when it comes around. It's time for all of us to get to bed. I have a nine o'clock class and your father needs to get to work even earlier. You've done enough to advance your career tonight."

Clara hugged her mother. "Good night. I'll see you in the morning. I have to get these pages of fact checking to the paper soon. I'm hoping I can phone them in. I wonder if anyone is still at the office tonight?"

She waved at her parents as they left for bed, and then gave the operator the number for the newspaper. She was relieved when Eugene Walker, the reporter working on the story she was fact-checking, answered.

"Gene, this is Clara. You left the theater tonight before I could give you the information you asked me to double-check. And on the way home I encountered a robbery at The White House department store—so I wanted to let you know about that, too, in case you want to cover it."

Clara was nervous that Gene might be annoyed that she hadn't contacted him sooner. However, he only wanted the facts and then quizzed her about the robbery. He asked, "Are you okay?"

Surprised at his concern since he usually paid little attention to her, she responded, "Yes, I turned my ankle but my dad already wrapped it. I'm sure it'll be fine. I can go with you tomorrow to gather facts at the Jack London home." She finished giving him the details as succinctly as possible and hung up.

In fact, she would do whatever was necessary to get to a former home of the famous author. It had been designated a state park in 1940, and Clara had never visited. While Gene was doing an interview, Clara planned to listen to learn all she could.

Although her goal was to become a famous author, she believed she had to advance her writing skills and hoped by becoming a reporter she could hurry along her writing career, like Mark Twain or Ernest Hemingway, both reporters before becoming famous authors. In the meantime, she was trying to learn all she could by working with reporters like Gene whom she respected as a superior writer—for a reporter, that is. She often wondered about his background but was never able to discover much.

Using the railing on the steps, she managed to pull herself upstairs to her bedroom. However, instead of changing, she closed the door and lay on the bed relieved to be off her ankle. She stared at the ceiling and closed her eyes, hoping for sleep. Instead, her mind started to replay the last few months of her life—a frequent occurrence.

She recalled the move to Santa Rosa from Ventura less than a year ago. It was not a happy time. She hadn't wanted to move. She had a part-time job writing for one of the magazines out of Los Angeles. However, it didn't pay enough to support her so she'd had no choice but to accompany her parents so that she could live with them. Although she'd won numerous writing awards from various clubs, she could not get a writing job in her new town. All she could find was a part-time job fact-checking for the local daily Santa Rosa paper.

But what she really wanted was to be an author. She'd been searching for the heart of a story ever since arriving in Santa Rosa. Her lack of success haunted her, and she was beginning to panic that she would never find it.

Chapter 2

Clara awakened the next morning, tired but ready to go. She had inserted herself into a trip to the state memorial of Jack London's house in Glen Ellen, by claiming she could track down needed facts about London and possibly uncover more information about his friendship with the murder victim, the subject of the article.

Gene was covering the story of a highly publicized elderly murder victim who'd been a close friend of London's when they were both young. The woman he was interviewing was the niece of the murder victim who had asked to meet at London's home to search for some relics she hoped might include information about the victim—her uncle.

As a budding author, Clara was eager to explore the life of any well-known author in the belief that it would help her to form her own persona and voice. So, when she heard that Gene was going to visit Jack London's home, now a state park, she practically pleaded with him to let her go along.

However, when she stepped out of bed that morning she quickly realized that her movement was curtailed. Her ankle was swollen, and putting her full weight on it was painful. She'd at least need some kind of cane.

Of all days for this to happen. How will I explore the area? I won't be able to walk much.

However, she underestimated her father's skills. He knocked on her door and appeared carrying more bandages and a walking stick retrieved from a neighbor. "How's the ankle today?" he asked.

"I was really looking forward to visiting Jack London's home. I hear the grounds are extensive. How can I explore with this ankle?"

Her father smiled. "Let me see what I can do." He rubbed the ankle with alcohol and then tied the bandage tightly around it. "Is that better? Try using the walking stick."

She stood up with the help of the stick and then gently stepped on her ankle. "That's better. Thank you."

"Stay off it as much as you can. And keep it elevated. But you should be able to do some walking. I've got to run. I need to drop off your mother at the community college, pick up Charlie and Bill, and then get us all to work."

"Your turn to drive?"

He nodded.

Clara knew that the three of them took turns and shared gas coupons. They typically used the car only to get to and from work. She hurried as fast as she could, and after eating an apple for breakfast managed to be ready in time to respond to Gene's honking outside the house.

Eugene Walker confused her. Despite having worked with him for almost a year, he never spoke about his personal life. Nor did he ask anything about hers. Their conversations were brief and only about work.

She barely knew anything more than that he was a reporter, he valued his car which he'd purchased with hard-saved funds, and he was friends with other reporters at the newspaper, which is how she found out about his car. She did know better than to mention that he was still working at the office at two in the morning and covering another story several hours later. He prided himself on his stamina. She took a deep breath pondering how they would interact during almost an hour on the way to Glen Ellen. Maybe they could discuss his car.

Carrying her walking stick and bag with her pencil and notepad, she hobbled down the steps and into his car.

"What happened?" he asked as he pulled out from the house.

"As I said on the phone, I ran into some thieves, and managed to sprain my ankle. It's hard to see with the dimout and when I got off my bike I tripped over a rock."

Gene said, "Oh. I hope you can walk to the house."

"How long do you think your interview will take?"

"Don't know. I depend on my fine-tuned reporter instincts." He smiled.

"What do your instincts suggest? Ten minutes or five hours?"

Gene glanced at her. "It won't take five hours."

"And I plan to make the most of whatever time we have there. You'll see. I'll check out their private library and any available press clippings. Are you doing the interview in the library at the house?"

"Yes."

"I'm surprised you haven't covered this sooner. The murder's been in the news for months." She tried hard not to sound snide.

"Because the niece of London's murdered friend wasn't in town. She lives on the East Coast. Her visit this week is the first opportunity I've had."

"Oh, I see."

"How did you manage to talk Stu into letting you come along?"

"Well, I'm familiar with London, who died in nineteen sixteen as you know."

"Yes, I'm aware of who Jack London is."

"Anyway, I might be able to find out interesting facts to add to your story. You know. By searching through the library and all the rooms and just looking around. That will save you time."

"And you'll get to explore the home of a well-known author."

"Well, yes. It's good for both of us."

They chatted for the remainder of the drive about last night's movie and what a great job the local Santa Rosa girl did, a new restaurant in town, a plane crash in the area—(there seemed to be one every week), and FDR's most recent edicts, but their conversation remained superficial. That seemed to be their normal approach—keep the conversation on a safe level with no commitment in it. But Clara felt there was more to Gene than he was willing to reveal. Someday, maybe he'd relent and actually talk to her. She'd learned not to try to discuss anything about her personal life with him. He would typically change the subject when she tried.

When they reached Glen Ellen and found the way up to the area near the Jack London home, they were both impressed with the splendor of the area with its hills filled with redwoods overlooking valleys. However, when it came time for Clara to follow Gene as he walked the remainder of the distance to the home after parking, she realized that she could never make it with her sprained ankle.

Gene looked at her almost sympathetically. "I could carry you"

"No, thank you. Drat."

"Do you want to try it? I can't wait for you. I'm due to meet her in ten minutes."

"Go ahead. I'll see how far I can get. I hope I don't disturb any snakes with my walking stick."

He looked concerned. "Be careful. Use your stick if you need it. If you're not here when I return, I'll look for you. Don't go too far. Okay?"

Clara smiled, surprised at his concern. "Yes."

She was disappointed she wouldn't get to see the house of the famous author with its library. But she decided to at least do what exploring she could. She chose a path that was relatively level and started to walk through it toward some kind of outbuilding in the distance. A few people were hiking and smiled at her as they passed by. One woman asked if she needed help. She shook her head, then asked, "Is there a fairly level path where I could at least see some of the area?"

The woman pointed to a nearby path and said, "That one eventually gets to an opening, but it's mostly trees. It's really pretty, actually."

"Thanks. I'll head that way."

Clara headed down what she hoped was a path she could navigate. The trees swished in the wind soothing her irritation. Although she was not accomplishing her goal, she at least was experiencing the environment that London appreciated when he built his home. She easily understood why. The surroundings were breathtaking.

She sat down on a log and listened to the quietness of nature. She imagined London sitting there penning one of his famous stories. What would he notice about the nature of the place? How would he approach the story? What would be his first words?

She stood up to look around, believing that's what London might have done. She decided to walk a little farther to see where the path went. It was fairly level although its unevenness caused some problems. But she didn't want the trip to be a waste. She could at least explore a little.

She was about to turn around when she spied something a few feet away near the base of a tree. It wasn't an animal. It appeared to be something made of metal. Using her walking stick, she prodded the ground, moving slowly to assure her footing. After a few minutes, she managed to get to the object. She struggled to turn it over with her walking stick. It was some kind of metal statue. She stared at it.

Wow! Maybe it belonged to London!

She leaned over to pick it up, but it was too heavy to lift with one hand. It was definitely some kind of heavy metal. She propped her walking stick against the tree and leaned against it so she could grab the statue with both hands. Once she moved it, she could tell it was a cow due to its head protruding from the earth. She tried to brush away some of the earth, but she found it difficult. She'd need to get something to scrape it.

How did it get here? What's its story?

She managed to put it into her bag and was able to walk slowly carrying it.

She turned around on the path to get back to where she started, elated she had maybe found the motivation for her novel. She barely noticed her ankle as she walked. How had a metal statue made its way into the forest near Jack London's home? What did it mean? Did he leave it there? What was its significance? Who was the artist? Did the statue mean something special to that person? Why was it there? It was unlikely that it got there by accident. Someone must have put it there. How old was it?

She reached the parking lot just as Gene honked his horn. She hobbled over to his car —and got in.

As he was pulling out of the parking place, he said, "How was your day? No snakes?"

"No, no snakes. And not as productive as I'd hoped. What about you? How was your interview?"

"Also, not too productive. She didn't know too much about her uncle or Jack London, or any of London's friends in the early days. She had heard stories from her uncle that they caroused quite a bit. She was more interested in talking about her uncle's murder. Seems she'd just seen him in New York. For an elderly man he liked to travel. I did get some interesting personal information about him."

"Does she think her uncle was murdered by his caretaker?"

"Yeah, she does. But I'm not sure. The evidence is really circumstantial."

Clara had to admit, according to everything she'd read, he was probably correct. The trial would be interesting.

"What did you do while I was interviewing?"

Clara said, "I actually walked on one of the more level trails. It's quite lovely. I see why London built a home here."

Gene frowned and shook his head. "How far did you get with your ankle?"

Clara laughed. "Not far. Fortunately, there was a log for me to sit on. Oh, and I found an old metal statue. I'll clean it up and maybe it will tell an interesting story."

"Maybe it belongs to the house."

"Not likely. However, I'll check with the curator when we get back to the office. But if it has a mystery about it, I can turn it into a story."

"Still looking to become the next Dorothy Parker, are you?"

Clara forgot that she'd revealed to him early on that she wanted to be an author. "Well, I don't know about Dorothy Parker. But writing is all I've ever wanted to do. That's why I longed to see what kind of place a famous writer like Jack London would live in."

"What do you know about him?"

"Well, of course, he wrote *Call of the Wild*—and maybe something you didn't know—he wrote a new type of literature called science fiction."

"Did you like *Call of the Wild*?"

"Not particularly. But I admired the writing."

"Did you know that London was a proponent of eugenics?"

Clara shook her head. "I don't know what that is."

"It's the study of creating so-called superior people by breeding certain human characteristics—predominantly white Caucasian."

Clara stared at Gene. "How do you know that?"

"We studied him at Berkeley."

"I didn't know you went to Berkeley."

"Well, I did."

"What was your major?"

"Pre-law. But when it came time to go to law school, I resisted."

"Why?"

"I looked at a law book. Not too interesting."

"So, what do you want to be?"

"Me?" Gene laughed. "I'm not sure I know what I want to do even now, although I'm sure the Army will be letting me know."

Clara winced at his tone. "What made you become a reporter?"

"Oh, my dad knew the publisher and he gave me the job. It's okay. It's better than farming, I guess."

Clara was surprised to hear him admit how he got his job.

They arrived at the newspaper office. Although she remained disappointed that she could not participate in the interview nor search any of the records at the Jack London home, she was excited about finding the statue. She wasn't sure what it meant, but she felt it was the time to search for its story.

But now it was time to return to the monotonous job of corroborating facts.

Chapter 3

After a few hours checking information for several articles, Clara got a ride home from Marjorie Baker, her friend and neighbor. Once in the car, Clara started to pull out the cow. "What do you think of this?"

Marjorie, focusing on her driving, said, "It looks dirty. Can you wait until we get home? Oh, there's Edward! He wasn't sure he'd be ready to go home, but there he is."

Clara said, "I'll get in back."

Edward Barringer, Marjorie's fiancé, got in the front passenger seat and gave Marjorie a peck on the cheek. He turned around to talk to Clara. "How's that ankle? Gene was telling me about it. Sorry you didn't get to be part of the interview. I thought it was interesting that the lady chose to meet Gene at the Jack London house."

"I think it was his idea. He took some photos and wanted to connect the London name with the interviewee. She was the niece of the murdered victim, and he needed a reason for the interview given that there have already been several stories about the murder and the upcoming trial."

"But she herself didn't even know London personally, I bet."

"No, she probably wasn't born until after his death."

Edward supported Clara and her goal to become a writer—just as he did Marjorie and her goal to become an artist. But similar to his friend Gene, he had no ambitions to follow in his father's footsteps to become a businessman and basically fell into the job of reporter.

"What else is new?" he asked.

Marjorie responded, "Clara found a statute today, and we're going to solve its mystery."

"Huh?" Edward looked confused.

Clara said, "When I couldn't walk up to the interview, I took a short path and came across this statue under a tree. It's amazing I even saw it. It was buried under some dirt and fallen branches." She showed him the cow. "I started to brush off some of the dirt. I think I see some letters on it that could give me a clue who might have owned it. But it was all by itself right there in the forest."

Marjorie said, "I wonder how long it's been there."

"I don't know. What should I use to clean it?"

"Start with soap and water. Get it really wet. That will make it easier to remove. Your mom might have some ideas, too."

Clara tried to remove some of the dirt again, but it was definitely stuck fast. On one part of the statue, near what looked like a rear leg, she could almost see letters, but couldn't make out what they were. She turned it over to check on the other side, but again the dirt was too thick for her to decipher anything.

Marjorie said, "Here we are."

Clara asked, "Can you come in and help me clean it up?"

Edward said, "It's okay with me. I can stay for a half hour or so. Marjorie?

"Sure. Let's help Clara with her mystery." She parked the car. Edward got out and assisted Clara. When he lifted her bag, he removed the statue. "This is really heavy. I wonder what kind of metal it is? Some alloy, maybe."

Clara nodded. "Let's take it into the kitchen and use the sink there to clean it. I'll put some towels down first to gather the dirt."

She led the way, and they gingerly placed the heavy statue on top of the towels in the porcelain sink. Clara pulled out a brush from under the sink and Marjorie grabbed a spatula, and they went to work. After about fifteen minutes of scrubbing, Clara said, "I see all but one or two of the letters. It looks like D-o-b-b-s- but I can't get the others. I'll have to chisel off the remaining dirt."

Marjorie made a face. "It's not a particularly handsome statue."

Edward said, "But look at the cow's face. I think she's smiling, and her eyes are friendly. This isn't an angry bull, it's a kindly cow. I wonder if it's from one of the Japanese farmers that got sent to the camps. I understand they tried to hide their valuables rather than sell them at reduced prices."

Clara shook her head. "But why would they hide something in the Jack London park? Although that's as good an explanation as I've thought of. But DOBBS...doesn't sound Japanese, although that could be the name of the sculptor, rather than the owner. Would the creator be a blacksmith? Anyway, thanks for your help. I better get this mess cleaned up before my mom gets home."

Edward interrupted, "We need to go. Let's clean up. Remember we're joining my folks for dinner at the Madrona in Healdsburg to check it out for our wedding."

"Oh. You're right." She giggled. "But I'm sure it's way too expensive. It's nice of your parents to want to chip in, but I doubt we can afford it."

"But it will be fun looking, won't it?"

Clara laughed. "You two go. I'll keep working on it."

She saw them to the door and returned to finish cleaning up. Since she was the first one home, she checked to see how much meat was available for dinner and found a chicken. She lit the oven and prepared the meal with onions, potatoes, and

18

carrots from her mother's "Victory" garden and placed the pot in the oven.

Feeling pleased with herself, she hauled her bag with its statue wrapped in a clean towel up to her room, and again started to chip away at it. After ten minutes, she grew weary and picked up the morning paper to see if any of her "facts" were included. She skipped the front page, which was packed full of tall heavy headlines about the latest war news, and went to the society pages. She resented being relegated to the social news, but at least the job paid enough that she could help out with food.

She was just ready to check out the sports page when she noticed an event at the Occidental Hotel that included a Cory Dobbson, an art connoisseur who was speaking at a luncheon at the hotel day after tomorrow.

Could he be part of her cow's story? Was he somehow related to the statue? She read more of the article, but it didn't give additional information. There was no byline, but she could check at the newspaper tomorrow to see who wrote the article to uncover additional information. If she couldn't find out more about him, she'd have to figure out how to attend his presentation. In the meantime, she'd check bus schedules. Or, maybe one of the reporters was covering the meeting who would let her tag along.

She heard the door opening and called out, "Mom? Is that you?"

Her mother responded, "Yes, dear. Oh, something smells good. I hope it's the chicken."

"It is. Is Dad with you?"

Her father said, "Yep, I'm right here. How's your ankle? And how was your trip to Jack London park?"

"Oh, I couldn't actually make it to his home where Gene was doing the interview. But I did find an interesting artifact in the woods. I'm going to try to track it down."

Her father glanced at her mother. "We need to tell you something. Have you talked to Ed or Marjorie recently?"

"Yes, they brought me home. Why?"

Her father put his hand on her arm. Clara felt her stomach flip flop. She knew what was coming. "Oh, no. He's been drafted, hasn't he? But they're going to get married. That's not fair! And why didn't they tell me?"

Her mother said, "Ed waited to tell Marjorie when they were alone. I just talked to her right before your father picked me up. But, yes, he's been drafted. And he considers it to be his duty, which is as it should be. They're planning to rush the wedding. But then he'll go to war."

"No, no. That can't be!" Clara shook her head.

"Marjorie asked for our help to move up their wedding date. They just found out and are already changing arrangements."

Mrs. Wilson turned away from her husband and daughter and started to set the table for dinner. Clara wasn't sure, but she thought her mother was crying.

Chapter 4

Clara managed to talk Gene into reporting on the meeting at the Occidental Hotel in Santa Rosa so she could meet the artist Cory Dobbson to see if he knew anything about the statue. Unfortunately, at the last minute, she was unable to accompany him because she was needed to fact-check a breaking story about a prisoner escape. But Gene agreed to take the statue and ask the speaker if he knew anything about it.

Following the lunch, Gene returned and handed the statue back to Clara. "I'm sorry, but Mr. Dobbson didn't know anything about it. I did get a little bit of information from him. He recommended a blacksmith who deals in metal art." He ripped a page out of his notebook and handed it to her. "Here's the name of the business. He believes the studio is in Petaluma. However, he didn't seem too impressed with the cow as a piece of art."

"Thanks, Gene. I appreciate the effort. It would have been quite the miracle if we'd uncovered its secret on the first try."

She studied Gene who was smiling at her. She asked, "You heard about Ed being drafted?"

He stopped smiling. "Yes. Unfortunate timing for them. I expect I'll get a notice sometime soon. I almost enlisted, but decided to wait to see what happens."

"I don't know how to feel about all of you going off to kill or be killed. I know it's necessary to stop Hitler, Mussolini, and Hirohito. Nonetheless, I fear for Ed and eventually you and everybody."

Gene shook his head. "It's tough, but it must be done. Maybe you'll write a story about it—about how difficult it is at home as well as on the battlefield. However, in the meantime I need to get started finishing the piece on the prison escape from San Quentin by that Santa Rosa guy. My car's out front. I'll drop you at the police station so you can get background information there."

He led the way to his car with Clara doing her best to keep up. He waited for her to get in and then pulled away from the newspaper office. She didn't understand why working with Gene was always a strain. She liked him, but he made her feel insecure.

Gene said, "I'll drop you off first. Unless you want to come with me to interview the wife of the escaped prisoner."

"No. That's good if you drop me off first. Take your time. If I finish before you, I'll find a chair and wait. By the way, are you sure you don't need to interview anyone at the Santa Rosa police or county sheriff's office here in Santa Rosa?"

"The police here wouldn't know anything beyond what's in the escape report. The people to talk to are at San Quentin over in Marin County. After I talk with the wife, I'll do a phone interview with them."

Clara asked, "What did this guy do? What was he in for?"

"He shot a guy and stole his car."

"Did the victim die?"

"No. I interviewed him last week. He just got shot in the arm. I think he provoked his attacker, but that's irrelevant in the eyes of the law. The guy got ten years for attempted murder." He pulled over in front of the police station.

"Here you are. I'll see you as soon as I can." He reached back to grab her bag and walking stick. "Want some help getting out?"

"No, I can manage. Thank you."

22

"I figured you could but just thought I'd check."

Clara winced as she turned to get out of the car. Using the walking stick and the car door she managed to stand, grab her bag, then close the car door.

She groaned when she faced the steps leading up to the police station. She felt that Gene was watching her, and was determined not to show any weakness. She grabbed the railing and used it to pull herself up step by step. She was panting by the time she got to the door, but proudly turned to wave at Gene who was watching her. He waved back and pulled away. She turned and entered the station.

She approached the counter separating visitors from officers and showed the attending officer her newspaper identification and that she was there to get the details of the escaped prisoner. He rifled through some documents and handed her a description of the escape saying, "Look that over and if you have questions let me know."

Clara found a chair that was fairly clean and away from a bench where two men were seated: a young man wearing a torn shirt and trousers with no shoes and an older man in a dirty blue shirt and grease-stained tan trousers and shoes with holes on both top and bottom.

According to the report Clara read, the prisoner managed to overcome a guard in the dispensary, then changed into his uniform. He locked the guard in a linen closet, and used his identity badge to get through the gates. The details were sketchy, leaving Clara to believe that they didn't really know how he got out. And they hadn't figured out what he did once he was outside the gate. Her mind churned: Did anyone accompany the escapee? When did they discover he was missing—how much time elapsed when he escaped and the time his escape was detected? Did someone pick him up?

She finished reading the report and returned to the counter. She asked her questions and received the answers to both, "We don't know. We'll have more information tomorrow. We figure he's gonna try to get home to the missus. We got that covered. And no one knows if he got picked up."

Clara stared at the officer. "We have a reporter going there right now to interview her. Will he be safe?"

"Nothin' will happen, little lady. He'll be safe. We got someone there."

Clara smiled. "By the way, has there been any progress in catching the burglars from The White House department store? I was the one who reported it that night."

"Nope. Nothin' yet. But we'll get 'em."

"I need to wait for my ride. Is it all right if I just sit here where I can watch the street for his car?" She pointed to a chair next to the door.

He nodded. "Looks like ya got a bum foot. Ya get that at the robbery?"

"Yep."

The clerk shook his head. "What's the world coming to beatin' up on little lasses like yourself. Ya just relax there till your fella picks you up."

Clara sat down, relieved to be off her ankle. She again reviewed the report covering the missing convict and thought how little information was available about this brazen escape from one of the most secure prisons in California. She pulled out the metal statue and, using her house key, again tried to scratch off some of the yuck that was on it. The clerk was dealing with the two men in the lobby. Clara listened briefly but didn't see a story in their conversation about a problem with a supermarket door. So, she tried to relax and think about the possible story of the cow statue.

A half hour later, the clerk said. "Is that fella of yours comin'?"

"Yes. I'm sure he is. Do you happen to have the phone number of the prisoner's wife?"

"Naw. She's doesn't got one."

"Oh. But he should be here by now."

"Well, they'll be changing the watch in about ten minutes. Mebbe he forgot to pick you up. I'll ask one of our guys on his way over to check on him. Okay?"

Clara nodded. "Thank you. He's probably just caught up in the interview."

She picked up her walking stick and sat back down on the bench where she could see Gene's car when he pulled up.

Suddenly, she heard yelling and banging doors and saw officers running out the door while sirens blared. She couldn't see the cars but definitely heard them. She jumped up and hurried—as much as she could—to the counter.

"What's happening?" she tried to yell over the din.

But the clerk was busy at the radio which was screeching and cracking faster than she could decipher the words. The clerk stopped and looked up suddenly, at Clara.

"Your reporter friend never showed, right?"

"No." Clara felt her stomach drop. "That's not about him, is it?"

"Mebbe. Don't know. Stay outa the way. I gotta tend to this." He interrupted himself to respond to whatever he heard, which sounded like gibberish to Clara. She ignored the pain in her ankle and watched the clerk to see if she could figure out what was going on. But she couldn't understand most of what was being said; and what words she could recognize, she couldn't comprehend the meaning.

The clerk asked, "What's the name of your reporter friend?"

"It's Gene; Eugene Walker."

"What kind of car was he drivin'?"

"Blue Studebaker."

The clerk repeated the information in the same incomprehensible jargon over his radio. No one responded. Clara clutched the counter. What was happening? Was Gene in an accident?

The clerk heard something and responded in the affirmative. Then said, "I'll let her know."

Clara stared at the clerk, who rushed over to her. When he reached the counter, he took a deep breath. "I'm afraid your fella's been beat up."

She stopped breathing. "What? That's not possible. He just went for an interview with the wife."

"I know. But the prisoner was there and took his car. Your friend tried to stop him."

"No. That can't be. You said he'd be safe!"

The clerk heard some screeching from the radio and dashed over to respond. "I'll tell her. Which hospital? Okay."

He turned and saw Clara with eyes and mouth wide open, shaking her head.

"Ma'am, he's still alive. They took him to the Santa Rosa General Hospital. They'll patch him up real good. Ya got someone to take ya there? Ya can come in and use our phone." He lifted the opening to the counter and Clara sleepwalked in ignoring her ankle. He led her to the phone. "Do ya know the number? Just tell the operator."

She gave the operator her home phone number, although it was early for her parents to be home. She let it ring, but the operator informed her no one answered. She gave the operator Marjorie's number, and was relieved when her friend answered. However, it took her a while to say anything.

The clerk gently took the phone from her and said, "Who's this? Okay. Your friend Clara is here at the Santa Rosa city police station. Her reporter friend was beat pretty bad doin' an interview and has been taken to the hospital. Clara needs a ride. Can you come get her?

"Good. I'll let her know."

He hung up and turned to Clara, "She's comin' to get ya. Be about twenty minutes."

He guided her back to her chair and helped her sit. "Are ya gonna be all right?"

Clara looked at him, first shook her head, then said, "Yes. Do you know how seriously he's injured?"

"No, ma'am, I dunno. I'm gonna get you some water."

He went back toward a water cooler, but got interrupted by more gibberish from the radio. He responded and after almost five minutes he returned to the water cooler and got a cup of water, which he took to Clara. She drank it quickly. "Thank you. That helped. I'm sorry I kind of lost my way there. You said Marjorie will be here soon to pick me up?"

The clerk nodded. "She said in about twenty minutes. I'm glad ya feel better."

Clara tried to smile as she watched the clerk return to his desk. She wasn't sure why the news of Gene getting attacked hit her with such force. She read the paper every day with its list of soldiers killed, but no one whom she actually was acquainted with. What she was visualizing was Gene in the car smiling. She wished they were together now. She would listen to him more carefully and try to understand him. And maybe try to make him understand her.

"Miss, I think your ride's here," the clerk said. "There's a car out there."

Clara saw Marjorie running up the steps. She stood up, grabbed her bag, and with the help of her walking stick

27

headed for the door, just as Marjorie came and took her arm. They started out the door together, but Clara stopped and turned to the clerk. "Thank you."

He waved.

She limped to the railing, grabbed it, and tottered down the steps with Marjorie beside her. Edward got out of the driver's side and came around to help her into the back seat. Clara mumbled, "Thanks." Edward and Marjorie got in the car and both turned to Clara. "Are you all right?"

"Yes, can we go to the hospital? I want to see if Gene's all right. If you can't stay, I can call my parents later."

Edward nodded. "Of course. It's not that far out of our way."

Marjorie asked, "What happened? Do you know?"

"Just that he got attacked when he tried to stop the prisoner from stealing his car."

Marjorie asked, "Have you eaten today?"

"I don't know. I think I had breakfast."

"Ed, let's stop somewhere and get her something— Victory Lunch should be open."

Edward said, "No, that'll take too long. Let's just go to the market. And, Clara, eating something will help you to think more clearly. You're going to want to phone in the story."

"What?"

"You'll be the reporter on this one," Ed said.

"But it's Gene! How can I do a story about someone I know?"

"Because he's a reporter for your paper, and you've got the scoop. You should call as soon as we get to the hospital and know his condition."

Ed stopped and told them to wait in the car. He went into a market and brought out some bread, cheese, cookies, and juice. Marjorie managed to fix Clara a sandwich and handed it to her. "Here. It's not perfect—might be a little dry." Clara nibbled slowly, but managed to eat half. She drank the juice that Marjorie put in her hand and admitted she felt better.

Ed pulled up to the hospital and said, "Why don't you two go in? I'll find a parking place and join you."

Marjorie got out and helped Clara with her bag. They entered and asked the front desk nurse about Eugene Walker.

The sympathetic attendant said, "I'm afraid he's still in surgery. He was badly beaten. You can wait in the second floor waiting room. Let the nurses' station there know you're there for Mr. Walker."

"Thank you," Clara and Marjorie said. They headed for the stairs and with the help of another railing Clara was able to climb to the second floor where Marjorie found the nurses' station and asked her for any updates on the patient's condition. The nurse repeated Gene's status: he was still in surgery, but she wasn't sure why or what injury required it.

Clara asked to use the phone and called the newspaper. She let her editor Stu White know what was happening and told him she and Edward were at the hospital. She filled him in on what she learned while waiting at the police station. She promised to call with any updates.

"Okay. And tell Ed to get over to the location of the incident and cover the rest of the story. We'll use your information and his follow-up. Can you give me the names of everyone involved right now? Oh, and tell Ed I'll wait as long as I can for his story. I'll be here for at least another hour anyway."

Of course, the editor would have Ed follow up and be the actual reporter. She was only the fact-checker. From her notepad, Clara read off the names of the prisoner and his wife and kids and provided the details from the police report of the prisoner's escape. And she also told him that Gene's blue Studebaker had been stolen.

She hung up and asked the nurse if she could make one more call. She reached her parents after one ring. She told them what was happening. "I might need a lift home."

Her father responded, "Of course. Are you all right?"

"Yes, I'm fine."

She hung up and sat down next to Marjorie just when Ed entered. "How is he?"

They both shook their heads. "Still in surgery or getting plastered for casts."

Clara told him, "Stu wants you to cover the story. I gave him my information, but he wants you to go to the scene and follow up."

"Okay. Got the address?"

"Yes." She gave him the address and the names of the prisoner and his wife.

"Do you have a ride home? I'll need your car, Marjorie."

Marjorie said, "We can take a bus, if necessary. But Clara's dad said he'd pick us up."

"OK. Call Stu with any updates on Gene's condition."

"Of course."

Marjorie stood and followed Ed to the door. He turned and hugged her and then left. She walked slowly back to her chair. "I'm scared, Clara."

Clara studied her, initially assuming her friend was referring to Gene's status.

"He'll be all right, I'm sure. The police are there, and the prisoner is long gone."

Marjorie shook her head. "No, I'm scared that Ed's going off to be a soldier. I'll be home waiting for the notice that he's wounded, or worse dead. I don't know if I can stand it."

Clara hugged her friend, not sure what to say. "For now, focus on your wedding and the next happy days."

"Yes, I suppose so."

What was happening? If Gene can get beat up so seriously here in his hometown, how likely is it that Ed will be shot in a faraway country where the goal is killing?

She patted her bag holding the statue. And was it really the time for Clara to be searching for the story of the cow statue?

Chapter 5

Clara sat in a chair next to Gene's bed admiring the flowers and candy he'd received.

"So, this is what you have to do to get all this." She motioned to the goodies.

"Jealous, are you?" Gene whispered. "Sorry it hurts to talk too loudly."

"Well, from my perspective that's better. I get to talk and you have to listen."

"I see."

"No, just listen. You don't have to see."

Silence. Then "Well? What are you going to say?"

"I'm not sure you're smart enough to understand." She laughed. "You know I'm teasing?"

"Really? You would take advantage of a man when he's down?"

Clara was surprised at how easy she found it to talk to him. They had begun to banter the third day she'd visited him in the hospital. He seemed to enjoy it. She still wasn't sure what to say next. "Okay. So, you know how I want to become a writer?"

"Yeah, I heard."

"It sort of consumes me. I don't let anything else in."

"Then how can you become a writer? You need to have experiences so that you'll develop a greater understanding about life and people."

Clara frowned. "You have a point."

"What? I made a point?"

"Yes."

"Do you know if they found my car?"

"No, I don't know. Ed's following up. You made the headlines."

"Of course, I did." He closed his eyes.

Clara swallowed and almost choked. Their banter had seemed quite natural, yet somewhat surreal. She'd spent almost two days waiting for him to regain consciousness, wondering if he was going to pull through.

She greeted the nurse with a smile. "He talked to me."

"Yes. Me, too." She put her hand by her mouth and whispered loudly, "Are you his girl?"

From the bed, they both heard a growl. "Hell, no!"

The nurse laughed. "Well, this young lady has been by your side off and on ever since you came in. It's a good thing, too. She needed to rest that ankle. How're you feeling?"

"Some guy clobbered me with a hammer several times. How should I feel?"

"You're a lucky man. The doctor was able to repair the damage. He saved your life."

Gene asked, "You don't happen to know if they found my car, do you?"

Clara interrupted, "I'll see if I can find out."

The nurse winked, and pulled the curtain.

Clara headed out to use the phone at the nurses' station. She hoped that her friend, Fred, the clerk at the police station was on duty. They were on a first-name basis since the incident. "Hi, Fred. He's awake and as ornery as ever. You don't happen to know if they found his car, do you?" She listened as Fred told her they hadn't found his car, nor the escaped prisoner.

"Okay, thanks. Any news at all?"

Again, the answer was no. "But I'm glad to hear he's gonna recover."

Clara hung up and asked the nurse, "Has Mr. Walker's family been notified?"

The nurse shook her head. "We asked him this morning who to contact, and he said he didn't have any family left."

Clara returned to Gene's room. When Gene saw her, he asked, "Well?"

"No car, no prisoner. Sorry."

"He'll destroy it."

"I'm sorry about your car."

"I guess I should be thankful to be alive. What story are you working on?"

"I'm headed over to the Chamber to confirm the names of all the new officers. Then I'm off to interview the owner of a new restaurant, then to check out the Rotary Club meeting."

Gene almost grinned. "Sounds exciting."

She ignored the sarcasm. "I might go check out a blacksmith who makes metal statues later if I have time. I'm able to manage my bike now. The ankle's better—just a little sore."

"I forgot your statue. Have you written anything lately?"

Clara hesitated.

"That's all right if you haven't. Things have been busy."

"Actually, sort of, yes. I'm just not sure if now's the time to search for the story about the statue or even to write— what with Ed going off to war and you hurt. And the war itself."

"So, tell me—why—not?" His voice was fading.

"You need to sleep. Remind me later, and I'll fill you in. I'm going to leave you now but I'll be back."

She wanted to touch him to reassure him, but she hesitated and decided that would be too forward.

She walked out of the hospital, retrieved her bike from the rack, and headed to the Chamber. She was surprised to discover she would have preferred to stay at the hospital with Gene.

Chapter 6

Gene went home from the hospital following almost a week of care. He managed to hire a nurse to visit him for a few days to help him around the house. Clara visited him when she could but the bike ride was a few miles beyond what she liked to do, although her ankle was much improved.

She continued to earn her small paycheck by gathering whatever facts Edward needed. With Gene out of commission, Ed kept her busier than usual. Stu, the editor, didn't want to hire another reporter in the meantime. He was already interviewing candidates to replace Edward.

Ed and Clara were just returning from a trip to Petaluma where Clara did some research at the Free Public Library of Petaluma while Ed conducted an interview.

Clara said, "We're early. Do you have time to stop at the Knick Knack store downtown? I want to see if they might know something about the cow statue."

"Sure. Marjorie won't be ready for me to pick her up for almost another hour."

They entered the store together and were greeted with several floor-to-ceiling shelves packed with porcelain, wood, and metal statues of various sizes, shapes, and figures. Clara whispered to Ed, "I should have started here first."

He nodded.

A young woman greeted them with enthusiasm. "Can I help you?"

Clara pulled out her statue as she approached the woman. "I hope so. Do you happen to recognize this cow?"

"What? Where did you get that?" She laughed.

"Oh, I found it and am trying to track down the owner."

"It's dirty. Where did you find it?"

"Over near Glen Ellen, in the wooded area by Jack London's place."

"Oh, I see. Well, then it most likely belongs to him."

"No. He's been dead for years. And this is a fairly modern piece of art. It has a partial name etched on it. See these letters D-O-B-B-"

"Yes, I see them, but I don't know whose they would be."

Ed interrupted, "Maybe someone named Hiram Dobberson?"

The woman's eyes opened wide. "Well, if you have the name of someone why don't you just ask him if it's his?"

Clara looked surprised and turned to Ed, "Where did you get that name?"

Ed turned to the clerk. "Hiram is a friend of Marjorie's and he appreciates art, so I'm sure he's visited here."

The clerk said, "I see. Well, I don't know anyone by that name. And I don't know this piece of, well I guess you'd call it a statue. It's hardly art." She wrinkled her nose and shook her head in distaste.

Ed asked, "Do you have any art at all that depicts cows? Have any customers requested cows?"

"No and no. We don't do cows." She smiled. "But we do have some lovely horses."

Clara smiled back. "Thanks. I appreciate your help."

She and Ed left the shop.

Ed said, "I think she knows more than she told us."

"I sensed that, too. But why would she lie about something as silly as a cow statue?"

"She recognized Hiram's name. Maybe she didn't want to spend time giving information rather than making a sale."

"I'll return another time. Maybe someone else will be there who's more co-operative. You need to get back to the paper so you can finish work, and I want to be with Marjorie tonight."

When they got in the car, she handed him her notes from the library, but her mind was racing. Why would anyone want to hide the ownership of a metal cow statue? Was there more of a story than even she envisioned? And, again, thinking about Marjorie and Ed's predicament, and the injured Gene, was this the time to be focused on finding the story of a cow statue?

Chapter 7

The next morning Clara peddled to Gene's house. Despite her misgivings about whether she should be focused on the cow statue, she was eager to discuss it with him. However, when she arrived she was startled to see a police car parked in front of his boarding house.

She decided to enter anyway, and if they didn't want her there, they could tell her to leave. She knocked on his door and heard him say, "Come in."

"Hi, Gene. It's Clara. Are you decent?"

"Yes, I'm talking to Sergeant Hastings. They think someone saw my car."

"Really? Where?" She turned to the sergeant and said, "Oh, hi. I'm Clara Wilson. We work together at the newspaper."

He nodded. "Yes, you were the one waiting for him to pick you up at the station house, right?"

"Yes, that's correct."

"One of our officers identified a car illegally parked out by the race track. When he reported it, our dispatcher recognized the plate number. But when they got back out to the track, I'm sorry to say it was gone."

"Oh, no."

"What's good about the sighting is it means the car is still in Santa Rosa."

Gene asked, "Was it still in good condition?"

"Mostly, although its condition's why he reported it so it may have some dents. Well, I gotta go now. Nice to meet ya, Clara."

"Nice to meet you, Sergeant."

After he left, Gene muttered, "Damn."

"I know. So close. I'm sorry, Gene. But it is good news that it's still in Santa Rosa."

"Yes, but it's been in Santa Rosa, and they didn't find it. So, what makes us think they'll locate it now?"

"I'm sorry."

"How are you? Any new stories you're working on?"

"First, how are you? Have you been walking?"

"A little."

"Do you want to take a walk now?"

"Oh, you mean gimpy you with your ankle is going to support me in case I start to fall?"

Clara lowered her head. She didn't want to banter today. "My ankle's almost healed."

"I'm sorry, Clara. I'm still angry about my car. I'd just as soon not walk now. I'm tired."

She struggled with what to say then decided to tell him about the trip to the Knick Knack store. "Ed and I are convinced that the clerk at the store was lying. She recognized Dobberson's name and knew something about the statue. But she wouldn't tell us."

"Why would she lie? It doesn't seem likely. She was probably just annoyed that you weren't going to buy anything. What are you going to do now?"

"I'm going to contact this Hiram Dobberson and see if it's his statue. Ed knows him, so I should be able to locate him."

"If it is, then what?"

"I'll ask him about it. And once I know its history, if it's meaningful, I'll write a story about it."

"Why don't you just invent a story? Call it fiction."

"I suppose, but I can't decide until I know its story." Again, she felt the pangs of guilt about spending time on the statue. She wanted to tell him he never seemed to understand but she stopped when she saw his eyes, still black and blue, and noticed him wincing in pain when he tried to move.

Instead, she said, "Thanks, Gene. I'll leave you now to get some sleep. Before I go, can I get you anything?"

"I'm sorry, Clara. I really don't feel well. Could you get me some water?"

"Sure." She went to his sink and filled a cup, then set it on the table next to him with a variety of things he might need, like a razor, soap, a basin of water, and some apples and bread. "I'm sorry about your car. I hope they find it. Do you think you'll be able to go to Marjorie and Ed's wedding? It's just a few weeks away. My dad said he could pick you up and you could go with us."

He shook his head. "I don't know. I really don't know. I'd like to sleep now."

Clara nodded. On some strange impulse that she later questioned, she kissed his cheek.

He opened his eyes and mouth wide. "What was that for?"

"Oh, I thought you needed it. I'll check on you again tomorrow."

She left him with an open mouth and eyes staring at her.

Once on her bike peddling back to the newspaper, Clara couldn't comprehend what she'd done. She still didn't believe that she'd kissed him. Okay, so it was only on the cheek, but their relationship did not warrant even that.

But since he was beaten up, she saw him as vulnerable, which made her re-think her image of him. But did that earn him a kiss?

Chapter 8

Clara finished helping Marjorie choose flowers for the bridal party and was on her way to meet the couple for lunch at Victory Lunch on Fourth Street. They planned to get a hamburger to take to Gene, whose diet was mostly fruits and vegetables given the rationing of meat. Clara had extra coupons for him, and was pleased to give them up. She took her bike rather than ride with Marjorie and Ed because she needed to do errands after lunch.

She arrived at the restaurant first and smelled the cooking burgers and fries even before she entered. She almost regretted giving up her own ration coupon, but she'd promised herself a salad and that's what she'd have.

She found a seat at the bar, and despite her promise of just a salad she ordered a side of fries to tamp down her hunger until Marjorie and Edward arrived. She told the waitress that there were two more coming—and that they were getting married in a few days.

The waitress smiled. "That's nice."

Clara said, "Yeah, but then he's got to go into the service. He got drafted. So, it's bittersweet."

"Sorry to hear that. My brother's on a ship somewhere."

"Oh, do you hear from him much?"

"Every once in a while we get a letter, but not often. And they're censored, you know, in case a spy here might read them."

"I see."

"Do you have anyone serving now?"

"No. Only my friend right after getting married. He'll be here soon."

Just then Marjorie and Edward entered the restaurant followed by a group of five young men dressed in work clothes and boots looking as if they'd just come from tearing down a building. Their clothes were filthy, and their shoes were full of holes. Hands and faces were covered with dust. Clara ignored them and stood to greet her friends, led them to the counter, and offered them her fries.

Marjorie laughed and said loudly over the din of the young men, "I thought you were going to resist and just have a salad!"

Clara shouted, "Well, I figured one or two wouldn't hurt me. And they're so good."

The waitress took the hint and walked over to the boisterous group of workers. "What can I get you fellas today?"

"Hamburgers with everything and fries, my fine lady."

Clara whispered to Marjorie, "At least they quieted down."

Marjorie nodded. Edward was preoccupied reading the newspaper.

Clara asked, "Anything in there of yours, Ed?"

"Oh, I suppose. I was checking to see the latest news about the war. It's not looking so good right now." He shook his head as if to shake the news away. "Hey, have you found out anything more about your cow?"

"No, not since we visited the Knick Knack shop down the street. I've been focusing on research for the paper. By the way, who's following up with the trial of the guy they arrested for the murder of Jack London's friend?"

"Gene and I are sharing it. Also sharing Gene's sports coverage. We're really short-staffed. You know what?"

Clara said, "What?"

"You should ask to be assigned some of these stories. You could write them. With so many guys off to war, you women are going to need to fill in."

"Really? You think so?"

"I definitely do. I'll talk to Stu."

"I doubt our esteemed editor will agree. But I'm willing. I hope Gene gets better soon."

"Even if he does, we're still short with me going off to war."

Marjorie let out a painful sigh. "Please, don't say that."

"Hon, we have to be realistic."

"Not until after we're married. Let's spend the next few weeks as if the whole world is about our wedding."

Ed stroked her hair. "Okay."

Just then their food arrived. Clara put in an order for a hamburger to go, and tried to imagine that her salad made her superior. She took several forkfuls and pushed it aside, grabbing one of the fries instead.

Laughter erupted from the table of young men. Clara tried to glare at them, but did not succeed in getting them to lower their voices. Several other people in the restaurant looked annoyed, but said nothing.

Suddenly, something struck Clara as if she'd crashed into a wall. She again tried to see the group without them noticing. She quickly turned back. The waitress was serving the group their hamburgers, so Clara couldn't see clearly. She leaned over to Marjorie and said, "I think one of those men is the one who robbed The White House store—the guy who chased me."

Marjorie tried to look, but Clara stopped her. Marjorie turned to Ed and whispered something to him, which Clara assumed was what she'd just told her. Ed jumped up and asked the waitress for a telephone. After confirming that it was a local call, she led him around the counter to the back into the kitchen area to the telephone.

Clara looked again at the group and saw that they were preparing to go. She motioned to Marjorie who followed Ed to alert him that the group was starting to leave. Clara was left alone at the counter. The waitress had also disappeared.

The group got up and moved in unison toward the front door. One of them broke off and walked over to Clara. She recognized him and grew cold. She called, "Ed, come quick."

The young man grabbed her arm, shielding it with his body so no one could see. "That won't do you no good, missy. You better keep your mouth shut. I'm warnin' you."

"Let go of me. Ouch! You're hurting me."

"You'll hurt more if you say anything."

He turned and lurched out of the restaurant just as Ed and Marjorie returned to the counter.

"Ed, he's getting away!"

Marjorie rushed to Clara, who was rubbing her wrist. "Are you all right? We called the police."

"He told me to keep my mouth shut. He *is* the same guy who robbed The White House store."

Ed came back into the restaurant. "They got away on their motorbikes before I could catch them."

Marjorie said, "He actually attacked her and hurt her wrist."

Clara shook her head. "I think it will be okay. Are the police coming?"

"Yes, but we don't know how long it will take them."

The waitress and two customers were hovering over Clara, while two other customers were talking with Ed.

"What was it he did, honey?" asked a fortyish woman wearing a nurse's uniform now sitting at the counter. She picked up Clara's wrist to examine it. "You might want a doctor to check that out. What doesn't he want you to tell?"

"He's the one I saw robbing The White House a while ago."

Ed said, "I'm not sure how he thinks he's going to harm you. He has no idea who you are or where you live. You don't need to be afraid of him."

Two policemen entered the restaurant with guns drawn.

Ed said, "They got away on motorbikes." He turned to Clara. "This is Clara Wilson the person who witnessed the robbery at The White House."

One of the officers left the restaurant, saying, "I'll see if I can track down a group on motor bikes. You check with her."

Clara gave the officer a description of the man and reminded him that she had also reported the robbery, so they should have that information on file. She'd gotten a much better view of him in the restaurant than in the darkness at the store.

"What about the others with him?"

Two of the customers gave their descriptions of the group, and the waitress filled in what she observed. It took almost an hour to note everything, and Clara was beginning to worry about Gene. She'd told him she was bringing him a hamburger, and it was close to one thirty. By the time they cooked it, and she rode her bike to his house it would be two o'clock.

She asked the waitress to prepare a burger with everything and fries, and told Marjorie and Ed to leave. But Marjorie was worried that the attacker would wait and follow Clara. "No, I doubt that he stuck around with the police showing up. I'll be fine. I'm worried about Gene. I promised I'd bring him a hamburger. He hasn't had much meat with it being so tightly rationed."

Ed said, "I think she's right, Marjorie. She'll be okay. We're supposed to meet the justice of the peace at two to go over the wedding plans, and I have to stop by the paper first and give them my story."

Clara nodded. "I'll be fine."

The waitress brought a bag with Gene's food.

Ed told them, "I paid for everything, so we can leave whenever you're ready. How about if we follow you over to Gene's? That will make Marjorie feel better."

Clara picked up her bag, still heavy with the cow statue and led the way to her bike. However, when she arrived at it she saw that the spokes were pulled out, the fender ripped off, and the handle bars stuck at an upside-down angle.

"Oh, no!" She tried hard, but could not hold back the tears.

Marjorie heard her and rushed over. "Oh, I'm sorry, Clara. We need to tell the officer."

Ed said, "I'll go back in and call him. Unbelievable."

Clara said, "I don't know what I'll do. It's hard enough getting around *with* my bike. How will I manage now?"

Marjorie said, "I know, and it isn't easy getting bikes right now. They're scarce. But maybe someone can fix yours."

"It looks beyond repair."

Ed came back out. "Let's put it in my car. We'll fit it in somehow. Then we'll take you to Gene's, go see the justice of the peace, then come back and pick you up. We can drop your bike off at the bike shop I know. They might be able to fix it."

Clara and Marjorie walked arm-in-arm to Ed's car and watched him stuff the mangled bike inside the trunk. Clara then got in the back. She hoped Gene's hamburger would be warm enough that he could enjoy it.

When they arrived at Gene's, she hauled her bag out of the car and carried it and Gene's lunch to the door. She hoped he was still awake. She knocked several times and finally heard him say, "Come in." She entered and was surprised to find him sitting in a chair in the living room area.

"Hi, Gene. How are you feeling?"

"Well, for one thing, I'm starving. I can smell that hamburger from over here."

Clara smiled and pretended to rush the burger over to him with long Charlie Chaplin strides. She found a tray and placed it on his lap and laid out the food. He gulped down his first bite of the burger and then turned to the fries. "How come you're so late?" he mumbled between bites.

Clara wasn't sure what to tell him. She hesitated, which made him stop chewing. "What happened?"

"I saw the guy at the restaurant who robbed The White House. He threatened me and destroyed my bicycle before the police got there. Ed called them and they came soon, but not soon enough."

"What's wrong with your wrist?"

Clara looked and realized it was swollen. "He grabbed my wrist when he was threatening me." She noticed the concerned look on Gene's face. She quickly added, "I know what you're thinking—weak woman can't even defend herself."

Gene shook his head and quietly said, "That's not what I was thinking at all. How did you get here?"

"Ed and Marjorie. Ed's taking my bike to get it fixed, although I doubt it can be saved. They'd have come in but they have an appointment about their wedding."

"I see. We're both without transportation."

"Yes, we have something in common. Finally!"

Gene almost smiled. "Thanks for the burger. Given what happened, you're nice to have brought it."

"I hope you enjoy it. I, on the other hand, had a salad. Watching my waistline, you know."

He took another bite, studied her, then said, "Stu came by today."

"And what did our esteemed editor want?"

"He asked if I thought you could be a temporary reporter. Could you?"

"I'm curious what you told him."

"I said if you wanted to, you could. And probably a good one. I'm laid up for at least another week. And Ed will be leaving in a few weeks. We're going to need someone to help out."

Clara constrained her excitement and said casually, "Well, I suppose if you men need some help, I could manage."

"This is serious, Clara. You'd need to focus on the stories you're reporting. For a while, at least, you'd have to forget about your novel and your search for the statue's story."

Clara kept quiet for a few seconds, although she already knew her answer. She was excited to be considered to be a reporter—certainly not the same as being a best-selling author, but better than being a fact-checker. "Well, I could probably do that for a while. Do you know what he's offering salary wise?"

"No, he didn't say."

"How should I proceed?"

Between munching on his burger and fries, he said, "I was going to tell you to go to the office right now, but do you have a way to get there?"

"There's a bus stop a few blocks from here that has a connection to the office. But it will take a half hour or more. I need to let him know I'm on my way."

"Okay. You're serious about this?"

Clara put on her most serious face. "Yes, Gene. I mean it. Thank you for helping me get the opportunity."

They both were quiet. Then Clara asked, "Have they gotten any closer to finding your car or recapturing the prisoner?"

"No. At least the police haven't told me anything. This burger is wonderful." He licked his lips.

"Should I follow up on that story?"

"Maybe, maybe not. Check with Stu. And don't forget to fill him in on what happened to you today. You might want to follow up your own story."

Clara stood, gathered her bag, and headed toward the door. "Could you call Stu and let him know I'm on my way? Also, Marjorie and Ed will be dropping by to pick me up. They planned to visit with you anyway. They should be here in half an hour."

She looked at him and saw him put his hands up in front of his face. "No, no kiss today. I couldn't take it again."

Clara laughed. "Then you better behave."

She turned and left, in a much better mood and looking forward to her visit with the editor. She was eager to get started and could hardly wait to tell her parents. For the moment, she wasn't thinking about her novel or the cow statue.

Chapter 9

Clara was in the courtroom with Ed on the second day of the trial of the accused murderer of Jack London's one-time friend. Stu had asked her to attend with Ed so he could show her the key points to include in her story. It was a good idea. Although it was not her first, Clara was fascinated with this trial, given that it was loosely connected to Jack London. She was so absorbed that she was slow to take notes. She noticed Ed jotting down things constantly.

The courtroom was filled, including the accused's wife and eight of his nine children. The prosecutor was asking for the death penalty. The defense attorney argued that the evidence was circumstantial and that there was no hard evidence that the accused had actually murdered the victim.

Clara started to take notes as fast as she could. She knew how to gather the correct names, however, so if she didn't get everyone correct in her notes, she could track them down afterward.

She was engrossed in the details and fascinated with what she could see of the defendant. He was dressed in a suit that was worn but clean. And all of the children and his wife were also dressed in worn but clean clothes. Clara suspected that the younger children probably were wearing hand-me-downs.

The district attorney's witnesses were compelling. They told how the accused carried on as caretaker of the victim's ranch where he lived with his family, drawing cash from forged checks during the time the victim was missing. The victim's body and that of his dog were eventually discovered buried at his ranch while the caretaker and his family were still living there. Clara noted one witness name after the other with little recognition, until she heard the bailiff call for "Hiram Dobberson."

"What?" she realized she said it out loud. Ed turned to her with a finger on his lips to shush her, even though he knew why she'd uttered the comment.

She hung on to every word of Dobberson's responses to the DA. It turned out he had seen the defendant and the victim together prior to the victim's plans to travel to New York to visit his niece. He claimed that he saw them at the Knick Knack store and that the defendant grabbed a bag full of items for his kids and handed them to the clerk, telling her that the victim would pay for them.

Ed turned to Clara again. This time he shrugged. When Ed and Clara had questioned the clerk at the Knick Knack store, she claimed that Hiram Dobberson did not do business there. Clara had to somehow talk to Dobberson to see if he knew anything about the cow statue. But how to do it and still write the story about that day's trial? It was big news. She couldn't screw it up.

Ed motioned and mouthed "me" then pointing to himself and then to Hiram. Clara nodded. She understood. He was going to talk to Hiram. He'd ask about the statue. He didn't have it with him, but he could describe it.

The DA finished with Dobberson and called his next witness. Clara focused on the testimony and continued to take notes. The story was beginning to take shape, and, although the evidence was circumstantial, it didn't look good for the defendant.

They broke for lunch, and Clara took the time to draft her article as a starting point. She understood that Ed would edit it and also that Stu would edit Ed's edits. She smiled when she thought about it. This would be her third story, and she might get a byline with this one.

She was just getting ready to return to the trial when Ed met her. "He said he doesn't understand why the clerk didn't recognize his name. He goes there frequently. But he doesn't know anything about a metal cow statue."

"Oh." Clara tried not to show her disappointment. "We better get back in there. I drafted my notes from this morning. I'll add this afternoon's notes to the story and give it to you at the end of the day."

"Good. For this round, don't try to reach any conclusions. We'll let Stu do the editorial about that."

"I'm not sure how successful I'll be at not reaching conclusions. I do have a mind, you know."

"In this case, I do it by putting myself in the shoes of both sides: the district attorney and the defense attorney. First write the DA's side and then the defendant's side and then put them together."

But Clara wasn't sure how she could keep her perspective out of the article. Nor was she sure she wanted to. Although she was enjoying reporting articles, she longed to get back to writing her own story, and that meant she needed to more fully unearth the mystery behind the cow statue.

Chapter 10

The name Dobberson plagued Clara the next few days as she ached to write the story of the statue. It interfered so much that she had to rewrite her first article on the trial three times, but finally got it to the satisfaction, first, of Edward, then, of her editor. But she continued to want to speak with Dobberson herself. Maybe he had some relatives who might be aware of the statue.

She fantasized about the cow: it was created by a metalworker as a symbol of his business to be given to his firstborn son. But the boy died of some incurable disease before he could receive it. So, the father discarded it in the forest so he'd never have to see it again.

Or, a Japanese dairy farmer had made it as a type of banner for his farm, but got rid of it when forced to move to one of the wartime relocation camps.

She wondered if maybe it was stolen by a criminal who might have thought it valuable and, upon discovering it was worthless, threw it away.

How did it get into the forest near Jack London's home? It couldn't have survived more than twenty years after his death and still been in the shape it was in when she found it.

"Clara, we need to go. Are you ready?"

Ed spoke sharply. He knew she was daydreaming.

"I'm sorry, Ed. Where're we headed?"

They were just leaving the courtroom. Clara had a first draft of her article ready for his review. But it was still early, so they had time to do another one. Ed had phoned the office for their next assignment.

"We're going to interview the parents of one of the most prestigious families here in Santa Rosa. They've just heard that their son was killed in the Philippines."

"Right." She pulled a sheet of paper out of her bag. "I've got the latest figures for the draft to add to the article. All men, ages eighteen to thirty-eight, except farmers are to be drafted. Twelve thousand men are being taken into the armed services every day. What's the name of the family?"

"You need to behave."

"What? What do you mean?"

"It's the Dobberson family."

"What? Your friend?"

"Yes, it was Hiram's brother."

Clara tried not to be elated that she'd get a chance to talk to him directly. Maybe the statue belonged to his deceased brother.

Ed said, "Don't say anything to them about the statue. Please."

"I promise. Are we going to their home?"

"Yes. This is my last story. From now on you're on your own."

"I know. You're getting married soon. Are the Dobbersons invited to your wedding?"

"Yes, of course. Marjorie and I are both friends of the family, although Marjorie knows the family better. I just knew Hiram for a year at school."

Clara was surprised to reach the Dobberson home in less than twenty minutes. The change in the style of houses was significant. Clara studied the Dobberson home. She decided it qualified as a mansion.

She admired the ornateness of its covered porch, stone railing with miniature columns at the front of the house, although the steps leading up to the porch looked prohibitive with no railing. However, she managed to reach the heavy front door without any help. Ed rang the bell.

It took a while for someone to answer, but eventually Hiram opened the door and said, "Hi, Ed. C'mon in."

Ed said, "I'm sorry about your loss, Hiram. I know you were close to your brother."

"Thanks. How long will this take?"

"Only for as long as you say. How's your mother?"

Clara did her best to be listening to the conversation but was busy eyeing the art work throughout the house. She didn't notice any metal statuary. Nor were there any painted cows. Instead, she saw pastoral scenes and a few painted portraits. The furniture—a sofa, a love seat, and three armchairs—was overstuffed and looked soft.

She felt Ed's hand on her arm. "I'd like you to meet Clara Wilson. She's an up-and-coming writer at the paper and will be taking over for me when I leave."

Hiram barely nodded. "When do you go?"

"Two weeks after my wedding. We'll be honeymooning at the Madrona in Healdsburg, a gift from my family."

Hiram smiled. "That will be nice. Look, could we get this interview over?"

Clara pulled her attention back to Hiram as Ed spent the next five minutes asking questions about his brother. Did he enlist? What did he feel about the war? Was he proud to be a soldier?

"Of course he was proud." A female voice interrupted. Clara hadn't seen the woman enter the room.

Hiram introduced his mother. Clara saw that she'd been crying but had put on makeup. Ed greeted her by reminding her who he was.

She said, "We'll miss him so, of course. But we're proud, too. I don't know what else we can say, except he would have made a great artist."

Clara asked, "Oh, was he an artist? Do you have some of his art that we could print along with the article?"

Mrs. Dobberson pressed her lips together, then nodded to Hiram, "Can you get her something? But I want it returned. I need to go now."

Ed glared at Clara, understanding her request was more out of her selfishness than it was to have art work to attach to the article.

Hiram said, "Follow me. You can choose from his art. But, Miss Wilson, there are no metal statues among his work." Clara was embarrassed. Of course, Ed had asked him about the statue and probably told him about her.

They followed Hiram into a back room which was filled with blank and painted canvasses. Clara stared at the paintings in awe. "Wow!"

Hiram nodded. "Yes, he was talented. What a waste."

Clara moved to study the paintings up close. "These are incredible." She turned to Ed, "Which one should we take?"

Ed also was stunned and slow to respond. "I'm not sure."

"Is there one he painted that might remind us of Santa Rosa?"

Ed pulled out a few and said, "Here's one of the court house. Oh, and here's one of this house."

Hiram shook his head. "No." He reached down and brought out a painting of the Sonoma racetrack. "He loved racing. This is more about him."

Ed said, "Thanks, Hiram. We won't bother you anymore. We really appreciate this. As will the people in Santa Rosa who know you and your family. I'm really sorry."

Clara also said, "Thank you," and turned to lead the way out of the home.

Once in the car, Clara studied Ed. He wrote insightful yet compassionate copy. She wished she'd had more time to learn from him. And more than anything, she hoped she would never have to write his obituary.

Chapter 11

Clara checked the invitation to the garden show at the home of the Dobbersons. Marjorie had handed it to her and told her she'd gotten it because she thought Clara and her mother would enjoy attending. Clara recognized the name, but was surprised that she was invited personally—even with Marjorie's influence—and that they were holding an event so soon after the son's death. Clara assumed she was included as a reporter to cover the event. As a fundraiser for local artists, they would be looking for donations and an article could help.

Regardless, she decided to attend and take her mother as a guest. Clara was not interested in gardening but her mother definitely was. One of the reasons they bought the house was due to the large back yard, big enough for an ample garden of tomatoes, string beans, onions, and other vegetables. Her mother was eager to research local gardens and was pleased that Clara was taking an interest.

"Are you ready, Mother? Dad's going to drive us there, and Marjorie will bring us home."

"Yes, let's go. I don't want your father to be late. Is he out front with the car?"

"Yep."

Mother and daughter headed out to the car and joined Mr. Wilson, who greeted them with a patient smile.

Clara said, "Drat. I forgot my bag."

Her mother said, "Don't worry about it. I've got mine. If we need anything I've got it covered. I even have a notebook and pencil if you have to take notes."

"Okay. You're right. I'm not sure if I'm invited as a reporter on this, but I'd like to be prepared."

They drove off to the mansion that Clara had visited a few days earlier. Clara said, "I can hardly wait to see how big the back yard is."

They said goodbye to Mr. Wilson and followed signs directing them and several others into the back yard, which as Clara surmised, was quite large. Mrs. Wilson moved eagerly from rows of string beans, cauliflower, broccoli, cabbage, peas and spinach.

"Oh, and look at the flower garden. I think those are sweet Daphne and look at those camellias!" Her mother handed her purse to Clara and ran toward the flower garden filled with multiple-colored flowers, where a young man was cutting small bouquets for visitors.

But Clara was yearning to again look inside the home to see more of it than just the main room she'd visited. She meandered toward an open door, which she discovered led to the kitchen. The stove was at least double the size of theirs at home. The table and chairs were oak. Three women were stirring pots on the stove, and a man in a uniform was arranging trays of food, which he was picking up just as Clara arrived. She backed out of the way as he approached her. "Sorry, Miss, but no one is allowed inside. Please step outside. The food will be served soon."

Clara was embarrassed. "Oh, I'm sorry. I was just curious."

She turned and started to walk away and at the same time she pulled out the notebook and pencil from her mother's purse and started to write down key items in the kitchen. "Oh, before you go, can you tell me all the different vegetables and flowers that are growing here?"

"No, Miss. Mr. Lowry, the gardener is the best person for that. But I believe there's a marker at the end of each row that provides that information."

"Is Mr. Lowry here?"

"Oh, yes. I'm not sure where exactly, but you can't miss him. He's the gentleman wearing a large straw hat."

"Thank you. I'll search for him. I'm planning to write an article for the Santa Rosa paper, and I need to talk to someone who is informed."

"Well, Mr. Lowry would be that person."

Having established herself as a reporter, Clara started to look for a "gentleman" in a straw hat. She spotted someone who met that description in the vegetable garden talking to a matronly woman dressed as if going to a parlor party rather than a garden party who appeared to be giving instructions to Mr. Lowry, who looked pained to be listening. The woman turned and headed for the flower garden, so Clara took advantage of this opening to approach the berated gardener.

"Excuse me, are you Mr. Lowry?"

The man jumped, seemingly startled that someone knew his name, but he managed a smile and responded, "Yes. How can I help you?"

"Hi, I'm Clara Wilson, and I'm a reporter. I'd like to write a story about this magnificent garden. Can you fill me in on the details?"

"I'll try, although I've only been here for a short time as an assistant. What do you want to know?"

"How old is this garden? I mean, did the current owner plant it originally?"

"I'm sorry. As I said I've only been here for a short time."

"Okay. Maybe I can get that information from the current owner. But what about what's planted here? I can see by your markers the identification of the vegetables and flowers. Do they sell the vegetables?"

"No, they mostly give them to their church to give to the poor people in the area. They also do, of course, keep some for themselves and their family."

"By the way, you said you were an assistant? Who is the principal gardener, and can I talk to him?"

"Well, it was my uncle, actually. He worked here for twenty years. I grew up in San Jose, and my family also grew vegetables, so I was familiar with gardening, although not as expert as my uncle. I've been helping him here off and on for about a year. When he disappeared, the family called me to take over. I'd just lost my job so I was available, but I'm not sure how long I'll be here."

"What do you mean your uncle disappeared?"

"Just that. One day he was here and the next day he was gone. No one knows what happened, although my mom, his sister, thinks he had a lady friend and just up and left with her." He looked around to be sure no one was listening, Clara assumed. "The family here said he stole some things from the house. But I don't believe it."

Clara shook her head. "That wouldn't be in character of someone who held down the same job for twenty years."

Mr. Lowry shook his head. "No, it wouldn't. Maybe you can find out as a reporter what happened. The family here doesn't seem to care. They've hardly tried to find him. I've stayed on to try to uncover what's happened to him. I hope I haven't said too much. You won't tell the family that I told you any of this, will you?"

Clara was excited. The disappearance of the gardener promised to be an interesting story. "No, of course not. How can I get hold of you?"

"Well, it's best to reach me at my parents' house in San Jose, south of San Francisco." He gave her the phone number, which Clara noted in her mother's note pad, which she put in her pocket.

Lowry nodded then said, "I need to go now."

Clara glanced in the direction where he was looking and saw the lady of the house headed their way. She moved quickly to intercept the woman and gushed, "What a beautiful garden you have! You may remember me. I'm Clara Wilson, a reporter with the Santa Rosa paper. We met last week about the passing of your son. Could you answer a few questions for the story?"

The woman forced a smile, but appeared not to be interested. "What kind of story?"

"About your garden and how you donate the food to the poor."

"No. I don't want people knowing I donate food. That will just encourage more. I'm not after publicity for this event."

"That's strange. I received an invitation, and I'm a reporter. I was surprised given your son's—, well, I'm sorry. Of course, I won't write anything if you don't want it to be published."

"Thank you. I would appreciate that. And this event had been planned for months, and it was difficult to call off. It's a major fundraiser." Another forced smile, and a retreat to the table now filled with food.

Clara's mother had approached the two at the end of the conversation. "That's unusual. I've never encountered a woman of her status who wouldn't want publicity to help raise funds. And it is strange that they went forward with the event, given her son's death."

Clara nodded. "Yes, I agree. I don't understand why I was invited if she doesn't want an article about the garden. And there's more. Apparently the previous gardener disappeared and they've made little effort to find him."

Clara noticed the flowers her mother was carrying. "What a beautiful little bouquet. The gift of flowers doesn't match that woman's disposition. I hope she doesn't accuse us of stealing them."

Her mother smiled. "Oh, I don't think so. She doesn't like reporters, but that doesn't mean she's a vile woman." Her mother laughed. "Let's go get something to eat. Is Marjorie here yet?"

"I don't know. With her wedding coming up so soon, maybe she decided not to come. We might have to find another ride home, or call a taxi. By the way, I tried to get a look inside but was stopped. I only got to see the living room when I was here last week."

"I bet the home is lovely with lots of antique furniture."

They joined the line for food just as Marjorie appeared, without Ed. They waved and she joined them in line. "Sorry I'm so late. My caterer had some last-minute questions. Trying to do this wedding in such a short period has been difficult. Ed is dealing with it so won't be joining us. I've always enjoyed this garden."

Mrs. Wilson asked Marjorie, "Do you know these people?"

"Oh, yes. I went to school with their son, Hiram. I don't see him here though. But I think he might be a bit of a disappointment to the family. He didn't want to go to college, like his brother, and he was always getting into trouble. Nothing serious. I think they assumed he'd grow out of it. I haven't seen him recently but the last I heard he was living off his family's allowance and didn't have a job."

"Marjorie, dear, how are you? Welcome, did you just get here?" Mrs. Dobberson hugged Marjorie and ignored Clara and her mother. "Do join us. I'm so excited for you and plan to be at your wedding."

Marjorie smiled. "Thanks. Have you met my friends, Clara and Mrs. Wilson?"

Mrs. Dobberson said, "She's a reporter, you know, and I don't want any publicity."

Marjorie looked startled. "I'm sure she won't write a story if you don't want one. Right, Clara?"

"Of course. Let me reassure you I will not write a story about this event."

The woman sighed. "Well, then. Let's get some food and join the others at the tables. Almost all of the vegetables were picked from the garden fresh today, or prepared from vegetables we canned when in season."

Clara, her mother, and Marjorie followed the matriarch to the buffet table and helped themselves to the squash—the vegetable du jour—along with some cooked chicken followed by apple pie. It was a balmy late afternoon and once the tension was broken with their hostess, she was quite pleasant, albeit distant.

They were just finishing when a young man, who looked familiar to Clara, appeared. Marjorie jumped up to greet him but Mrs. Dobberson reached him first.

"May I have your attention, everyone? This is my son, Hiram."

Clara then recognized him as Hiram Dobberson, whom she and Ed had recently interviewed.

He waved to the group. "Hello, everyone. Please enjoy yourselves. We're pleased to see you all here today. You'll have to forgive me, but I have some business to do. I'll be back in a little bit." He turned to his mother and said something to her. She nodded.

Marjorie rejoined Clara and her mother. "I hope you're enjoying this. I thought it would be a pleasant evening for us, which is why I asked Mrs. Dobberson to send you an invitation."

Mrs. Wilson said, "I've had a wonderful time. I love exploring gardens. Thank you so much for including me. But I believe we are ready to go home."

"I'll meet you out front. Give me about five minutes. I'm not parked too close."

She left them clearing the table of the food and carrying it and dirty dishes to the kitchen door, where the man thanked them and reminded them of the location of the exit to the front of the house.

Still won't let me inside.

They rounded the corner to the street and were about to step onto the sidewalk when suddenly a burly man with a bandana over half of his face rushed at them and grabbed her mother's purse from Clara's wrist, pushed her down toward her mother so that both fell to the ground.

Clara yelled and tried to get up but heard her mother cry out, so she turned to help her. "Are you all right?"

"My purse! He took my purse!"

"I know. I'm sorry. I forgot I was carrying it. Normally I would have had my bag, but I just kept carrying yours after we got together. Oh, Mom, you're bleeding."

Someone came around the house just as Marjorie drove up. She stayed in the car, not realizing what had happened. Meanwhile the man from the kitchen helped them both up and asked, "What happened?"

Clara answered, "Someone stole my mother's purse. I was carrying it. They came out of the bushes. He had a bandana on. I couldn't stop him. We need to call the police."

"Oh, no, Miss. We can't do that. What will the Missus say?"

Marjorie, realizing the situation, joined the group. "But we have to. Surely she'll understand if there's a thief. Was it someone from the party?"

Clara shook her head. "No. He was big, heavy. I didn't notice anyone like him there. I can't identify him, Marjorie. He had a bandana over his face." She turned to her mother. "Did you have much money in your purse?"

"Maybe twenty dollars, but my license and identification for the college is in it."

Clara said, "We have to tell the police, so they can search for it. The thief will probably throw it away after he takes the cash."

The kitchen man said, "Please. Let me go tell her, and then I'll phone them. You both all right?"

Mrs. Wilson said, "I need to sit down."

Marjorie led her to the car and opened the door so she could sit. Clara also felt shaky, but wanted to stay standing to watch in case the thief returned. Barely five minutes passed when the matriarch joined them. She looked concerned and seemed frightened, instead of her previous stern self-assuredness. "Are you both all right?" She walked to Mrs. Wilson seated in the car.

Mrs. Wilson said, "Yes, I'm just shaken up. I do hope you'll understand why we must call the police. I need to get my purse back. I have identification. I know I won't get the money back, but it will help me to get the identification."

"Of course, you poor dear. I'm so sorry. Alfred is calling the police. They'll be here soon."

She walked slowly to Clara. "You won't put this in the paper, will you?"

Marjorie interrupted, "No, she won't but whoever monitors the police reports might. We'll do what we can to keep it out of the paper, but it isn't your fault, so no one should care."

"Yes, I know. Of course, you're right."

Just then a police car drove up behind Marjorie's car. An officer got out and joined the group. "What happened here?"

Clara took the lead and told the story. She admitted to the officer that they had little hope of recouping the cash, but if possible were hoping for the return of the purse with its identification cards. He took down their names, noted the address, and asked people who were filing out of the backyard of the house if they saw or heard anything. But no one had.

Clara said, "It happened so fast. I didn't get a chance to react."

The officer nodded. "Probably better that you didn't. He mighta hurt ya more. Is your mom gonna be all right?"

Marjorie said, "If not, we'll take her to a doctor. I think she's just shaken up."

"All right. Go home now. I can reach ya at your phone. If we find your purse, we'll let ya know."

Clara said, "Officer, many of us were departing from the party. I guess I'm curious why you think he picked us to rob?"

"Two women alone most likely. Easier than if there's a man. But, who knows? Mebbe he got here and saw ya, and he just did it."

"Of course. That makes sense, I guess. Please let us know if you find the purse."

He nodded and left. Clara thanked her hostess and joined her mother and Marjorie in the car. She said, "Well, that was quite an afternoon, all in all."

Clara patted her mother on the shoulder, but she was disturbed by the incident more than she let on. It was just by chance that she was carrying her mother's purse. What if she hadn't forgotten her bag? What if she'd had her bag and the thief had taken it along with the statue she prized as the inspiration for her story?

Chapter 12

The next morning both Clara and her mother felt their bruises. Mr. Wilson ordered both of them to stay home and rest. Clara studied her mother, noticing several bruises on her face and arm, which caused her concern. She couldn't leave her, and felt responsible for her pain, since she'd invited her to the garden party.

She told her father, "I'll stay home with her. I can phone people for interviews and then phone in my stories."

Mrs. Wilson said, "Didn't you promise not to write about last night's incident?"

"Yes, I did. And I won't. But if my editor hears about it, I won't have much choice. I'll let our hostess know if that should happen. In the meantime, I'm working on other articles."

"All right. I'll stay home. I must admit that I don't feel up to teaching today."

Her husband said, "I'll call them and let them know that you need to rest."

Clara watched as her mother shuffled back toward the bedroom, stooped over and wincing. She hurried to help her and supported her into the room. After she'd put her in bed, she asked, "Can I get you something for breakfast? Coffee? Toast?"

Her mother smiled. "That would be nice."

She joined her father in the kitchen. He'd just hung up from talking to the community college. "They're going to see if one of the other teachers can take her classes today. I said I didn't know when she'd be back."

"Dad, something about last night is really bothering me—and not just the robbery."

"Tell me. But I promise you if I get my hands on whoever did this to your mother, I won't be merciful."

"I know. It's hard to see her like that. I think I've always thought of her as, well, indestructible."

He reached out and hugged her. "None of us is indestructible. Especially these days. But tell me what bothered you about last night."

"There were several things. First of all, why didn't the Dobbersons cancel the event? Everyone would have understood that the death of a son surely qualified as a good reason. Mrs. Dobberson said it was too late—and that it was a major fundraiser. But the garden wasn't at its best.

"And Mr. Lowry, the gardener, was new and couldn't answer questions other than being concerned that his uncle, the previous gardener, had disappeared. He didn't seem to care about the garden at all. And if they didn't want publicity, why was I invited? And, I know Mom and I were alone with no male escort, but why would a thief try to rob us outside the house where people are coming and going?"

"Do you think that the thief had something to do with the family?"

"Well, I don't know. But that doesn't explain the other issues. I've been trying to think about why someone would go after Mom or me."

"It sounds like your reporter instincts are working overtime. I need to go. We can discuss it more tonight. You'll stay with your mom all day, right? And don't go outside."

"Yes. I need to call my editor right now to see if he needs me. Ed's not available. As you know, the wedding is soon. But I can do interviews and writing from here."

"By the way, how's Gene? Have you seen him lately?"

"I've been busy, but I understand he's more mobile. We're hoping he'll be back at work full time any day now. I should call him, too. Thanks, Dad."

"For what?"

"Mostly for listening."

"Look after your mother today. I'll be home for the weekend so you can help with the wedding, but today I really need to get to work."

He gave her a peck on the cheek and left Clara standing in the kitchen wishing he didn't have to leave. The previous evening's robbery had shaken her up more than she realized. It didn't feel good to be alone protecting her mother.

She picked up the phone and called the office. Without revealing too much about the previous evening, she said she needed to care for her mother. However, she had a story regarding a sideline of the murder trial that she needed to read over the phone to someone. And if she was needed, she could pursue other stories using the phone.

"That's okay. Gene is here today—for a half day. Read your story to him. He can take it from there. Hold on. I'll get him."

Clara pulled her bag out with her notes and prepared to read him her brief story about one of the neighbors who had helped discover the body of the missing friend of Jack London who'd been murdered. She explained to Gene about the story and then read it to him. He made a few suggestions she agreed to, then said, "Tell me something about this man. Did you learn anything personal about him?"

"Actually, I tried but he wasn't forthcoming. He seemed to really care for the victim, and I think it was difficult for him to talk about it. He was in a hurry, anxious to get away. I felt sorry for him, so I didn't press too hard."

Gene was silent.

"Gene, are you there?"

"Yes. Good job, Clara. You've come a long way."

Clara was taken aback. Gene had never said anything positive to her about her work. She was surprised and pleased and not sure what to say. Finally, she uttered, "Thank you." And then to cover her lack of poise she asked, "Will you be going to the wedding?"

"Yes, and I'll be at the rehearsal, so I'll see you there if not here at the office. I definitely feel up to it, but still need to take it easy. By the way, why aren't you coming in today?"

"Oh, my mother fell, and I need to stay with her. Dad had to go to work."

"I hope she's all right."

"Me, too. I've never seen her like this. She's bruised and, well, that's why I'm staying home. If I need to get her to a doctor, I can call a taxi, but we didn't want to leave her alone."

"Have you had any progress finding the owner of your statue?"

"Not much, but I'd like to discuss an incident with you that happened at an event yesterday. I don't think it has anything to do with the statue, but it was somewhat peculiar."

"Can you do a phone interview with one of the high school students from the production of *Arsenic and Old Lace*?"

"Sure. Do you need me to track down the phone number?"

"Actually, could you get in touch with the faculty director? They already sent us photos, so a phone interview should be sufficient."

"Will do. Thanks, Gene. Take care of yourself. See you tomorrow."

Clara hung up feeling rejuvenated and not understanding why. From their first meeting, she and Gene spoke only whatever they needed to communicate about work. Perhaps his beating by the escaped convict turned him into a more conversational co-worker. On the other hand, she'd been more considerate of him following his injuries. Maybe she had changed, and he was responding to her.

She looked at her notes from their conversation and asked the operator for the faculty number at Santa Rosa High School. When she reached the school secretary, she asked for the faculty advisor of the play and, after explaining her circumstance of needing to stay home with her mother, left her number.

She heard her mother in the next room and hurried to reach her. "Are you all right?"

"Yes. It's just a little difficult walking." She smiled. "It's nice to spend some time with you, Clara. We always seem so busy we don't get much quiet time together. Of course, you are growing up, that's for certain." She smiled.

Clara felt guilty although not sure why. "I seem to have drifted away. I want so much to write a best-selling novel. It's most of what I think about when I'm not working. Although I'm enjoying writing articles for the paper. It's so much more rewarding than fact-checking."

Her mother smiled. "I understand. You'll get there."

The phone interrupted their conversation. Clara answered and was pleased to respond to the faculty director. She spent ten minutes learning about the play, why she'd chosen it, and who the leads were—jotting notes as quickly and accurately as possible while holding the handset of the phone. The faculty advisor provided information about the photos so Clara could pass it on to Gene.

She thanked the woman and turned to find that her mother had gone back to bed.

She went back to thinking about the mystery of the statue. Still unanswered was why the clerk at the Knick Knack store had lied about knowing Dobberson.

And what if there really was no story attached to the statue?

But, if there was no story, why was it buried in a forest where few people would visit? It must mean something.

The phone interrupted her again. She was surprised when the caller identified herself as Mrs. Dobberson.

"Is this Clara? I was calling to see how your mother is doing."

"Thank you. She's resting, and I'm here with her. I think she'll be fine. How's your son doing?"

"My son? Oh, Hiram, He's fine. He's helping Marjorie today get ready for the wedding."

"Oh, that's kind of him. She had to rush preparations when Ed got drafted. Will he be at the rehearsal?"

"Yes, I believe so. Will you be there?"

"Yes. I'm a bridesmaid."

"Did the police find your mother's purse?"

"No, not that I'm aware of. They haven't telephoned if they did."

"Well, let's hope it turns up. Bye now."

"Thanks for calling."

Clara was not good at casual conversation, and was sure that the woman had called her strictly because it was the appropriate thing to do, because her conversation was also stilted.

She spent the next half hour writing the interview of the faculty member about the upcoming drama production. She looked forward to calling Gene and giving it to him. Unfortunately, he was out when she called. She read the story and the photo captions over the phone to a typist.

Then she went back to her reflecting about the statue—her so-called inspiration— and her novel. The gardener, Mr. Lowry, had said that the family had accused his uncle of stealing things. Would it be possible that the statue was part of what he stole? If so, wouldn't Hiram have identified it? However, everyone she'd contacted said the statue was not valuable, so it was unlikely.

The story of the Lowry's missing uncle was intriguing Clara. She now doubted that it had anything to do with the statue. However, it was too interesting not to follow up. She wrote down everything she remembered about the conversation with Lowry. She was eager to research more about the family where he worked, about him, and whatever was stolen. Did they report the theft to the police? If so, could she get a list?

She turned to the page in her mother's notepad where she'd placed Lowry's number and called it. However, when she asked for him, the woman at the other end said that he wasn't home. She didn't expect him for another week, but, yes, she'd tell him that Clara called. Or, she recommended that Clara might want to try to reach him on the following Saturday. Clara left her name, address, and number, and thanked the woman.

She'd just hung up when Marjorie called. "Are you and your mother all right?"

"I'm in better shape than Mom. I stayed home with her. She didn't go to work."

"Hiram is here helping me this morning. He wanted to know all about you. Apparently you made quite an impression."

"Really?"

"Well, maybe it was his mother who was impressed. Anyway, I'm glad you're all right. You're coming to the rehearsal, right?"

"Yes, I wouldn't miss it. And I'm so happy that Gene is coming."

"I am, too, and so is Ed. I so wish we could somehow stretch the next week to last forever."

"When does Ed have to check in?"

"A week after the ceremony. He thought he had more time, but he doesn't."

Clara didn't know what to say.

"Thanks, Clara. I'll see you tomorrow. Tell your mother not to worry. I've got plenty of help."

Clara hung up, wishing she could have said something more comforting. She slammed down her book of notes and shook her head. Then she checked on her mother, returned to her chair, and started to read today's paper willing herself to be productive in order to shake off her despondency.

Chapter 13

Clara was surprised at how moving she found the wedding. She'd always envisioned herself as a single person dedicated to becoming a best-selling author. It never occurred to her that she'd appreciate or become involved in a wedding ceremony that would touch her. However, seeing Marjorie and Ed say their vows and knowing that their future was jeopardized by war left her feeling first tearful and then numb. She surprised Gene by noticing his expression, which reflected how she felt.

She and Gene followed the bride and groom to the reception area. Gene made an emotional speech in which he tried to provide some humor, but the room was filled with a lull given the circumstances. Nonetheless, when it came time for a dance the bride and groom looked joyous and encouraged others to join. Gene invited Clara and they pirouetted around the floor as if they'd always been paired to do so.

Clara saw her mother and father get up to leave and motioned to Gene, who led her over to them. "Are you feeling all right?"

Her mother nodded. "Yes, but I'm tired. I think everything is under control. Marjorie's parents are still here, and the food has been served. I'll see you at home."

Her father nodded.

"All right. See you later. I'll stay around in case Marjorie needs something. They're going to change before going to the Madrona for a few days."

Her father responded, "Call me when you're ready to come home. I'll come back and pick you up."

Just then Mrs. Dobberson and Hiram joined them. "Oh, I do hope you're feeling all right," said Mrs. Dobberson. "I've been so worried."

Clara's mother said, "Yes, I'm doing fine."

Hiram asked, "Did you get your purse back?"

"No, not yet. I hope they find it, but I'm prepared to get new identification cards if necessary. Goodbye now."

Clara watched her parents leave and turned when Mrs. Dobberson asked, "I understand you're trying to reach my gardener, is that correct?"

Clara was surprised that the woman was aware of this. She wasn't sure what to say. "Yes, that's right."

"Why, may I ask?"

"Oh, well, I was interested in learning more about the disappearance of his uncle and his possible theft of some items missing from your house."

"Oh, I see. Well, we're not sure where Mr. Lowry's uncle is. He left us without informing us. And as for the missing items, they're not missing. We found them moved to a different room.."

Clara gulped. "Oh. I'm curious, did Mr. Lowry complain that I called him?"

"No, his mother called the house and explained that someone was looking for him, and gave me your name when I asked."

"Okay. Well, I'm sorry to have bothered you."

"Oh, no bother at all, so long as you don't write a story about us. I'm glad to see that your mother is all right."

Clara noticed that Gene was holding onto a chair and looked pale. "Are you okay?"

"No, I need to go home."

"Sit down. I'll call my dad." She placed the call hoping that her parents had had time to reach home and was relieved when her father answered. She explained the situation quickly, and her father responded that he was on his way back. "Does Gene need to go to a doctor?"

"I don't know."

"I'll be right there. Look after him."

Clara turned to Gene and helped him sit. She looked for some water, and found a decanter and poured a cup for him, then hurried back. She handed him the water and said, "My dad's on the way. Do you need to see a doctor?"

"No, I just overdid it today. I'll be all right."

"Would it be better if you stayed at our house overnight? We have a spare sofa."

"Maybe. Let's see how I feel once your father arrives. Now tell me about your call to Mrs. Dobberson's gardener. Did it have something to do with your statue?"

Clara smiled. "No, I don't think so.." She told him about the missing gardener and missing stolen items that had been found.

Gene's face had gotten even whiter. Her father walked in just as Clara was looking for someone to help. The two of them got on either side of him and half-carried him out to her father's car. He sank into the seat and closed his eyes.

"Dad, I think we should take him to our house and let him sleep on the sofa. I'd give him my bed but it's upstairs."

"Agreed. Gene, how do you feel? We're going to take you to our house. If you think you need a doctor, let us know."

"No, I just need to rest. Oh, and Mr. Wilson, your daughter is starting to have the makings of a good reporter."

Clara wasn't sure if that was a good or bad thing.

Chapter 14

Clara just finished preparing an egg breakfast for Gene and her parents when the phone rang. She was surprised to hear Hiram Dobberson greet her. "I hope I'm not bothering you. I was wondering if you had any luck tracking down the owner of that statue you found."

Clara thought this a strange question since they'd just talked about it the day before at the wedding. "No, I haven't. But I'm still trying to locate other people whose name begins with 'Dobber.' So far, you're the only local one."

"Well, I might be able to help you there. I have two Dobberson cousins who live nearby. I doubt that they know anything about it. However, I was curious if there's any other writing on it, like maybe a date to give us a clue about its origin."

"I don't know. Hold on a minute. I'll get it and look at it more closely." She put the phone down and ran upstairs to her room to retrieve the statute, and hurried back to the phone. On her way she told Gene, "It's Mr. Hiram Dobberson. He's calling to see if there's a date on the statute or some other kind of identification besides a partial name."

Gene shook his head. "I don't recall seeing anything, but let's check it out." He picked up the statue and started examining it closely while Clara returned to the phone.

"We're examining it now. Gene Walker, a reporter from my paper and a friend of Ed's, is here at the moment. We're working on a story." Clara wasn't sure why she added the last sentence about working on a story. She just didn't want

Dobberson to think she and Gene were, well, together or anything.

Gene said, "Well, I don't know if this is a date, but there is a number on it: 252."

Clara repeated the number to Dobberson who responded, "I'm not sure what that might mean—maybe the number of statues manufactured. Does it appear hollow? I was thinking maybe it was Chinese, and they might have smuggled heroin or something into the country in it."

Clara said, "Oh, that would be an interesting story, but it's awfully heavy, so I doubt it's hollow. What do you think, Gene? Could it be hollow?"

Gene shook his head.

"Nope," Clara said.

"Oh, well. I thought I'd give it a try." He gave her the names of his two cousins who lived in the area and their phone numbers and suggested she check to see if they might be the former owners. "But I doubt it. Also, I checked myself with the Knick Knack store and they claim they've never seen anything like it, but I'd recommend speaking to the owner of the store rather than the clerk. She's new to the store, but the owner used to run it herself, before she hired her."

"That's a great idea. Thank you."

She hung up just as her parents appeared, so she didn't have time to wonder why Hiram Dobberson was suddenly so helpful. She pointed to the toast on the table which she'd set, and prepared eggs for them.

Her mother was still limping, but she'd definitely improved. "Who was that on the phone?"

Clara said, "Oh, you won't believe it, but it was Hiram Dobberson who, as you know, I originally tracked down as a possible owner of the cow statue. He seems to have become interested in helping me identify the owner. He had some suggestions. He seems as eager as I am to find out who owns it. I think maybe he's trying to deter me from looking into the theft at their home."

Mr. Wilson asked Gene, "If you're ready to go home, I can take you this morning on my way to work."

Clara interrupted, "Actually, can you drop both of us off at the office?"

Gene said, "Yes, I feel much better, and we both have stories to finish. There should be a verdict today on the murder trial."

Mr. Wilson nodded. "The murder trial? Oh, that's the caretaker of the owner of the farm who used to be a friend of Jack London. He's got to be guilty. I mean, cashing checks that he forged while the poor man was missing—and probably dead."

Gene nodded. "It certainly looks like he's guilty, but there's no definite proof."

Clara said, "I wonder if he had anything to do with the statue?"

Her father shook his head. "That's really reaching. If you'd found it on the victim's farm, that might be relevant. But you found it near Jack London's old home. What has the suspect got to do with that location?"

Gene said, "And who would know? The old guy was probably the last person around who knew London."

"But London's wife is still around. She was much younger. She might know something. How stupid of me. I checked with the curator, but I should have also asked her. I'll track her down and send her a letter."

Gene shook his head. Her father and mother just rolled their eyes.

"I know. I'm being obsessive about this. But something's making me do it." She grinned.

Her parents finished eating, and Clara did a quick cleanup. They were just ready to leave when someone knocked. Her father answered the door, and both Clara and her mother jumped when they saw who it was.

Clara said, "Hi, Mr. Lowry. Come in. Dad, it's all right. We know him."

Lowry said, "No, I can't stay. I'm getting back to you" He stepped inside, but continued to look around outside. "Here's a list of all the things that were stolen from the Dobbersons. You asked for it when you called. Please don't tell any of the Dobberson family that I gave it to you. I'm not sure what they'd do to me, but there's more going on in that house than I want to know."

Clara took the handwritten list and glanced at it, wanting to learn more. "How did you get the list?"

"My uncle left it in his bedroom. I found it in one of his books. Look, I gotta go now." He opened the door and again scanned outside, then ran out and down the street leaving Clara holding the list, and Gene and her parents staring after him.

Her father was the first to speak. "Well, are you all ready to go? I need to get to work."

Gene said, "I'm ready. Thanks for the loan of the clothes, Mr. Wilson."

Clara said, "Hold on. I need to get my bag, and I'm taking the statue today. Maybe I'll get a chance to go to the Knick Knack store and track down the owner. Dobberson suggested she might know more about the statue."

She ignored the "tsk tsks" from her mother and the shaking heads of her father and Gene, and ran upstairs to grab her bag. Her inspiration was calling her.

Chapter 15

Using a borrowed car from their editor, Clara and Gene were headed to the Victory Lunch restaurant. This was the first time she'd been there since her bike had been demolished.

She was uneasy about returning, but it was convenient. "I sure hope things go better this time than the last time we visited."

Gene said, "Oh. I forgot. We can go somewhere else."

"No, there isn't time. And what are the chances that the same thing could happen again?"

They entered the restaurant and sat at the counter. The smell of cooking hamburgers called to Clara, and she ordered without hesitation with Gene requesting the same. They both pulled out notes from a previous interview and were studying them when a middle-aged man dressed in a blue work shirt and khaki pants approached them.

"'Cuse, me, Miss. You here time ago? When bad men broke *bicicletta*?"

Clara said, "'*Bicicletta*', oh, yes, my bicycle, yes. Were you here?"

"*Sí*, I know those men. They bad men."

"Do you know their names?"

"*Sí*, I know. I tell you. You tell *policía*. I no get involved. But you get them."

Gene interrupted. "If you know who they are, you must tell the *policía*."

The man shook his head leaving no doubt he would not speak to the *policía*.

Clara said, "All right, tell me their names, and I'll tell the police without involving you."

The man pointed to Clara's notebook and pencil. "I write."

She nodded and handed him the pencil and notebook and watched as he slowly printed two names. "You take to *policía* but no tell where you hear." He smiled, and hurried out the door. Gene got up and followed him, but he disappeared around the corner before Gene could catch up. He returned to the counter as their hamburgers arrived, and greedily began enjoying his.

Gene said, "We'll go to the police station after we eat. I need to check on the bastard who beat me up and stole my car. They called to let me know they might have a lead. We can give them these names as well."

"But how reliable do you think that poor man is? I mean, he could hardly speak English. Why does he know the names of the two guys who attacked me here?"

"I don't know but we'll let the '*policía*' figure it out. This hamburger sure tastes great. I'm happy that the Victory Lunch is able to get enough meat to keep us in hamburgers. We might want to write a story on how they do it."

They finished lunch and drove to the police station uneasy about what they would encounter. Clara did not recognize the officer on duty. Her friend Fred was not there. However, the duty officer helped them as soon as they entered, and was eager to check out the names of the two who'd attacked her at the restaurant, especially when Clara reminded him that one was the burglar from The White House store.

He checked his records and came back to them, shaking his head as if he'd discovered something he couldn't quite believe. He looked at them and said, "You're not going to believe this."

Gene asked, "What?"

He looked at Gene. "One of these names is related to the convict that beat *you* up."

Gene grabbed the paper with the names from the clerk's hand. "What? Let me see that. I don't believe it. Yes, this is the name of the convict who beat me up."

Clara shook her head. "How is that possible? You mean the thief I saw robbing The White House, and the guys who attacked us at the restaurant, and the escaped convict are all connected?"

The officer nodded. "That's exactly what I mean. Where did you get these names? We need to talk to them for more details."

Clara shook her head, "I don't know how to reach him. He approached us at the restaurant and offered the names. He hardly spoke much English. I know a little Spanish."

The officer said, "We need to find him. He's probably scared for his life."

Gene said, "Can't blame him."

The officer nodded. "Agreed. But this is the first lead we've had on these guys. Can you wait here while I check with the detective on this? He might want to get in touch with the County sheriff."

They both nodded. While they waited, neither spoke. Clara was recalling the night she encountered the thief outside The White House and then later at the restaurant. She assumed that Gene was remembering the horrific beating he took when he went to interview the wife of the escaped convict. They were not pleasant memories.

The officer returned leading a stocky balding man in a suit with an eager but cautious expression that caught the attention of both Clara and Gene. He did not introduce himself, but simply said, "Tell me how you got these names."

Clara told him about the man at Victory Lunch and how they were related to the attack outside the restaurant and the department store robbery. Then Gene filled in how he'd been beaten up while attempting to interview the convict's wife and had his car stolen.

The officer said, "I just connected the names to these two here on this list that the Mexican wrote."

The detective pursed his lips, leaned on the counter, and said nothing. He then stood. "I need to follow up on this. You both should stay clear of either of these crooks, and don't go back to that restaurant unless you hear from me. We might want to track down the Mexican."

Gene said, "I don't suppose there's any chance you've recovered my car?"

"Not that I know of." He turned to the officer. "Any cars been found in the past day or two?"

"I'll check." He turned away toward a stack of papers, which he pawed through until he came to a group he started to read page by page. "Nope. Nothing that looks like yours."

Clara saw Gene's disappointment and felt his pain. She recalled again how hard he'd saved for it—forgoing such necessities as heat for his one room, new clothes, and using the bus or walking for most of his early interviews. She reached out and touched his arm and was rewarded when he didn't pull away.

"We need to go, Gene. Deadline."

The detective was already reviewing other pages he'd uncovered on a desk. The officer nodded at them. "We've got your phone numbers. We'll call you if anything comes up. Be careful. If these bums are together and they realize you're connected, well, they might come after you. Try not to be out alone at midnight again, Miss."

Chapter 16

Clara had forgotten about the list of stolen items from the Dobberson home Lowry had given her. She was preoccupied with assigned stories that she and Gene had divided between themselves. The murder trial of the man being tried for killing Jack London's friend was coming to an end, and one of them had to cover the verdict. The US Government had just announced the latest "freezes" including forty percent of the nation's butter to add to that of rubber, radio and typewriter production among others. And, the Army was having a parade down Fourth Street to rally home spirit.

So, it was easy to have forgotten Lowry's list of the items stolen from the Dobberson house, supposedly by his uncle.

Gene said, "You take the Army parade and I'll cover the trial verdict. Whoever finishes first can get the latest list together from the Feds."

Clara would have preferred handling the trial, but Gene was the senior reporter and she realized he would do a better job at pulling together an article. She pushed the Lowry list back into her bag and headed downtown to cover the Army parade.

She hoped to finish her coverage in time to get to the meeting in Sonoma of the League of American Pen Women, who were hosting artists, writers and musicians living or visiting in Sonoma County. She had befriended the president of the League in a previous meeting while she was gathering facts about the organization for an article that Ed wrote. The woman had welcomed her to the local chapter of the national organization whose membership included First Lady Eleanor

Roosevelt and encouraged her to continue writing. She was aware that Clara had been recognized by the Los Angeles chapter of the group for her outstanding writing as a high school student.

Although Clara was eager to explore opportunities for her novel, she also considered the meeting an opportunity to inquire of more artists about the statue.

She showed up for the parade an hour in advance of start time and was able to interview the sergeant in charge along with several Santa Rosa young men and families who were there to watch. She touched base with the photographer who got photos of all her interviewees and gave him their names. She had to stay for the entire parade in case anything happened, sitting on a bench and writing her story, so she could be ready to meet with a member of the League to catch a ride with her to the town of Sonoma for the meeting.

When she finished writing, she looked up to see the men marching by in step together shouldering rifles. It seemed to Clara they were too young to be giving up their lives, but their faces wore expressions of pride and willingness. She welcomed their emotion and tried to capture it, but all she felt was sadness and an emptiness wondering how many of them would return.

Suddenly, there was a break in the lines as a new group entered the parade. Clara stared at one of the onlookers across the road from her. Was it the thief she saw rob The White House store who later destroyed her bike? Or was she just seeing him everywhere now that he was in the forefront of her mind? She searched for the photographer, but he was not nearby. When she looked back at the possible thief, she was surprised to see Hiram Dobberson talking to the man she believed might be the thief. They didn't notice her, and just then the ranks closed in the parade, and she couldn't see them any more—nor could they see her.

Was that really Hiram? What was he doing talking to a known criminal? And who was the other man talking to them? And why would they be attending a public parade?

She could not get across the road to check out what she'd seen, and by the time there was an opening, neither of them was in sight. In their place was a family of six who were waving flags. Clara searched the crowd but did not locate them. Her stomach felt heavy, and she now wondered if they'd seen her. She again searched the crowd, and waved at the photographer who was bringing up the end of the parade. They got together, and he drove them back to the newspaper office where she filed her story.

She searched for Gene at the office but could not find him. He would understand her anxiety.

She was interrupted by the receptionist who let her know that she had a visitor, Hedda Johnson. Clara ran to the lobby carrying her bag with the statue.

She greeted Hedda, who she'd met at a previous writers' gathering. Hedda had offered to drive her to the Pen Women's meeting. "Hello, I'm ready to go. Thank you for coming here to pick me up."

The young woman who Clara estimated to be her own age smiled. "I'm happy to have someone to ride with me. And I have directions to the home where we're having the meeting. It should be easy to find. It's a home facing the Sonoma town square."

"Oh, good. The last meeting was here in Santa Rosa."

"I was hoping my boyfriend would be able to join us, but he had to go out of town on business. I think you might know him, Hiram Dobberson? I believe I saw you at their garden party, but I couldn't get to you. I was helping out."

Clara wasn't sure how to react other than first feeling confused, and then uneasy at the coincidence of meeting a friend of Hiram's. Was she stalking Clara to make sure the reporter didn't pursue a story about the missing items at the Dobberson house?

"Oh, Hiram wasn't going to go to the meeting. He had some business or something in Sonoma, and wanted the ride. But it would have been nice to have him along."

Clara recovered enough to say, "I didn't see you at the garden party. Have you known Hiram long?"

"Oh, yes. We went to school together. I knew Marjorie Baker, too. I believe she's also a friend of yours?"

"Yes. I didn't see you at the wedding, either."

"No. I was out of town visiting my brother in Sacramento. His wife just had a baby."

Clara decided it was time to change the subject. "Do you know Mr. Lowry, the gardener?"

"No, I knew his uncle. Sad case."

"Do you believe he stole the things that are missing?"

Hedda shook her head. "You know, I never did believe it. Of course, it turned out that nothing was actually stolen. But he certainly seems to have disappeared, and none of us knows where he's gone. Oh, I think we're here. I hope I can find a parking place nearby."

Hedda found a parking spot not too far from the home of the head of the local chapter of the Pen Women League. Although carrying her bag with the heavy statue weighed her down, Clara found it an easy walk.

The first half hour of the meeting was a social; people mixed together to get to know one another. Clara used the time to show several artists the statue, but no one recognized it. She had almost given up when a young writer queried her about why she was seeking information.

"I found it and am looking for its owner to uncover its story."

"I see." The young woman looked puzzled and moved on to the next person.

The chapter president walked to the front of the room where a dais had been placed, but a loud conversation between two women erupted from the rear of the room. "You can't just take away a citizen's rights and incarcerate him!"

"It's not incarceration. They're living well and have everything given to them."

"What? They had but a few days to sell everything and pack a single suitcase to take with them!"

"They sneaked up on us at Pearl Harbor. How do we know they won't attack again. It's safer for us and them that they be somewhere we can watch them."

"Excuse me, excuse me," the chapter president interrupted. "It's time for our meeting to begin. If everyone will gather around, we'll have a short business meeting, then discuss our literary and art projects, and we'll finish with a number of selections to be played by their composer. As everyone here should know, we've been around as a national organization "linking creative women" since 1897. So, I want to be sure that all of our different creative arts are represented."

Clara, however, was more interested in reaching out to the two women who were arguing about the relocation camps. She didn't want to take sides on the argument—she'd been terrified like most Americans when the Japanese surprised the country by bombing Pearl Harbor. On the other hand, she knew several Japanese American families in Ventura before she moved to Santa Rosa who were every bit as American as she was. She'd tried to track one of her friends down, but could not locate her and assumed she'd been sent to the Manzanar relocation center in south eastern California. She'd given up trying to find her.

She inched her way over to the two combatants and reached them just as the business meeting ended. The young author, who had earlier questioned her about the statute without much interest in Clara's response, was reading a poem, followed by an artist showing paintings of the ocean and beach, and wood carver and sculptor pointing to their pieces. Finally, it was time for the pianist to play her compositions. Clara made sure she was standing close to the two she wanted to meet so that they would have to speak to her.

When the music ended, she approached them and said, "Excuse me. I couldn't help but hear you talking about the relocation camps. Could I ask you to look at a statue?" She pulled it out of her bag. "I've been trying to track down the owner of this piece with little luck, and a friend suggested that maybe a local Japanese farmer might have buried it. Does it look familiar?"

The woman who'd argued that the relocation camps were a violation of the Japanese American citizens' rights said, "What? Relocation? Don't you mean internment? Why do you think it belongs to a Japanese farmer?"

"Well, no one else has claimed it."

"It looks like a piece of junk anyway."

"Oh, are you an artist?"

"No, I'm sorry. I didn't mean to be rude. I'm just very emotional about this topic. It doesn't look Japanese. Where did you find it?"

"Over in the Jack London park in the woods. Do you know how I could approach the people in the camp and which camp is the closest here?"

"Well, I'm not sure that would help. They didn't get sent necessarily to the camp closest to their homes, but I suppose either Manzanar in Southern California or Tule Lake up north would be the closest." She studied Clara a few seconds before saying, "And I have no idea how you'd get hold of anyone. I guess you'd just go there and see if they'd let you in."

Her friend laughed. "Not likely. They're dangerous spies."

Clara felt the need to defend her friend from Ventura. "Oh, my friends from Ventura were hardly spies. They really loved being Americans."

"That's what they'd have you think. But look how sneaky they were to bomb Pearl Harbor."

The chapter president reached them just as the argument was heating up again. She said quietly but firmly, "Please. That's enough. We're here to celebrate art and women's creativity. Both of you stop your arguing."

Clara pulled out the statue again. "Oh, I'm sorry. It's my fault. I was hoping to find the owner of this statute and thought maybe it might have belonged to someone who'd been relocated. I was just asking if it's possible to maybe go to a camp and ask them."

The president shook her head. "That's probably naïve thinking. Furthermore, it doesn't look valuable or particularly artistic—just a friendly cow. Why bother?"

"Well, I'm a writer, you see. I want to discover its story for inspiration, you know. Surely, as a creative woman, you could appreciate that."

Out of the corner of her eye, Clara noticed three women breaking off from the group and going into another room. Most of the group members were gathering their books or art pieces and going outside. Clara asked the president, "Are we finished for tonight?"

"Yes."

"Thank you. As you know, I'm writing for the Santa Rosa paper and would appreciate a list of the artists so I spell their names correctly."

"Of course." She pulled a sheet of paper out of a folder with names typed on them. "Here you are. And I've included the titles of the compositions played by the composer. You won't include anything about that argument, will you?"

"No, of course not. Thank you for the list."

Clara looked around for Hedda and found her approaching the door to outside. She felt satisfied that the trip had been interesting and worthwhile. She planned to pursue writing about the relocation or internment camps, if her editor would allow it, so she would need further research, and that would give her the opportunity to ask about the statue. Also, it was interesting that Hiram Dobberson had a girlfriend—and one who quickly offered to reinforce the Dobberson claim that the robbery did not exist implying that Clara should drop the story.

All in all, an invigorating meeting.

Chapter 17

Clara had put off long enough examining Lowry's list of stolen items. It was time. She'd submitted her story on the Pen Women's meeting and was caught up with all of her other articles. She was sitting in the press room waiting for Gene, so had some time to work on a possible story about the Lowry disappearance and possible theft.

The list of stolen goods included seven printed items in large, all-capital letters with annotations on several of them. The first was an oil painting of several blooming red crepe myrtle trees labeled, "McDonald Ave." The artist's name was included. She didn't recognize the name. Second, was a statue of a Dobberson ancestor. Clara shook her head at that one. Why would anyone other than the family want it?

Third was a crystal vase. Fourth, a tapestry that had been hanging in the dining room. Fifth, a photograph album of old photos from Dobberson family trips. Sixth, two silver candlesticks. And, finally, a copy of Charles Dickens' *A Christmas Carol.*

Clara read and re-read the list. What would Lowry's uncle want with any of those items? Further, who, other than the family, would want them? She needed to talk to Lowry or Dobberson. Other than maybe the silver candlesticks, surely there wasn't anything of significant value among the stolen items.

She was mulling over the list when Gene entered. "Why so pensive?"

"I was checking out Lowry's list of stolen items from the Dobberson house—if they were indeed stolen. There's

98

nothing of high value. I don't understand why these things were chosen, and I also can't comprehend why they'd fire an excellent gardener rather just asking him to return the stuff. And why not rehire him when the items were discovered."

Looking at the list, Gene shook his head. "I agree. Maybe the gardener was unwilling to confess—or maybe he didn't steal anything. Maybe he disappeared for other reasons. Are you ready to go home?"

"Yes, thanks. I appreciate the lift."

They headed out to Gene's borrowed car. Clara asked, "Have you heard anything from the police about your car?"

"No, I've given up. I guess I'll just have to save and buy a new one, which won't be easy with all the war restrictions and shortages."

"I know. I haven't been able to find a new bicycle even. I've been riding an old one from one of my dad's friends, since mine couldn't be fixed. But I have a question. I'd almost forgotten about this. Do you happen to know how or if I could see people at one of the relocation camps to ask any of them if they lost the statue?"

"What?! Clara, you need to give up on the statue. You can write a fictional story about it if it's that important, but you're wasting time and effort trying to track down its owner. Now isn't the time to be searching for the story of a mediocre piece of art. And, no, I think it highly unlikely that you could visit anyone at a relocation camp. And who would you talk to out of the thousands there."

"I know. You're probably right."

"I am?"

"Yes, but I'm also interested in the relocation camps. I had good friends in Ventura who were Japanese American. I'd like to write their story."

"That's not a good idea. You could be accused of sedition."

Clara said, "That's why I thought I'd use the statue."

"Let's focus on one story at a time. What are you going to do about Lowry's list?"

"I don't know. I've been trying to reach him for a couple of days. I'll call again."

When they arrived at Clara's home, she was surprised to see Hedda sitting on the porch.

Gene asked, "Who's that?"

"She's Hiram Dobberson's girlfriend who drove me to the Pen Women meeting. I wonder what she wants? Maybe I left something in her car. Thanks for the ride. See you tomorrow."

Clara got out of the car and waved to Hedda. "Hi. Did I leave something in your car?"

Hedda got up and walked to Clara. "No, no. I was wondering if you'd been successful figuring out how to visit any of the relocation camps or if you found an owner to your metal statue."

Clara opened the door. "Come in. The answer is 'no' to both questions. Did you happen to figure out a way?"

"Oh, no. I just wondered, and then Hiram asked me so I thought I'd stop by—I was going by here. And hoping we could get together for dinner or something."

Clara was surprised. The two had little in common. Hedda appeared to be from a wealthy old Santa Rosa family. Clara wasn't, although she was close with Marjorie. But she responded, "Of course. I guess my parents aren't home yet. My mother teaches at the junior college and my dad is helping manage an oil project in Petaluma."

"I see. Where did you find the statue? I'm not sure I ever heard the story."

"Oh. I was visiting the Jack London park over in Glen Ellen and walking in the forest and there it was. It seemed to call out to me, and I've adopted it as sort of my muse—or at least my inspiration. Remember—I want to be a writer, you see. But it can't be my inspiration until I uncover its story."

"What made you think it might be from a Japanese family?"

"I'm not sure. Maybe because it was buried in a forest. I haven't eliminated other options yet, but most of them haven't been successful. I have a question for you. I was reviewing a list of the items stolen from the Dobberson house and none of them seemed too valuable. Why did they fire the gardener? Was there more to it than just a robbery?"

"Where did you get a list of the stolen items?"

Uh oh. I shouldn't have mentioned that.

"Well, I'm a reporter so I can get things like that."

"Why? Are you writing a story about it? I was told you'd promised not to write any stories."

Clara was annoyed at the woman's bullying and retorted, "I said I wouldn't write about the garden party or the theft that caused my mother's injuries. I wasn't aware of this earlier theft at the time, but I won't write about it if the family doesn't want it public."

"Well, you better not publish it. Hiram wouldn't like that."

"Did you say you'd like to have dinner somewhere?"

"No. But I'm warning you. And stop trying to find the owner of that statue. You shouldn't be trying to see Japanese families anyway. You'll just get them or yourself in trouble."

Clara was flabbergasted. This Hedda was so different from the Hedda whom she'd befriended at the Pen Women's League meeting. Her eyes were wide open and her mouth curled when she threatened Clara. "I think you'd better leave." Clara opened the front door.

Hedda shoved her way through the front door.

What was that about?

The phone rang pulling Clara away from the confrontation with Hedda. She answered, "Hello?"

"This is the police. We're lookin' for Gene Walker. You're a friend, right?"

Clara hesitated. She didn't recognize the voice. But then she probably didn't know every policeman at the station. She said, "Yes."

The voice enunciated each word slowly. "We think we discovered his car—although it might have disappeared again, but we're not able to reach him. His phone seems to have been disconnected. Do you think you could get hold of him and let him know?"

"I'm not sure. I'd have to get a taxi. Does it have to be tonight?"

"Yes, ma'am."

Clara knew how important Gene's car was to him. "All right. I'll get word to him somehow. This is at the Santa Rosa city police station?"

"That's right."

"We'll be there as soon as possible."

She called the taxi company, gave them her address, and then left a note for her parents. The ride to Gene's house took about fifteen minutes, but by then it was dark. She asked the cab driver to wait, but he had another call, so she paid him and ran up to Gene's door and knocked loudly. She glanced through a window. His room looked dark. She pulled out her notebook and left him a message to call the police regarding his car. She pushed it into the crack in the doorframe and turned to leave when someone grabbed her and pushed her down to the sidewalk.

She wasn't sure what was happening but knew she needed to free herself from the arm smothering her. When she looked down, she saw a foot in a dirty brown leather shoe. She gathered all the strength she could into her free leg and stomped the foot as hard as she could, breaking free.

"Hey, what's going on here?"

She recognized the voice. "Gene, help me!"

But the arm was gone and she felt herself falling.

"Clara, what are you doing here? Who was that?" He helped her up. "You're shaking. Of course, you are." He unlocked the door.

Clara shook her head. "I don't know. I came to let you know they might have found your car. The police called and need to know right away if it's your car so they can hold the guy who was driving it."

"Why didn't they call? I've only been gone for a short time. I've been here most of the day."

"They said they did. But something's wrong with your phone."

He helped her inside. "We'll need to report this to the police anyway."

He poured her a glass of water and then picked up the phone. "Operator, has this number been in service this evening?"

He listened to the response and then continued, "All right. Would you get me the police—"

Clara interrupted, "At the Santa Rosa station—not the Sheriff's."

"At the Santa Rosa station. Thanks."

"Hi, this is Gene Walker. Were you trying to reach me tonight?" He listened. "No? You didn't find my car?" He shook his head.

"Then we need to report an attempted mugging. My friend Clara Wilson received a phone call at her house from someone claiming to be the police." He finished repeating what Clara had told him. "Yes, she's all right, but this sounds like she was targeted. Someone planned to attack her. Well, can you send someone out right away? He could still be around here." He gave the police his address, then hung up.

He turned to Clara. "It was all a ruse to get you out of the house. I got a call earlier about a possible robbery at the Victory Lunch restaurant. When I got there, the restaurant was closed. My god. They must have lured me away to get you here alone. Do you think they were planning to attack both of us?"

Clara was still shaking. She said, "I don't know what's going on. You remember the woman you saw on my parents' porch when you dropped me off?"

"Yes. You said she was Hiram Dobberson's girlfriend."

"Well, I let her in, thinking she wanted to become friends, but then she turned on me and threatened me after I said I was investigating the robbery at the Dobberson house and to see if I could talk to a Japanese at one of the camps."

"She threatened you?"

"Yes. I had to almost push her out of the house. Then the phone rang and that was the call about your car. You mean that call was a fake?"

Gene nodded. "So, this is either about the stolen goods from the Dobberson house or about the statue. I find it hard to believe it's about a lost statue."

Clara said, "I bet Hiram himself stole those things and doesn't want his mother to find out."

"More to the point, he doesn't want YOU to find out."

A loud knock interrupted their conversation. Gene asked, "Who's there?"

"Police."

He opened the door to a uniformed officer. "We've looked around all the nearby streets, and didn't see anyone suspicious, although it's hard to say. Are ya both all right? Neither of ya was harmed?"

Clara answered, "No, but he tried to force me to go with him. I was lucky that Gene showed up when he did."

"And to add to the story, I was lured away by a phone call that turned out to be a false lead. So, we don't know if this was about both of us or just a way to get Clara."

"Are you sure you don't want to get checked out?"

Clara responded. "No, I'm fine, really. But I wish I could understand why it happened."

Gene asked, "How did you get here?"

"Oh, I came in a taxi."

The officer made some notes. "Ya said ya got a call at your house from someone claiming to be a policeman asking ya to come here because they couldn't reach Mr. Walker on the phone?"

"That's correct."

"Can you identify the man who accosted you?"

"No. I didn't see him. I can tell you he was taller than me by at least a foot."

Gene added, "But he wasn't big—just tall with dark hair. I only saw him from the back."

Clara said, "And he wore dirty brown leather shoes— that's how I got him to let me go. I stomped on his foot."

The policeman nodded. "Good for you. I'll report this tonight, but you should both go into the station tomorrow and tell them everything you can remember. Get a paper and pencil right now and write down anything you remember. We'll cruise around here for a little while. Do you need a ride home?"

Clara nodded, "Yes, that would be helpful."

"We'll pick you up in fifteen minutes."

"Thank you."

"And, Mr. Walker, be sure to lock your door. We'll continue to drive by every hour or so, but we can't stay outside your house all night."

After they'd gone, Clara turned to Gene and said, "What should we do? Is it too late to call the Lowry house?"

"I think that can wait. Let's plan what we're going to do. None of this makes sense. Why would the Dobberson family care if you wrote a story about the robbery? And why would your friend threaten you about it? And why did the Dobbersons report the theft and then retract it?"

Clara nodded. "Good questions. You know what else doesn't make sense? Why did Hedda care so much that I was going to go to one of the camps to identify the statue? She was almost as upset about that as she was about the stolen stuff."

All of a sudden, Clara yearned for Gene to hold her. She swallowed and then coughed to fight off the temptation.

Gene jumped up for more water. "Here, drink this. That should help your cough. Are you sure you're all right? That man really was leaning on you hard. He didn't choke you, did he?"

"Thanks for the water. No, he didn't choke me. Do we have any details to add to our report?"

"No. It was too dark to see much of him, and I was more concerned about you."

Clara smiled. "Thanks."

The officer returned to take Clara home. She told Gene, "I'll call you when I get there so we both know each other is all right. Then we can decide tomorrow when to go to the police station."

He nodded and watched her open the door. She greeted the policeman, said good night to Gene, and got into the back of the patrol car. She hoped her parents wouldn't panic when they saw her being dropped off by a police car.

Chapter 18

Clara and Gene finished at the police station before noon. The same detective who was working on Gene's stolen car case took their statement. "I'm glad to see ya weren't hurt. But ya need to be careful. Ya musta done something to make someone mad, cuz this was planned—out to get ya. Be thinking about who that might be and what ya done to 'em."

When they got outside, Gene stopped her. "Why didn't you tell them about your friend threatening you?"

"Because I don't believe she had anything to do with this. And I want to continue to check it out myself."

"I know you're starting to think of yourself as an investigative reporter, but that kind of thinking could get you hurt—or worse."

"Oh, for heaven's sake, the Dobbersons aren't spies or anything. They're just trying to protect their reputation."

"Maybe. But I think we should pay the family a visit."

Clara nodded. "Also, I left another message for Mr. Lowry. This time the woman promised to make him call me back."

"What number did you leave for a call-back?"

"The office number for reporters."

"I'll drop you off there now. I have to get to the courthouse. The final verdict and punishment are due today in the murder trial. If the defendant is found guilty, the jury has to decide whether to give him life imprisonment or the gas chamber."

"I'll pick up anything else that comes in. I wonder what his wife and children will do if he's found guilty. They'll have to move out of the house, of course. But the poor family."

"Yes, you're right. We'll need to cover them, too." He started to leave and then turned back. "Clara, be careful. Don't go anywhere alone."

She nodded, the impressions from the previous night's encounter still fresh. "I'll be careful, but the first chance we get, let's go to the Dobberson house to interview them, especially Hiram."

"All right. But promise me you won't go there alone."

"I promise."

Gene studied her. "I wish I could believe you." Then he was gone.

Clara pulled out a short article she was writing about the latest war rations, and typed up her notes into coherent sentences, then took it down to her editor. She returned to her desk—or what was currently her desk—and rifled through a pile of news stories to see if any needed more research. She was getting ready to add some background facts she'd gathered from county sources to one of them when the phone rang.

She answered and was pleased to hear Lowry's voice. "Hello, Mr. Lowry. Thank you for getting back to me."

"You need to stop snoopin' around for the stolen stuff. They don't want anyone looking for them."

"But what about your uncle? Don't you want to clear him?"

"He had nothin' to do with taking them. You're just makin' it worse for him."

"I appreciate your predicament, but I don't understand why the Dobbersons are so upset about this?"

"That's just it. They're not upset any more. Just drop it."

"Did Hiram take them and they just don't want it known that he's a thief?"

"Lady, just drop it. You're right. It's not a big theft. You're only making things worse. I should never have given you that list. I just didn't know."

"You didn't know what? I'm sorry if I've gotten you into trouble."

"Well, you did. I got fired. You hear that? You got me fired. Now drop it so I can get my job back."

"Oh, I'm so sorry that you got fired. Is there anything I could do to help you get rehired."

"Yeah. Knock off your snoopin'!"

"Mr. Lowry, do you know Hedda Johnson?"

"I don't think so."

"She's Hiram's girlfriend."

"I don't know her. I don't know much about the family." He hesitated, then said, "I'm not saying nothin' more. You got my message. Just stop this. I gotta go now."

He hung up leaving Clara with more questions than before. Why did he say he didn't know Hedda? Surely that wasn't a secret. Hedda certainly was open about the relationship. Why would Lowry deny it? He would obviously know the couple if he was around the house.

And why was he so frightened about her investigation? She'd barely started it. All she'd done was mention the list to Hedda without further exploration. She'd never mentioned it to the police or to her editor—just to Gene. She'd barely glanced at the list and only enough to believe it was not a list full of valuables.

Maybe one or more of the objects had something secret hidden in them, and the family didn't want it known.

And maybe her desire to create a story was overcoming her common sense.

Regardless, Lowry's and Hedda's insistence that she stop "investigating" only encouraged Clara to move forward.

Chapter 19

Clara was disappointed with her trip to the Army office that regulated the relocation camps. She hoped to at least be given a procedure to follow in order to visit any of the camps or Tule Lake specifically. However, the answer was "*no.*" And no exceptions. Being a reporter writing a story was not enough of a reason. She needed more information in order to have the "correct" reason to get in.

Or, she could show up at the gates at Tule Lake and plead her case. However, the relocation center was almost four hundred miles away, and that was a long trip to make if she couldn't get in.

In the meantime, the man accused of murdering and burying Jack London's friend and his dog on the grounds of his home had been found guilty. But the jury still had to decide punishment: life in prison or the gas chamber. Gene was covering the decision which was scheduled to be final that day.

She pulled her used bike—a gift from a friend of her father's— up onto Marjorie's front porch. Ed was due to leave for training that evening. She wanted to say good-bye but didn't plan to stay long, knowing Marjorie and he would want as much time together as possible.

She knocked and waited. She was getting ready to leave when Ed answered the door.

"Hi, Ed. I don't need to come in. I wanted to say goodbye. I'll miss you—especially your editing my prose." She made her best effort to smile.

"No, come on in. Marjorie will appreciate seeing you." He held the door open for her.

Marjorie was curled up on a chair in the small living room of her home. Clara ambled over to her, trying to think of what to say. However, no words came to her when she saw Marjorie's puffy eyes and wet cheeks.

"Hi, Marjorie. I just came to—"

"I know. To say goodbye. Go ahead."

Ed said, "Listen, Marjorie. I think it would be a good idea if Clara spent tonight with you."

"I'm glad to do it, Marjorie. I can be here as soon as Ed leaves."

"Sure. Why not?"

"Okay. I'll go away now and come back." She turned to Ed and hugged him. "Take care of yourself."

He nodded. "You, too. Let me know if you ever track down the story about your statue."

Clara nodded and left—with cheeks as wet as Marjorie's. She lugged her bicycle off the porch and started toward the Dobberson house. Although she was not in the mood, she'd promised herself she would visit the house and interview Hiram or his mother about the robbery. She didn't want to give them advance notice, so she was just going to show up.

She was pulling up to their house when she spotted Hiram and someone get into a car parked in front. She diverted her direction and managed to get behind a truck parked next door. Hiram's companion got in the passenger side before Clara could study him, but he looked like the thief she'd seen at the department store.

She waited for them to leave and then pedaled to the front of the Dobberson house, walked up to the door, and rang their bell. She didn't have long to wait. The man she'd met in the kitchen during the garden party opened the door and said, "You. What are you doing here?"

"I want to see Mrs. Dobberson, please."

"Sorry. She's not here."

"I don't believe you."

"Quite frankly I don't care if you believe me. Leave us alone."

"All right. But I want to understand about the items that were stolen. The police said they never received a report about them."

"It was all a misunderstanding. We have the items. They were not stolen. Now leave us alone." He slammed the door.

Back on her bicycle, Clara headed toward the police station. Given the door man's reaction, she decided to check it out. However, when she arrived—even after explaining who she was—they refused to show her the report.

"Can you at least tell me if there was a report of stolen items from the Dobberson house?"

"No. The Dobbersons explained it was an error."

"Thanks. So they did file a report and then took it back, which confirms what they're saying."

The clerk asked, "Is there anything else?"

"No, thanks. No reason to write about it, I guess."

Clara headed back to the newspaper office to finish some small stories about local club meetings. She was surprised to find her editor, Stu, in the reporters' room rifling through papers on their desk.

"Where've you been? I need your stories."

"Sorry. I have them all ready." She pulled them from her bag and handed them over."

"Did you cause trouble at the Pen Women's League meeting?"

"Me? No. There was a ruckus between two women arguing about relocation camps, but I had nothing to do with it."

"Well, I got a message from the League president that someone named Hedda Johnson complained that you caused a problem."

Clara started to shake in disbelief then anger at what appeared to be an attempt to smear her reputation by someone she thought was a friend. "What? Not true. That's a lie. Hedda has a problem with me over something else. She was my ride to the meeting, but she thinks I'm interfering with a personal situation. That's rather nasty of her to take it to you."

"What was the relocation camp argument about?" Stu seemed interested.

"One woman said it was an infringement of the rights of American citizens even if their ancestors were from Japan. And the other said, well, that given Pearl Harbor all Japanese are sneaky."

"What do you think?"

"I had some good friends in high school in Ventura of Japanese ancestry. They were as American as anyone I know."

"Draft me an editorial on the two sides and bring it to me as soon as you've finished. It'll go out under my name if it gets printed, so you won't be risking yourself. I'll have to run it by the owner of the paper."

"What? Really? Would you be interested in a story about them?"

"About whom?"

"I was hoping to track down a Japanese most likely at Tule Lake, but I got a blunt "no way" from the Army about visiting."

"Write the editorial for me, and we'll go from there."

He left the room with Clara bewildered. Their newspaper was just a local paper. He was risking his job and the paper by printing an editorial opposing a wartime policy. But she spent the next two hours drafting a two-paragraph editorial that she hoped presented both sides of the issue.

She was getting ready to walk to the editor's office with her copy, when the phone buzzed. It was Stu. "Where's Gene?"

"I don't know. He was working on the trial story."

"I need his story. I hear they didn't give the murderer the death penalty, only life. I need his copy now."

"All right. I finished the editorial. I'll bring it to you first. Then I'll try to track down Gene."

She called Gene at home. When there was no answer, she grabbed her bag and the editorial, and rushed into Stu's office, dropped it on his desk and hurried out to her bicycle. She decided she'd start at the courthouse, which is where he'd have been to cover the trial. She wasn't sure where she'd go after that. Maybe to his apartment.

She parked her bike and ran inside the courthouse. She tracked down the sentencing courtroom, it was empty. She looked for the bailiff or a guard and found the latter standing outside the door.

"Excuse me, have you seen Gene Walker? He's the reporter who—"

"I know who he is. He left right after the sentencing—he and another reporter."

"Another reporter?"

"Well, I assumed it was another reporter. They looked chummy, although the other fella looked kinda scruffy."

"Can you describe him?"

"Not too tall. Kind of straggly long hair. Not too clean, neither."

"Did you see which way they went?"

"Nope. Reporters have special parking spaces out back."

"Yes, I know. I'll go check. Thanks."

She headed outside and ran to the back of the courthouse. She looked for Gene's borrowed car, but did not see it. The press spots were all empty. She got back on her bike and pedaled as fast as she could to his apartment. But when she pounded on his door, no one answered. And she didn't see his borrowed car parked anywhere around.

Where else could he be? Maybe at the police station. She got back on her bike and again pedaled at top speed. But again, no Gene. The officer on duty asked her if he was missing.

"Yes and no. We're not sure. But he was supposed to have handed in a story earlier today, and he hasn't. And I can't find him at home or anywhere he might be."

"Is he the reporter that got beat up by that escaped convict?"

Clara nodded. "Yes, and he lost his car."

"Well, maybe that's where he went. There was a report that they found the bum and had him surrounded out at the racetrack in one of the buildings there. Mebbe he went out there to see about his car or somethin'."

"Oh, no. I hope he doesn't get hurt again. I bet you're right."

"Now, don't ya go out there and get yourself hurt. I'll radio the detectives there and tell 'em to keep a lookout for him."

"Thanks." Exhausted from her ten miles of accelerated bicycling, Clara pedaled a more reasonable speed back to the newspaper. She stopped by Stu's office first and let him know what she'd discovered. Then she went to the news office and

116

asked if anyone had heard from Gene. All she got were blank stares and shaking heads.

Stu followed her and told her to confirm the verdict, which she did with a quick phone call. The paper could then print the story under a large headline with details to follow.

However, Clara was more concerned about Gene. Where was he? Was he actually out at the racetrack trying to help capture the convict who'd almost killed him? And who was the man who left the courthouse with him?

Oh, no.

Clara realized that it was time for her to get to Marjorie. Ed would have left by now, and Clara promised not to leave her friend alone. She called her parents to let them know she would be staying with Marjorie all night. Then she left a note on Stu's desk with Marjorie's phone number in case he needed to reach her. Feeling somewhat helpless, discouraged, and exhausted, she got back on her bicycle and pedaled as hard as she could to get to Marjorie's house.

When she arrived, she knocked on the door and waited for an answer without a response. "Marjorie, it's Clara! I'm sorry I'm late. Let me in." She pounded again on the door.

Finally, Marjorie let her in. "He's gone, Clara." And she turned and sat down on the sofa showing little life, her face without emotion. She sat motionless, staring straight ahead, hands folded in her lap.

Clara looked for some water and managed to get her friend to drink some. But she remained still with no expression or movement. She didn't even react when the phone rang.

Clara answered. "Clara, it's Ed. I had to call to be sure you're there. Don't tell her it's me. One goodbye was hard enough. Take care of her. She'll be all right, eventually. But look after her."

"I will. Sorry I was late."

They hung up. Clara stared at Marjorie, her best— perhaps her only friend—in Santa Rosa. At that moment, she hated the Germans, the Japanese, and Hitler and all his soldiers. How could she not? She put her arms around Marjorie and did her best to hold her. But the woman remained stiff and lifeless.

"Marjorie, I know it's hard, but Ed is strong and smart— and they'll train him well. He has so much going for him."

Eventually, Clara managed to get her to lie down on the sofa and covered her with a blanket. Then she sat and watched her finally fall asleep.

And where was Gene? Was he all right? Ed was gone to war, and Gene was missing. Marjorie was oblivious for the moment. Maybe that was best for her.

The phone rang again. Clara answered. "Hello?"

Her mother responded. "How is she?"

"Not good. But at least she's asleep. She hasn't said much since I arrived. And I was

late, which didn't help. But Gene's missing, and I bicycled all over trying to find him."

"What? Where is he?"

"That's the point. We don't know. He was supposed to file a story on the trial and he didn't. I tracked him down to the courthouse. A guard said he left with someone, and then an officer at the police station said he might be out at the racetrack. Apparently they've cornered the escaped convict who beat him up and stole his car."

She heard her mother explaining what she'd just told her, and soon her father was on the line. "Do the police know he's missing?"

"Not really. Because we aren't sure he *is* missing. He might be trying to help catch the guy. It's too far for me to try to get there on my bike. I let my boss know, so he'll take it from there."

"I'll drive out and see what's happening. You stay with Marjorie."

"Dad, be careful."

"I will. Don't worry. I'll just check it out to see if I can spot Gene. Do you know who he was with when he left the courthouse?"

"No. The guard thought it was another reporter, but he really didn't know. He said they seemed chummy."

"All right. I'm on my way. Stay by the phone."

Clara returned to Marjorie who seemed to be sleeping. She sat at a small table close to the phone, and pulled out her notebook to see if she needed to finish anything for the late deadline. She hadn't heard more from Stu about the proposed article on the relocation camps, and was feeling uneasy about even doing the research. She'd submitted all her "club" updates. She wasn't sure what to do about Gene's update to the trial—the sentencing was big news, but she'd have to re-interview the relevant sources.

She couldn't concentrate on any of her stories. She was uneasy about Gene and fearful for Marjorie. And it had started to rain, large drops and plenty of lightning. She hoped the thunder wouldn't wake her friend. The storm intensified her dark mood and made her restless. She started to pace, hoping that would settle her.

When the phone rang, it startled her and woke up Marjorie, even though Clara rushed to answer it before the second ring. "Hi, Clara. It's Stu. Have you heard anything?"

"No, nothing. My dad drove out to the racetrack to try to find him, but I haven't heard back. Anything from the police?"

"No. And this storm looks like it's gonna be a big one. The creeks and river were already high from the last one."

"Are you still at the office?"

"Yes. I'm calling the police every fifteen minutes. They said that's all right, but they'd try to get back to me as soon as they hear anything. Let me know if your father has any news."

"Will do."

She hung up and moved to Marjorie, willing her to go back to sleep. Clara stayed quiet, saw Marjorie blink and then close her eyes.

Whew.

Clara wondered what could have been so compelling that Gene drove to the racetrack. Only the return of his car would cause him to miss a serious deadline like the sentencing of a high-profile murderer. He was too much of a professional to simply blow a deadline.

She resumed pacing and was relieved (or anxious, she wasn't sure which) when the phone rang. She snatched it and whispered, "Hello?"

"Clara, it's your father. I drove around the racetrack several times and didn't see anyone. I did notice some parked cars, however."

"Weren't there any policemen there?"

"No. The place was deserted."

"Was there a blue Studebaker?"

"No. I didn't see Gene's car. I would have recognized it. How's Marjorie?"

"Sleeping."

"Maybe you should try to get some rest, too."

"I'm not sure I could. What could have happened to Gene? He'd never miss an important deadline like the sentencing. Something's wrong."

"It's up to the police now. Let go of it and get some sleep."

Clara hung up. She wasn't sure what to do next. She wasn't going to sleep. She needed to update Stu. He answered on the first ring. Clara said, "My dad says he saw no activity at the racetrack nor did he see Gene's car. I'm afraid something serious has happened to him."

"Agreed. Be prepared to re-trace his interviews first thing tomorrow morning. We'll put out a special edition. I've got his list of interviews. Show up here as early as you can. I'll get everything ready."

Clara had never handled a big story. She knew that Stu must have been desperate to ask her to cover it. Her concern for Gene minimized the pride she might have felt for receiving the responsibility. She said with little emotion, "All right. I'll be there as soon as I can."

The rain had not let up. If anything, it had increased along with the lightning and thunder. If it was raining this hard in the morning, Clara would have to arrange for transportation or risk running into flooding on her bicycle. Maybe it would be a good thing to divert Marjorie's mind if Clara were to ask her to drive her to the newspaper office.

Clara propped herself up in an easy chair and closed her eyes, but her mind was full of unanswered questions. And she was worried about Gene.

Chapter 20

Marjorie was more than willing to drive Clara wherever she needed to go. She'd slept most of the night—which Clara hadn't—and wanted to get out of the house and have something to do.

They left before seven the next morning and went directly to the newspaper office. Clara asked Marjorie to go with her. Stu greeted them looking as if he'd spent the night there—he was unshaven, his shirt was mussed and partially untucked, his suspenders were slipping, and he was in his stocking feet.

"Oh, sorry how I look. Give me a couple minutes to get myself together. You haven't heard anything, have you?"

Clara shook her head, and then introduced Marjorie. "She's agreed to drive me around at least part of the day."

"That will help. I'll be right back." He left them carrying some clothes and a razor.

Marjorie shook her head. "What does his wife think about him staying out all night?"

"As far as I know, Stu is single—unless you can call being married to a newspaper having a wife."

Marjorie smiled—a little.

Stu re-emerged and handed Clara a list. "Those are the interviews that Gene was going to do, but I don't know if he reached everyone. He's got phone numbers on there for some."

"I can track down phone numbers. I'll start with the district attorney and defense attorney. We definitely need a quote from them. When do you want something?"

"As soon as possible. It will be a one-page special. I'm pulling together previous articles to review the evidence and trial."

Clara sat down next to the phone and got out her notebook. She reached the district attorney's office first, quickly explained the problem, and asked to talk to the district attorney for a quote. Since he'd requested the death penalty, he was disappointed with the sentence. The defense attorney planned to appeal. Clara next called the wife of the convicted murderer who she'd learned was staying at a local hotel during the trial. She summoned up as much empathy as she could muster and gently asked the poor woman for her reaction to the life sentence. The wife and mother of nine wasn't sure how she would care for her children now without her husband.

Interviews complete, Clara typed the story and rushed it to Stu. It wasn't as good as Gene's, but she was satisfied that it would be enough for the start of an article. She waited for Stu's edits, and then asked if he needed more interviews.

"No, this is good for now. Gene was going to get comments from the jury, but I think this is enough." She started to leave. "Clara, good job, by the way." Then he went back to editing.

Clara returned to Marjorie in the reporters' room and was relieved to see her friend showing interest in reviewing the pile of possible stories on the desk.

Marjorie looked up and said, "Wow. You've got an interesting job! Did you see this one about another robbery at the Dobberson house?"

"What? No, I didn't." She grabbed the sheet of paper.

"It looks like some valuable objects were stolen."

Clara nodded. "I wonder what they'll say this time. You know, this is the second robbery they've had but didn't want to report. It looks like more of the son's artwork and more photos. That's still not particularly valuable stuff. I wonder why they reported it, given their previous lack of interest in getting the police involved."

"I don't know. Should we go check with them?"

Clara nodded. "Let me check with Stu before I leave the office. He might want me on standby."

But Stu said all right and told her to return by one that afternoon.

They left and drove directly to the Dobberson home in the continuing downpour. They ran from the car to the front door to avoid getting too wet, and rang the bell. The kitchen domestic opened the door and first saw Marjorie and smiled, but upon seeing Clara said, "You're not welcome here. I thought I made that clear."

Marjorie intervened, "We saw that you had another robbery."

Clara added, "Do you think Lowry committed this one, too?"

"I'm not at liberty to make any comment. Miss Marjorie, you are welcome to visit. But we'll not have that reporter here."

Clara was learning not to take rejection personally. But she had to try to get some kind of response. "Why would anyone steal a dead soldier's paintings? Surely you have some idea of what's going on here, and if not, why did you report the theft?"

"I did not report the theft. A new member of the staff did. It's not a theft. We simply moved some things around, like the paintings. We've corrected the statement to the police, so do not print anything. Good-bye."

And he closed the door. Marjorie looked at Clara and mimicked the man, "Goodbye."

Clara was happy to see remnants of the old Marjorie back and laughed heartily at her imitation. "We'd better get back to the car."

After they'd settled into Marjorie's two-door green Chevrolet, Marjorie asked, "Where to?"

"Let's go by Gene's house just in case for some reason he's there *incommunicado* and then head back to the newspaper."

"Sounds good." She choked and put the car in gear and drove them through puddles, thunder, lightning, and downpour to Gene's house. As they drove up, they saw another car pulling away from in front of his house.

Clara said, "Follow him."

Marjorie almost squealed. "Really? Let's go!"

Marjorie did her best to follow the car, but her windshield wipers were not good, and she had difficulty even seeing the car ahead of her, much less following it. "With all this rain, I can't even tell what color it is!" she said.

They lost it somewhere on Fourth Street, so decided to return to the office.

Clara said, "We don't even know if that car had anything to do with Gene."

"I know. But it was fun following it."

"Glad you enjoyed it."

"Thanks, Clara. It was good of you to stay with me last night, and I appreciate being involved today."

"You're welcome." She grinned. "I'm glad it's helping you, because it sure is helping me! By the way, Ed called last night to make sure that I was with you."

"Of course, he did."

Marjorie smiled, but tears were forming.

"Let's go see if Gene has checked into the office. And, if not, we're going to have to figure out a plan to search for him."

"Right!"

There were no messages from Gene when they returned to the office. But there was a report of flooding in the area. Clara gathered the pieces of information that were dribbled across her desk and wrote an article on the storm and the various sightings of flooding. She typed it up and rushed it to Stu.

When she got back to the reporters' room, Marjorie was reading a handwritten note. "Did you see this?"

Clara took it and read, "Flooding of Santa Rosa Creek near Fourth Street deposited debris—sighted are statuary, papers, books, bicycle, auto parts, and more."

Marjorie said, "Should we go see if there's a statue of a cow or anything similar to the one you found?"

"It's still pouring. We might get wet."

"So?"

Clara looked at Marjorie's eager face and realized her friend just wanted to keep busy. She let Stu know they were exploring a story about the flood. They'd return—if they didn't get washed into the Russian River.

"That's fine. This story you just gave me about the flood is good. If you can add anything, we can follow up tomorrow if you don't get it back in time for tonight's deadline."

Clara hung up and said to Marjorie, "Let's go." They grabbed their rain coats and Clara's notebook and pencils and marched to Marjorie's car full of purpose. Clara was pleased that her friend was almost euphoric about the danger they might be encountering. Also, she didn't believe they'd uncover anything of much value to add to the story. And she wasn't even sure they'd be able to find the so-called "debris."

But there was always a chance of finding a treasure! And the diversion seemed helpful to Marjorie.

They drove directly to Fourth Street and then to the Santa Rosa creek side. Pools of water stood in all of the roads, but seemed particularly deep as they drove further along the creek.

Clara said, "We shouldn't go farther. We might get stuck in the water."

"Where's your sense of adventure? You can write a story about this! Oh, look. There's some junk."

Clara saw a mound of silt filled with a variety of paper goods, auto parts, and, yes, some small statues. She began to absorb some of Marjorie's excitement.

Marjorie pulled the car over as close as she could to the pile, and they both got out—fighting wind and rain. They pushed their way to the main pile. Marjorie shouted over the storm's noise. "We need something to prod with! I might have something in the car." She returned to the vehicle.

Clara nudged at some of the silt with her foot, but nothing moved. The thick silt held firm.

Marjorie returned, carrying an umbrella. "We might ruin this, but I can always get a new one."

She poked at the section with the metal statue similar to Clara's cow. Clara stepped closer to it to help bring it out, but slipped and fell into the mud.

"Are you all right?" shouted Marjorie above the roaring wind.

Clara's previously injured ankle complained, but otherwise she felt no pain. However, she was covered with mud.

"Can you stand up?"

She tried but got sucked back into the silt. "At least let me see if I can get the statue while I'm down here."

Marjorie shouted, "All right. I'll push it toward you."

Clara shoved herself as best as she could to reach the metal object. Suddenly she felt herself being submerged as a wave of water poured over her from the creek. She gasped and tried to swim with it and keep her head above water, but the swirl grabbed her and carried her back toward the creek. She heard Marjorie screaming. The water ripped Clara out of the mud, while at the same time immersing her head. She felt like she was being torn apart.

She grabbed a branch, but it snapped free, so she let go. She could still hear Marjorie screaming. She managed to get her head above water and keep it there long enough to take a deep breath and get a view of her situation.

Not good.

A wave was advancing toward her and the mud continued to suck her down. She took another deep breath. As the water approached, she saw a heavy auto part that appeared immovable. She reached out and grasped it just as the water flowed over her.

It held as the water receded. She gasped for breath and used the object to pull herself back and took advantage of the water to jerk her feet from the mud. She shouted at Marjorie, "I'm over here."

"Hold on, Miss. We're getting a rope." Clara didn't recognize the voice but it sounded male.

Marjorie yelled, "We've got help. Hold on!"

Clara wasn't sure how long the heavy auto part would stay put. She got ready for the next wave while she waited for a lifeline. It seemed to take forever. The next wave hit her. She panicked as she felt her savior auto part start to shift.

She shouted, "Hurry up. I can't hold on much longer!"

A rope landed nearby, but not close enough for her to grab. She saw it disappear as it was pulled back. A second try got closer and she took a chance and let go of her object and pushed her way to the end of the rope. She managed to get hold of it just as the next wave hit her, but she held on tight.

She tightened her grip on the rope and as the wave subsided she felt herself being pulled ever so slowly. She wasn't sure where she was going, but she was glad to be heading away from the pile of silt and trash and the creek.

She felt arms around her and heard Marjorie crying, "Oh my god! Are you all right?"

"I'm all right. I don't think anything is broken."

A tall man with a beard, blazing eyes and carrying the rope approached them and said, "What in blazes wuz you misses doin' messin' with them floodwaters? You coulda got kilt."

Clara turned to him. "Thank you for saving my life. I don't think I could have held out much longer."

"Yer welcome."

"We were trying to get that metal statue." She pointed to it still stuck in a pile of trash beyond where she'd slipped. Somehow trying to explain about her muse didn't feel right.

"Why would ya want one of Smithie's old things?"

Marjorie and Clara both said, "What?!"

"Well, we call 'im Smithie. I cain't remember his real life name. He made a bunch of them things—sheep, cows, even made a goat. He thought mebbe people would want to buy'em. As I recollect, he ended up givin' most of 'em away."

Dripping wet and covered in silt, Clara asked, "Is he still around? Where does he live?"

"I don't know if he's still livin' but he used ta live on a farm up north of here. His wife was the breadwinner in that family. Believed she passed away though."

"Can't you remember his name or anything else about him? We'd really like to talk to him."

"Well, had somethin' ta do with a dog, mebbe. No, not a dog. But it started with a 'D'."

Clara smiled. "Could it have been Dobberson?"

"Yup. That's it! Not Dobberman but Dobberson. How'd ya know?"

"Part of the name is on the back of another statue I found. Did he ever have a shop, or how did he sell them?"

"Well, as I said, he didn't sell many of them—just peddled 'em in his car. He'd go place to place."

"When was this?"

"Oh, mebbe five years back."

Marjorie said, "We might be able to track him down by putting an ad in the paper."

"That's a great idea. Thank you, Mr., I'm sorry, what was your name?"

"I'm Charlie Bastien. I got a little farm a couple miles from here."

Clara said, "Could you wait a moment?" She limped to Marjorie's car and pulled out her bag and with cold shaking hands searched for some dollars, which she offered to him. "Please accept this as a small reward for helping us. I can't thank you enough."

"No, Miss, I couldn't 'cept nothin'. I'm just glad you be all right. You might want to check to be sure your car starts so's you can go home now."

Marjorie slushed her way to the car and choked and put it in gear. All three were relieved to hear the engine running. Clara got in, and they both waved to their life-saver, who was busy wrapping his rope in a coil on the way to his truck. Marjorie drove slowly through the flooded road.

Clara said, "I ruined your seat. I'll pay to have it cleaned. I'm sorry."

Marjorie laughed. "What an adventure! And we even got a great lead for your cow statue."

Clara was soaked throughout to her underwear, bruised on every part of her body and cold. She realized her shoes were gone—she'd been slushing her way through the water and mud in bare feet. But she, too, started to laugh. "Wow! That *was* quite an adventure. And you're right. We even got a lead to solve the mystery of the statue."

Regardless, Clara viewed the future with trepidation, partially influenced by Ed's tenuous life as a soldier, and heavily impacted by Gene's disappearance. She appreciated Marjorie's enthusiasm, but doubted her friend's exuberance.

Chapter 21

Clara and Marjorie informed Clara's parents about her near-drowning when they arrived home. However, Clara and Marjorie had both put on dry clothes and appeared fine by the time Mr. and Mrs. Wilson arrived. Clara's father said, "I hope you won't do something like that again."

Clara nodded in agreement. "No. It wasn't too smart, but we didn't appreciate how dangerous it was."

Her mother looked doubtful, but didn't pursue it.

Mrs. Wilson prepared a substantial dinner with chicken, fried egg plant, mashed potatoes, and apple pie for dessert. Whether it was their adventure or just plain hunger, both Marjorie and Clara ate double portions of everything.

The next morning Clara moved slowly as a result of the scrapes and bruises all over her body. Marjorie had spent the night with the Wilsons. Clara convinced her that she needed Marjorie's help. However, she simply wanted her friend to be surrounded by people. Both of them slept well—Clara in her bed and Marjorie on the sofa.

Before breakfast, Clara called Stu to see if he'd heard from Gene, but he had not. She let him know she'd be at the office within the next hour. No, she didn't believe there was a story about her trip to the flooded area.

She called the police, but they had not found any clues regarding Gene's whereabouts, and they had still not uncovered either his missing borrowed sedan or stolen Studebaker. They agreed with Clara that they should be concerned and had circulated a flyer with his photo, which they'd gotten from the newspaper.

Clara sat down for breakfast thankful that Marjorie was helping her mother. She didn't feel much like moving. But she did enjoy the pancakes. "I love it when we have company. We get pancakes. Marjorie's going to take me to work today, so you don't need to. It's still raining really hard."

Her father asked, "What's being done to find Gene?"

"Besides the police and the newspaper looking for him—not much. I don't know where else to look. I mean, if he's all right and simply on a story, he would have let us know. I'm afraid he's been hurt or maybe even kidnapped. And I don't know what to do about it."

With little emotion, her mother said, "You might check the hospitals."

Clara nodded. "Of course."

They all departed the house about the same time. Marjorie dropped Clara off at the newspaper office and said she'd come back to have lunch with her.

Clara nodded. "Meanwhile, I'll do whatever stories we need—and check nearby hospitals for Gene."

Clara walked, taking as few steps as possible and guarding any friction with her arm, which was scraped raw. When she finally reached her desk, she was out of breath and shaking. She sat on the hard-backed chair to calm herself and then called Stu to let him know she was in the office. Neither of them asked the other about Gene. They both assumed the other would mention if he'd been found.

Clara called several hospitals in Santa Rosa and surrounding towns with no luck. She asked both for Gene's name as well as any unknown victim. Then she rounded up some additional information about the flooding. Stu was handling national and international or war news. The night reporters and the wire service gave her some leads which she followed up: additions to the rationing list from the government, two more Japanese submarines sunk off the Coast by bombing planes; a train wreck in Petaluma.

Stu burst into her office with a pile of papers he handed her. "Here are some notes we found on Gene's desk. See what you can make of them. Maybe there's a clue about where he went."

Clara nodded, handed Stu the rewrites of her current articles, and delved into Gene's notes. She'd never noticed what a meticulous note taker he was. Each page included a title of the lead topic and the date followed by scribbles were separated by lines preceding each idea. She struggled to keep from worrying about Gene, so she could focus on the notes

She started to read the most recent one which was labeled: "Escaped Convict"—and dated a week ago.

Looks like recent escaped convict knew previous one who got me. Cousins?

Should check with wife of previous escapee to see if she's heard from either.

Police record.

Clara raced through the other lists barely noticing what they said. She speculated that the convict had something to do with Gene's disappearance. Why didn't the police realize this connection? Why didn't they mention it to her? Maybe Gene never got a chance to talk to them.

She called Fred at police headquarters and asked, "Was there a recent prison break by a convict related to the one who beat up Gene?"

"What? I don't think so. We'd know about it. But let me check both San Quentin and Folsom."

"Maybe not even local—maybe, I don't know, San Jose or down south."

"I'll let ya know. Why do ya ask?"

"I'm reading some notes Gene Walker left and he mentions that a recent escaped convict might be related to the one that got him. He made a note to check with the previous convict's wife to see if she knew anything."

"That's news to me. I'll let ya know if I find out anything."

"Thanks."

Clara hung up and walked to Stu's office, thinking of how a connection might have been made. Gene could have visited the wife and then gone to the trial. The wife could have alerted her husband who in turn sent someone to pick up Gene. But why would it matter if they were related?

She laid out what she'd discovered to Stu and saw him, too, questioning a connection. "Did you call the police?"

"Yes, they're checking to see if anyone related to the previous escapee also recently escaped from a prison somewhere in the area."

The editor shook his head. "We certainly seem to have a lot of prison escapes. Did you see the one last week where the guy killed a husband and wife for their car?"

Clara responded, "You don't suppose that could be the same one, do you? Oh, god, I hope not! But why would they feel threatened by Gene? He's not the police, and all the wife had to do was say she didn't know anyone."

"When you've been a reporter for a while, you'll know that people don't trust us. Neither do the police. I hate to ask you to do this, but could you please write the story of Gene's disappearance? For the front page."

"All right, but I'll refer to the previous convict with his name and include Gene's beating."

"Of course. We can't put it off any longer."

Clara trudged back to her desk, her scrapes and bruises yelling at her and depressing her further.

He can't be dead. He just can't be.

She spent the next hour working on the story about the disappearance of a fellow reporter—and, she realized—a friend. She thought it ironic that she had difficulty keeping her emotions out of the story—something that Gene had suggested she needed in order to add depth to her writing. But she did her best to simply describe the facts as she knew them. When it came time to include information about the second escaped convict, she hesitated. She didn't have any facts to back it up. She could simply state that among his notes was reference to another escaped convict.

The phone rang, causing her to jump. She'd been deep into the story. She answered and heard Fred, the police clerk. "You're right. I have his name, and he escaped a week ago from Folsom."

"Was he the one who killed the husband and wife?"

"Yes. They were from Vallejo. Probably no need to have killed them. This guy is more dangerous than the first one."

"Are they related?"

"I don't know. We're checking."

"Have you contacted the wife of the first escapee?"

"We sent a patrol car to her house. No phone. I'll let you know what we find out."

Fred called back within ten minutes to let Clara know that the police found the house deserted—no wife or kids.

Clara was reviewing her notes when Marjorie called, eager to tell her what she'd found. "I went to the library— they have so much information and are so helpful. I got the address of the blacksmith our rescuer told us about."

Clara asked for the address, which she wrote in her notebook. "I don't know if I'll have time to get to it today. I just wrote an article about Gene's disappearance. I'm really concerned."

"Of course you are. We all are. Have you heard anything helpful from the police?"

"No, the only new piece of information was a reference in Gene's notes about another escaped convict and that he might have been related to the one who beat Gene so badly. The police are trying to verify the relationship, but the convict's house is deserted."

"You don't suppose the wife joined him somewhere?"

"I don't know. The police are checking. That second convict that escaped killed the husband and wife driving the car that he stole."

"Oh, no."

"I need to get back to work. Thanks for the address of the blacksmith."

"Yes, I looked on a map and it's up in the mountains somewhere. Actually, I think it's near where that murdered friend of Jack London's used to live. When we go there, we might want to see if your dad or someone could go with us."

"No, my parents believe I'm being unreasonable about the statue. If you don't mind driving, we can check it out on our own. We'll be cautious about who we talk to and won't allow ourselves to get caught alone with anyone we don't trust."

"Sounds all right to me. Who knows what we'll find! I'm ready for another adventure!"

Clara sensed that Marjorie was a little too eager, but wanted to make the trip and needed her car for her to drive. "I'd still like to see if we could check out one of the relocation camps in case someone there buried the statue to dig up later."

"Let me know when you want to go the blacksmith's place. Saturday is best for me. I'm about to start back with my volunteer work with my fellow artists but my hours are flexible."

"I will."

Clara hung up, and sat staring at the wall, not sure what to do next. She noticed that she had not completed going through all of Gene's notes, mostly because he'd labeled the remainder as low priority. She picked up the packet and started pawing through them. None of the notes looked helpful—one about a new restaurant, another about a possible interview with the new president of the Chamber of Commerce, and a new book of interest.

However, one list did pique her interest: a list of addresses with no title about their relevance. Why would he simply have a list of addresses? She reviewed these carefully and checked references on pages before and after to see if they were mentioned. But it was nothing more than a list of addresses.

Then suddenly Clara sat up and pulled out her notebook. One of the addresses was the same as that of the blacksmith that Marjorie had just provided. Was Gene trying to help Clara track down the source of her metal statue? Otherwise, why would he have this address? If it was related to the convicts, it would have been on the page with the convict information. Why this particular address?

Clara wasn't sure what to do with this information. Nothing about the notation suggested it had high priority. Nor, for that matter, low priority. It was simply part of a list of addresses. And this list was less documented than his other notes. It had no date, nor was there any notation about which story the addresses referenced. It was simply a list of addresses without names.

Stu interrupted to ask for a story on the new Chamber of Commerce president and more details on the wine industry.

The Roosevelt administration had just ordered California's wine and brandy industry to turn over twenty percent of its copper stills for the nation's synthetic rubber industry. Given the increase in demand for California wines due to Hitler's invasion of France, Stu wanted to estimate the impact of this new edict on the California wine industry.

Clara spent the rest of the day gathering facts for a comprehensive article. She talked to the California Wine Institute who represented the more than one hundred California wineries. She also called several local wineries. Her heart wasn't in it. Due to all of the cutbacks, rations, even starting daylight savings time so there'd be more hours of daylight to support the war effort—all believed to benefit the country's need for supplies, which would help win the war. She wasn't sure it mattered what impact any of the sacrifices would make.

She finished typing her notes into a coherent article with quotes from local wineries and the Wine Institute and rushed to Stu's office. He wasn't in, so she left it on his desk and returned to her own to check other wires and articles from reporters that had arrived while she was working on the winery piece. She edited a couple of called-in stories, and then drafted a few brief articles on local social activities.

She gathered them and returned to Stu's office. He was on the phone and motioned to her to stay. He hung up and said, "Your winery story is good. Thanks. What are these?"

"I followed up on a couple of news items that came across my desk."

He glanced at them and nodded. "Good girl." He looked at her. "Any news about Gene?"

"No. The police didn't get back to me. And there's nothing in his notes to suggest where he might be—other than the possibility that he might have tangled with the most recently escaped convict."

Stu hesitated, then said. "I understand you want to be a writer."

Clara was surprised. Stu never talked about his employees' private lives. "Yes. I've always wanted to be a writer—for as long as I can remember."

"Me, too."

"Really?"

"Yep. Still plan on it, if this job doesn't eat me alive."

Clara wasn't sure what to say. "Have you written anything?"

"Uh, yes. I've written several short stories, and I'm almost finished with my first novel. So far no one has wanted to publish my short stories. You can imagine that I'm not anticipating a huge reaction to my novel. I understand you've won some prizes for a couple of your short stories."

"Yes. However, I really want to write a novel, but I can't quite focus on the topic."

One of the night reporters entered the office so Clara returned to her desk, not sure where her conversation with Stu was going about her goal to become a writer, but hoping they'd continue it. Several others were in the room typing their stories to meet the deadline. No one was talking.

Clara again reviewed Gene's notes but nothing new stood out. She was still thinking about Stu's comment that he wanted to be a writer. She had no idea. She'd always just thought of him as a boss.

The phone rang and she picked up the receiver. Several of the reporters in the room looked, but Clara let them know by shaking her head that it was for her—Fred was calling to let her know that the police had little new information. They'd checked with some relatives and friends of both convicts and sent officers to their locations, just in case the convicts were hiding with them.

"I saw your article in the paper today about your missing reporter. I hope we find him."

"Do you think the convict has him?"

"Unless ya got a better idea. It ain't usual for him to go away like this, is it?"

"No. Exactly the opposite. He's careful to keep his boss informed and after his last confrontation, he even kept me informed."

"And ya don't know of any relations we could check with?"

"No. He was private about his family."

"Sorry we don't have news about him. Sure don't need more bad news."

"No, we don't. Thanks for letting me know."

She hung up and decided it was fruitless to call Stu.

Where was Gene? Why had he disappeared? Was he safe but unable to contact them? And given the article published about him, why hadn't anyone come forward with information?

Chapter 22

Clara was waiting for Marjorie to pick her up. At first, they weren't going to tell Clara' parents where they were going so as not to worry them, but they decided not to deceive them. They were headed to the blacksmith's place to check out his metal statues to see if they could track down the owner of the cow statue. Although concerned, Clara's parents were learning to trust their daughter's instincts.

It was Saturday morning. The past few days revealed nothing new about Gene's whereabouts. The other stories she wrote meant little to her. She tried to care but she was preoccupied with the missing reporter. She hoped the trip to explore the source of her statue would temper her anxiety about Gene.

Since Marjorie was driving, Clara prepared some sandwiches and vegetables and nuts—anything she could find in the refrigerator. Her mother gave her bottles of water, and her dad told her to be careful.

Clara put her bag with the statue along with the food in the back seat and jumped into the front. "This will be a respite from all the trouble in the world and wondering about Gene and Ed."

Marjorie smiled. "I didn't know you thought about Gene that way."

"What way?"

"You know. You miss him. Like I miss Ed."

Clara gasped. "No, no, no! He's a fellow reporter who's missing. That's all. And it's depressing that someone could just disappear off the streets of Santa Rosa and no one has seen him. I certainly don't feel about him the same way you feel about Ed—I mean like marry him?! Oh my gosh, no."

"I think the lady does protest too much."

Clara rolled her eyes and shook her head. "No. Really. He's become a friend which is more than when we barely carried on a conversation a year ago. We got better when he was mending from the attack. And I felt sorry for him losing his car."

"All right. I won't mention it again. And I do hope we find him. Where did you tell your parents we're going?"

"I told them we were going for a drive to get away, but were also searching for the blacksmith. I mentioned a park in the mountains near where we're going. However, I didn't tell them there might be a connection between the convict and the blacksmith, because I'm not sure there is—just because Gene had the blacksmith's name in a list of addresses."

"That sounds plausible. By the way, have you heard anything more from the Dobberson family?"

"No, nothing since Hedda called my boss about me causing a ruckus at the Pen Women League meeting, which was not true."

"You know, I really think the Dobbersons are hiding something. And I've known them for a long time."

Clara nodded. "Me, too. Why are they so ambivalent about the stolen things? First, they report it stolen; then they deny they're stolen; then they ask police to keep it quiet. Why report it at all if they want to keep it quiet? And why did Hedda turn on me? We were friends one day and then she threatens me as if I'm her worst enemy."

"Do you think that those robberies could have anything to do with Gene's disappearance?"

"I hadn't connected them, but it's possible, I suppose. Although I can't picture Mrs. Dobberson holding him hostage.

She'd have to use her umbrella or something to hit him to keep him hidden." They both giggled at the thought of Mrs. Dobberson whacking someone with her umbrella.

Clara looked at the directions Marjorie had copied from a roadmap of California at the library. "I think we missed a turn. We should have come to the next road several miles ago. You need to turn around. How's our gas?"

"Doing okay. This will use up all my gas coupons for the month, however."

"My dad said he'd donate one of ours to you since you've been driving me around so much."

Marjorie turned around and they backtracked with Clara scanning the side roads for the missed turn.

"There it is. Turn right here."

"Really? This doesn't even look like a road. It's so narrow. How far do we go on this road?"

Clara studied Marjorie's written directions. "Looks like seven miles. Then we turn again." She continued to study the page. "You know, I'm uneasy about this. Something's nagging me."

"Like what?"

"Like why did Gene have this place listed? If he thought it was a source for my statue, he would have come to me with it."

"Why do you think he had it?"

"Is there room to pull over here?"

"Not really. But there's no cars coming. So out with it."

"What if this is one of the addresses he noted to check on for the escaped convict?"

"You're just thinking about that now?"

"Well, I nixed that option because Gene had organized notes about the convict and this wasn't with them. It was by itself."

"And what's made you change your mind?"

Clara fiddled with the directions and looked out the window and finally said, "My intuition?"

Marjorie shook her head and then laughed. "We came all this way and your intuition is just now acting up."

"No, I've been uneasy since we planned it. Let's just suppose the convict is here. He probably wouldn't show himself, and all that would happen is that we'd discover the creator of the statue. I could ask him the story of the cow, and we'd leave."

"Or, the convict could decide he needs our car, kill us, and throw us off a cliff."

"Well, yes, I suppose that could happen." Clara smiled.

"So, what do you propose?"

"How about if we drive up to the place and you stay in the car with your foot on the accelerator. I'll get out and call to someone. If no one appears, we'll leave. If someone appears, I'll pull out my cow statue and ask him if he's the one who made the statues. You stay in the car and be ready to pull away."

"That's silly."

"You got a better idea?"

"Yes. Let's turn around and go back to Santa Rosa and ask the police to investigate."

"But wouldn't you feel silly if someone official came up here and only a blacksmith lived here."

"I might feel silly, but I'd still be alive."

Silence.

Marjorie said, "All right. Let's try your plan. But I'll drive in, and while I'm turning around you call out if no one comes out to greet us."

"All right. That sounds safe."

Marjorie restarted the car and they continued on the road that began to climb abruptly up into the mountains.

Clara said, "We're about ten minutes away, I'd guess. Here's your next turn. This is the road that goes to the address."

"It's even narrower than the other one! I hope there's room to turn around at this place."

"Me, too. The bumps on this road are bad. I hope your car holds up. However, the redwoods are quite impressive."

"We won't be able to get out of here quickly. And I'm not enjoying the drop-off on my side of the road. I'm not feeling the picturesque part of it."

For the next few miles, both of them hold on to whatever they could reach to survive the bumps from the ruts and holes in the dirt road. They couldn't have turned around if they wanted to—the road was narrow and dropped off on one side to a steep hillside. Large redwoods faced either side of the road, creating a corridor that restricted movement.

Marjorie gripped the steering wheel. Clara discovered she was gritting her teeth. They crawled along without speaking for several miles until they reached a clearing with a barn that had a partially collapsed roof and a small, unpainted shack with boarded up windows and tall grass in front of the door.

Marjorie said, "Well, at least I can turn around there, but I don't look forward to the return trip. We probably don't need to worry about them needing my car. That one looks pretty nice." She pointed to a green four-door Chevrolet coupe parked next to the barn.

Clara stared at the parked car, nodded silently, and pulled out the cow statue. Leaving the car, she called out. "Hello, is anyone here?"

Marjorie turned the car around and waited, engine running.

"Hello? I'm looking for a blacksmith who might have made this statue."

The door of the shack opened and she saw a bent-over man in overalls with suspenders, shirtless, and torn shoes and a long white beard and greasy gray hair.

"What ya want?"

Clara walked toward the man and said, "Hello. I'm from Santa Rosa and a gentleman there told us that you might have been the one who created this statue and might know its history. He said you made several of them."

Clara was sure that Marjorie would notice that her voice was high-pitched and shaking a bit. She trusted that her friend was keeping the engine running and her foot ready to go.

"Yes'm. I did make some a while ago. Don't know nothin' about the cow though. Kin I see it?" He limped his way toward Clara, and she took a few steps toward him. "I believe your name 'Dobberson' is on the bottom." She handed him the cow and noticed that his hands were full of grease and dirt, and his beard was tattered with remnants of what had probably once been food. The odor from him was unpleasant.

"Yep, this is one of mine. I forgot I made a cow."

"Do you remember who you made it for or who bought it?"

"Well, now, that was a long time ago. Let me see. There was that Japanese farmer that bought some. He said he was gonna put 'em in his barn—some religious purpose, ya know. I bet he was the one that got the cow."

"Do you remember anything else about him?"

"I 'member he had the bills to buy 'em. His farm musta been nearby. He come all the way out here, like ya. Ya must care much about this here cow to come all this way."

"Well, you see, I found it, and I want to return it to its owner."

"I reckon it ain't worth much." He handed it back to her.

She didn't think he'd understand about muses, so she stuck to her original reason.

"Do you still sell these?"

"Na. I stopped makin' them when my son left. He's in the army now."

"Oh. I see. Did he help you?"

"He made most of 'em. He liked to play with the smelt, ya see."

"You don't happen to remember which farm the Japanese man was from?"

"Na. Them names all sound the same to me. Couldn't tell ya. Just that he had—"

"The bills." Clara finished his sentence. "Well, thank you again."

She walked to the car, smiled at the man, got in, and told her friend, "Get the hell out of here as fast as you can."

Marjorie, sensing a tone she'd never heard from Clara, obeyed without hesitation. She drove back down the road faster than they'd driven up until Clara told her to slow down.

"Why did we have to get out of there so fast? I thought you got the information you wanted."

"All right. Don't freak out."

"Why would I freak out?"

"That was Gene's borrowed car parked there. We have to get to the police as soon as possible. You have to drive us to the nearest phone."

"Whaaaat?!"

"Keep your eyes on the road. Take it easy. Take some deep breaths."

"How did you manage to talk to him when you knew—"

"I had to. If we'd driven up and then away, he'd have known something was up. I had to pretend I didn't even notice the car and ask him the original question."

"I can't even imagine how you did that. I hope we don't run into any cars heading in the other direction."

"Me, too. We're almost to the first turn."

"Are you sure?"

"What do you mean?"

"You're just saying that to make me feel good."

"There it is. Turn."

But as they turned another car approached them and wouldn't allow them to pass.

Marjorie said, "What should I do?"

"Keep driving toward him, and pull over and around at the last moment. Look! There's a spot up ahead that should give you enough room, but don't pull over until we get there."

"He's not going to pull over."

"We're almost there."

"He not going to pull over."

"Now!"

Marjorie obeyed and managed to pull the car into the small space while the other car did pull aside. She downshifted for some extra pull-away power and they escaped without injury.

The other car continued on its way honking the horn.

"I bet he's laughing his fool head off at those dumb women."

"Marjorie, that was some great driving."

"Ed taught me, you know."

Clara patted her shoulder. "Incredible driving." She took a deep breath. "Are you all right?"

Marjorie said, "I don't know. But let's go find a phone."

"I think I saw an inn at that last little town we passed through. I think it was Herferdton. Do you remember it?"

"I remember the town. And maybe they have a police station. We could go there and have them get in touch with Santa Rosa police."

Clara nodded. "Let's try that. I was so scared, I didn't even think about what might have happened to Gene, and why the old man had his car."

"Probably the convict got it and maybe he's related to the old man." She stopped. "But I don't know what they'd have done to Gene."

They drove in silence the rest of the way to Herferdton in search of a phone or a police station. Clara had always assumed that Gene was alive and would return to his job at the newspaper—things would go back to normal. His disappearance was simply temporary. It never really occurred to her that he might have been killed. However, the probability of his death was now quite real, and she felt like she'd entered a dark cave with no way out.

Marjorie pulled into a gas station and asked for directions to police headquarters. The friendly attendant gave them directions, but said he wasn't sure that anyone would be there this time of day on a Saturday. He offered to call, and both Clara and Marjorie said, "Yes, please."

They followed him into the station and stood quietly watching. The attendant explained to the officer what was happening and turned the phone over to Clara. She provided the details, gave them the address, and suggested ways to get in touch with the Santa Rosa police. But definitely the car she saw was the one being used by the missing Gene Walker. And he'd been investigating the missing convict. "So, it's possible that the old man doesn't know the convict, but, approach with care. The convicts already killed two people that we know of. We'll wait here."

The attendant found chairs for them. "Can I get you something to eat? I've got some apples from my tree out back and some cheese from a local farm."

Clara smiled. "That sounds wonderful. You've been so kind."

"My pleasure. I heard what ya said. Wouldn't s'prise me at-tall if that old geezer's nephew didn't come back. They caught him onct before, but old Charlie he couldn't see nothin' bad in that bum. I heard he'd escaped but no one's seen him 'round here. We'd a reported it."

"Well, we don't know if he's there, but we do know that the car parked there was being driven by our friend who's been missing for several days."

"I don't know how long it'll take for the sheriff to gather some local officers. You might be more comfortable at our local hotel. It's just down the street. You can't miss it. If'n you'd like, I ken call and make you a reservation."

Clara and Marjorie looked at each other, shrugged, and Clara answered, "That would be kind. A room with two beds, if you don't mind asking."

"Sure thing." The kind man asked the operator for the local hotel and asked for a room with two beds. "Excuse me, could you tell me your names?"

They gave him their names, which he repeated over the telephone. When he hung up he said, "No problem. T'aint much but it's clean. I'll let the sheriff know where you are."

Clara asked, "Do you know if he's gotten in touch with the Santa Rosa police?"

"No, I don't. But he's a good feller. He'll be careful. He knows about them Dobberson boys."

They thanked him, and got into the car and drove to a hotel that Clara estimated had been built too many years ago to estimate. Its small porch overhung the street, and displayed "Hotel" written above the door on a sign that was leaning partially to the left.

Clara said, "Maybe we'd be safer staying at the filling station."

"Aw, c'mon. Where's your sense of adventure? Besides he said it was clean."

"Right."

Marjorie found a parking place around the corner, and they walked back up the street to the front door and entered. Once inside, Clara's trepidation increased. The walls were cracked and the rug worn, what there was of it. But the middle-aged man at the desk, who was dressed in long-sleeved white shirt and black slacks, welcomed them with a wide smile. "Hi, I'm Herbert Jones, the owner. You can call me Herb. Everybody does. Are you Clara and Marjorie?"

Clara answered. "Yes, we are."

"I have a room with two beds for you. Will you be wanting dinner? We can bring you something from next door if you'd like."

Both of them said, "Yes."

"Chicken pot pie okay?"

They nodded.

"Good. I'll call up to you when the food arrives. You can eat there in our dining room."

They looked at an alcove that had three small tables. Clara said, "That will be fine. Thank you."

"Sorry, we don't have no entertainment tonight. Our guitar player's wife is havin' a baby. Normally we would have music since it's Saturday night."

Marjorie answered, "Oh, that's all right. We're kind of tired. We need to call our parents, which might be long distance. Can we do that from here? We'll pay you, of course."

"Yep, just let me know when you're ready to do that, and I'll get the operator for you."

Clara said, "Maybe we should do that right away. I can talk to my dad. He'll stay calm."

Marjorie bit her lip. "Yeah, and ask him to get in touch with my parents, just in case they're trying to reach me."

The hotel owner got the operator. and Clara gave her the number of her parents' house. She was relieved when her father answered, but she wasn't well prepared to explain what was happening.

"Hi, Dad." She explained where they were and that they were fine. "It took us longer than we thought to find the blacksmith. And then, well, other things happened. We're planning to spend the night here in Herferdton and wanted to let you know not to worry about us."

Her father responded in a stern voice. "The police just called here. They wanted to know if you were really the person responsible for possibly tracking down an escaped convict. We weren't sure how to respond."

Clara hesitated and grimaced then whispered to Marjorie, "He knows about the convict." She turned back to the phone. "We're fine, Dad. Honest. We may have found a lead to Gene, although we weren't looking for it. I don't know about a convict. But I can't stay on the line too long. I'm calling from a hotel. Let me give you the number here in case you or the police need to get hold of me." She gave him the phone number.

"Thank you. Now tell me what happened and why."

Clara told him of their trip to track down the blacksmith who'd made the cow statute, and how she'd found the same address in Gene's notes thinking that he'd also tracked down the blacksmith for her to find the statue's creator. And then when they arrived they discovered Gene's car as well as finding the source of the statue. "We had no idea that the blacksmith was the one who grabbed Gene. I assure you we wouldn't have gone there."

"Are you all right?"

"Yes, we're fine. As soon as we saw Gene's car, we got out of there as fast as possible. We really didn't know that the blacksmith would be related to the convict and that we'd find Gene's car. But, it's a good thing, right? And we're fine. There's no need for you to worry. And could you call Marjorie's parents and let them know?"

"Of course. We'll talk about it more when you come home. Do you know when that will be?"

"We're just staying here tonight rather than drive back late. Also, the sheriff might need us. But I'll let you know tomorrow when to expect us."

"Be careful. Hope to see you tomorrow."

Marjorie asked, "Was he upset that we came here?"

"Yes and no. I think he was worried. The police had already called him to confirm that I was the one who saw the car, except they told him we'd found a convict."

Clara turned to Herb. "When will our dinners arrive?"

"I already ordered them so they should be here pretty soon. You can wait right at the table if you want. I'll bring you some water."

"Thanks." They sat at the table and each drank a glass of the cold water. It was close to five o'clock and although they'd brought snacks neither of them had had anything substantial

154

to eat since breakfast. Herb went outside and within five minutes returned with their chicken pot pies and salad with lots of vegetables. Both of them attacked the food.

Herbe watched them and then disappeared out the door. They both finished their food and were getting ready to leave when he entered again carrying two pieces of apple pie with ice cream. The girls sat back down and attacked what was surely the best apple pie Clara had ever had.

"Wow!" said Marjorie. "Thank you. I guess adventures make you hungry."

Clara laughed. But she wasn't sure that this had been an adventure she'd want to remember. Where was Gene? Was he alive? And, on a minor matter, except to Clara, what was the story behind her statue? She was disappointed if it was only a story about a cousin of a criminal out to make some money. She still needed to know who bought the statue and, if it was the wealthy Japanese farmer, where was his farm and what was his name? She had to track him down.

Chapter 23

The rooms were clean as promised, and both of them slept well. Marjorie pointed out that not only were adventures good for appetites, but also for sleeping. Clara nodded in agreement.

The next morning, they dressed in their previous day's clothes not having anticipated an overnight stay and went downstairs for coffee and toast. Herb pointed to one of the tables which was set for a morning breakfast. "We don't have much but coffee and toast, homemade orange marmalade. The place next door doesn't prepare breakfasts, so we make do. We squeeze fresh orange juice, too."

Clara said, 'This is perfect, and orange juice sounds great. Listen, I have a question. Do you happen to know if there was a large ranch nearby owned by a Japanese farmer? He'd probably have sold it by now and been sent to some kind of camp."

Herb looked at his feet and then back up. "I'm not sure I can answer that. Let me get your juice."

He disappeared behind a door.

Marjorie said, "Clara, you shouldn't have asked him that."

"Why not?"

"He's obviously upset. Most of us are scared of the Japanese."

"I understand. Me, too, of the Japanese from Japan. But most of our Japanese

friends who were born here are Americans, aren't they?"

"But they're still connected to their home country."

"Marjorie, where were your great grandparents from?"

156

"Germany."

"Are you still connected to Germany? Should we send you, an American citizen, to a camp because your great grandparents came from Germany?"

"It's different."

Herb interrupted their conversation with a tray full of toast, marmalade and orange juice, which he set in front of them.

"The name of the Japanese farmer is Osaka, and we were friends. Our sons grew up together. They took him to Tule Lake. Why are ya askin'?"

Clara glared at Marjorie. "Thank you for telling me. You see, I found a metal statue . I have it in my bag upstairs. I'll show it to you later. And the reason that we went to the Dobberson blacksmith was to find out who made it or who owned it. Mr. Dobberson said he thinks he sold it to a wealthy Japanese farmer."

Herb smiled. "Which one did you find?"

"It's a cow."

"Osaka bought many of them. He just wanted to help out old Dobberson, but he put them all over his barn. They was kinda, well, happy. They made the barn a happy place. New owner probably got rid of them."

"Have you visited Mr. Osaka since he was, well, taken to the camp?"

"No. It would be dangerous for both of us. I'd be accused of being a spy or somethin' and Osaka would suffer from the guards and his own people inside. Besides I'm not even sure you can get in to see him."

"Who's the new owner of his farm?"

"Someone I don't even want to talk about. He's no farmer, that's for sure. Place is run down somethin' fierce."

The phone ringing interrupted them. Herb answered it and turned to them and asked, "Which one of you is Clara?"

Clara stood up and walked to the phone. "Hello?"

"Hi, Clara. This is the local sheriff. Your Santa Rosa police friends asked me to let you know that we've got blacksmith Dobberson in jail, but no sign of his nephew or your friend."

"What about the car?"

"We have that, too, but it's empty. We couldn't find any signs that anyone else was there, although the place was in poor shape—kind of cluttered, if you know what I mean. I'm real sorry we didn't find your friend. But I want to tell ya to be more careful. Don't go off investigatin' on your own. That nephew of Dobberson is a mean boy."

"Did you find anything in the car? I mean, was there any blood or anything like that?"

"Nope. That car was the cleanest thing on the farm."

"Are you looking for him in the area? Maybe he escaped and fell or is walking somewhere."

"I wouldn't get your hopes up, but we're searching where we can. We've got the dogs out. We found some of his clothes in the trunk for the dogs to sniff. But, again, don't count on us findin' him. Of course, we're also searching for that convict nephew of Dobberson's."

"Thanks, Sheriff. Do you need us to stay here any longer?"

"No. If we find anything, we got your Santa Rosa number. We'll call there."

"Thanks."

Clara looked at Marjorie and shook her head. "No sign of either the convict or Gene."

Marjorie said, "I bet he got away and is hiding somewhere in the mountains. We should go look."

Herb shook his head. "Excuse me for listening, but no, you shouldn't. They've got the dogs out, I'm sure. They'll be much more likely to find someone than the two of you. And the worst that could happen is that the two of you would fall and they'd have to rescue you."

Clara nodded. "He's right. We pointed them in the right direction, now it's time for the experts to take over. We should go home." She turned to Herb. "Can you tell me the location of the farm we were discussing? I'd just like to drive by."

"Sure." He gave her directions and returned behind the door again. They finished eating and retreated upstairs to get their belongings, including Clara's bag. She wanted to show the cow to Herb to be sure it was like the ones his Japanese friend had purchased from Dobberson.

They arrived back downstairs at the desk just as Herb returned. They paid the bill. Then Clara pulled out the cow and said, "This is what I found and want to return to learn its story. I'm a writer, you see. And this cow has come to mean something special. I know it isn't much but I feel, well, compelled to search for its story."

He nodded. "That looks like one of the ones Osaka had. Like I said, it made for a happy barn. Look, I know you're planning to try to visit his farm, but be careful. That new owner can be kind of nasty, sometimes."

"Thanks. I just want to drive by. We don't plan to get out of the car even."

Herb missed the knowing glance Marjorie gave Clara. But Clara caught it and smiled at the clerk. "I think we've had enough adventure for now. Thank you again for your great hospitality. We'll have to come back some day when it isn't an emergency."

"You do that. We love gettin' visitors here."

They left the hotel feeling uneasy but pleased that they had at least uncovered the source of the cow and maybe even gotten closer to finding Gene. Clara was certain he was still alive—or at least that's what she kept telling herself.

As they got in the car, Marjorie asked, "We're going to get out and knock on the door at that farm, aren't we?"

"Well, of course, not if you don't want to. But I'd like to ask to see the barn."

"Are you going to give him your cow?"

"Depends on how nice he is, but maybe I'll ask him if I can keep it until my book is finished."

"So he shouldn't be in a huge hurry to get it back."

Clara laughed. "Aw, c'mon. Once I know the story of the cow, I'll write faster than you can believe. Remember, as a reporter I write thousands of words every day."

"Just kidding. Where do we turn here?"

Clara checked her directions to the farm. "We stay on this road until we see a couple of windmills. And then there's a dirt road up to the farmhouse. He said the grounds used to be immaculate but the new owner isn't quite as meticulous."

"How far to the windmills?"

"About ten miles."

"We've gone three."

They spent the next seven miles in silence until Clara spotted the windmills. "There they are, but I don't see the road. But there's a house, and I bet where those trees are, there's a road."

Marjorie followed Clara's advice and turned into what was indeed a narrow but solid road. She steered between the apple trees whose crop appeared neglected with rotten apples piling up among tall grass and weeds—all spoiling what would have been a pastoral lane leading to the home.

It turned out that the bushes and grass around the home were also unkempt and weeds were growing all around the barn as well.

Marjorie said, "That's a shame. I bet this place is beautiful when it's kept up."

"I don't see too many crops growing either. I wonder what he grew here. Maybe that orchard across the way belongs to this farm. Those look like cherries."

"I really wish you wouldn't knock on the door."

"What could happen? They'll either listen or slam the door in my face. It's happened before, believe me. People aren't always friendly to a reporter."

Clara picked up her bag and got out and walked up the steps (also full of weeds growing between cracks) and knocked using the ornate knocker on the heavy redwood door.

After a few minutes and Clara's repeated knocking, the door jerked open to reveal a red-faced, unshaven bald man in a dirty shirt with the straps off his shoulders of a pair of coveralls meant for someone smaller. "What d'ya want?"

"I'm sorry to bother you but I was wondering if you could identify this statue. I believe the previous owner might have had others, and I'd like to see them if possible."

"What the blazes? Go away." And he slammed the door.

Clara looked at Marjorie and then at the barn. She motioned with her head that Marjorie was to follow her with the car, and then started walking as fast as she could toward the barn. The door was open, and the barn area was as slovenly as the rest of the place, but she wanted to see if the other statues were still there.

She'd almost reached the door when she heard the man scream, "What the blazes do you think you're doing?"

She hesitated. She was so close, and he was moving slowly. She ran inside the barn, where she found dozens of boxes, which she ignored. She moved toward a stack of hay and was delighted to find a statue of a sheep similar to her cow. She discovered a stunning horse and a rooster, which appeared to have been painted at one time.

Old man Dobberson might have been ornery, but he certainly knew how to create barn animals—or his son did. And they were indeed happy-looking.

"Get the hell out of my barn. I'm gonna call the sheriff."

"I'm sorry. I only wanted to see the barn animal statues. I'll buy them from you if you don't want them."

"What?"

She pointed to the sheep, then the horse, and finally the rooster. "I'll buy them if you don't want them. I don't have a lot of money, but here's $20 for all of them. Is that enough?"

"Who the blazes are you?"

"My name is Clara Wilson. I live in Santa Rosa, and I found this statue of a cow and would like more. Mr. Dobberson—the man who made them—said the former owner of this house bought them, so I was hoping you wouldn't mind selling them to me."

Seeing the money settled him down. "Well, now, if'n they're worth twenty bucks mebbe they're worth more than that."

"It's all I've got. As I said, I'm not rich."

"All right. Take 'em." He grabbed the twenty from her hand. She snapped up each of the statues and was able to get one into her bag, but had to carry the other two. She passed by the red-faced farmer as far from him as possible, and would have run if the statues hadn't weighed her down. Marjorie, in the meantime, had turned around and was ready to leave as soon as Clara was back in the car. "Or at least I hope she'll wait for me," Clara muttered.

The man said, "If'n I find any more of them, do you want them, too?"

"Oh, yes. Tell Herb at the hotel in Herferdton if you find any more. He knows how to reach me."

She had to set down the statues in order to open the door, but she was quick to pick them back up and get them and her bag and herself in the car. Marjorie barely waited for the door to close before taking off.

Marjorie screamed, "What have you done now?"

"I bought three more of these statues. They're kind of cute. Look at them."

"Why?"

"Well, I'd like to take them to Mr. Osaka as a gift in exchange for the story behind them."

"You think they're going to allow you into Tule Lake to give him those statues?"

"Well, I won't know if I don't try. He placed these statues in his barn to make it a happy barn. I want to understand why. This has been such a successful trip.

"Now if we could only find Gene. I know he's somewhere."

Chapter 24

Marjorie and Clara returned to Santa Rosa late that afternoon. Marjorie left Clara at her parents' house after helping her carry the newly purchased statues into the house. Both parents held their comments until after Marjorie departed.

Clara expected them to make some comment about their trip, and why she wasn't more careful. To her surprise, neither one said anything until her mother asked, "Have you had dinner?"

"No, actually we didn't have lunch either. But we had a great breakfast at a small hotel in Herferdton where we were staying. It's this little town with a hotel and the nicest man named Herb."

Her father shook his head and then smiled. "It's all right, Clara. We understand this compulsion you have in the search for the statue's story, and we certainly understand your drive to find Gene."

Her mother added after giving her a hug, "There's some cold chicken in the refrigerator and some fruit. We're going to a movie. See you later."

And they left.

Clara wasn't sure if she was relieved or hurt, but decided that they were showing her respect. They were treating her as an adult. But they didn't even ask her about the new statues, and she was eager to discuss them.

She scrounged in the refrigerator to find the chicken and enjoyed it and some cherries. She set all four statues on the table, and had to smile at them. They were happy farm animals. She was getting ready to take them to her room when the phone rang.

"Hello, is this Clara Wilson?"

"Yes, who's this?"

"This is Deputy Tucker from Santa Rosa police letting you know that we found your friend Gene Walker. He's hurt and in bad shape but the doc thinks he'll make it."

"Oh my god! Where did you find him?"

"The sheriff up in the mountains with their dogs—amazing dogs—found him down a steep hill off a road near some blacksmith's house. They're not sure how he got there. They brought him here to our General Hospital, but he's not likely conscious yet."

"Do you know if he'll be all right? You said he wasn't conscious.

"Yes, ma'am. The doctors think he'll be fine but it'll be a day or so before they know for sure if there's any problems."

"I'll let everyone know. And thank the sheriff. He was so helpful."

She hung up and immediately gave the operator Stu's home number, hoping it was okay to call him there. He answered on the first ring. Clara gave him the news. She explained that they probably wouldn't know more until the following day.

"And, yes, I'll write an article about his rescue. I probably know more details now than anyone. I'll even get the names of the dogs who found him."

Next she called Marjorie and gave her the same news. "And it's all because we went in search of the Dobberson who created the statue."

"Well, and noticed the same address on Gene's list. I got a letter from Ed."

Clara hesitated, unsure if the news was good or bad. "Oh, that's great. How is he?"

"He says he's fine but he couldn't tell me where he is. It's a short letter telling me not to mope and to have fun. I'm going to write to him about our adventure. I think he'll enjoy it."

"Oh, yes, unless he's annoyed at me for putting you in danger."

"I can just hear him giving you a lecture." She laughed.

"Now I have to write the story about finding Gene. Let me know if you want to go on any more car trips."

"I don't have enough gas coupons to go much of anywhere. See ya!"

Clara spent the next few hours drafting her article. She called the sheriff's office and got the story of the dogs which she sidelined. And she did get their names, and how they sniffed along the side of the road until they located Gene. Then she added the story of how the emergency crew loaded him onto a stretcher and pulled him up to an ambulance. She was able to add a few words about the treacherous road that the ambulance and all the crews had to drive to get to where Gene was lying. It turned out to be a story about a heroic rescue effort. She didn't add that its success came from an initial clue being discovered by one junior reporter, Clara Wilson, in search of the source of a statue's creator.

After she called in the story to a typist, she felt her body almost collapsing under her, and started to cry big, loud sobs. Over the past few days, she buoyed herself into believing everything was fine. That Gene was okay and would return soon. And she realized that she believed the same about Ed. He would return soon and everything would go back to normal, the way it was.

In a way, it was that false certainty that enabled her to push toward convincing Marjorie to help her search for Gene. Perhaps in the same way that Marjorie used the search to displace it for her agony of missing her new husband. Clara's feverish energy propelled her to the Dobberson blacksmith and then to the Japanese farm house.

But now the sense of well-being was gone. Instead, it was replaced with exhaustion. Tomorrow she would return to her energetic self. Tonight, she had to sleep.

Chapter 25

Gene was propped up in bed and although the nurse had warned her about his appearance, Clara gasped when she saw him. His face was covered with bruises and wounds, his head was encased in a bandage, and one of his arms was in a cast, while the other one also showed bruises and scrapes. His closed eyes were swollen and black and blue. She couldn't see his legs; they were covered.

She took a deep breath, and said, "Hi, Gene. Are you awake? It's Clara."

He struggled to open his eyes and had difficulty focusing, but finally settled on her. "Hi, Clara. Thanks for figuring out where I was."

"I think the dogs figured that out."

"How did you—" he stopped, out of breath.

"You won't believe it. And sometime you need to tell me how you got there. But I was there for two reasons. I got a lead the blacksmith—old Mr. Dobberson—made my statue. But then I was going through your notes and found that you'd jotted down the same address. And when we arrived, and I saw your car, I got in touch with the local police as soon as we could. And we made the trip because I was also trying to keep Marjorie from missing Ed." Clara finished almost choking to keep from crying and not letting Gene know. He'd closed his eyes again while she was speaking.

"Your story was good. You'll get to be a great reporter yet."

"Thanks."

"Now do you want my side?"

Clara pulled her notepad out of her bag. "If you're up to it."

"I'll try." He stopped. "Can you give me some water?"

Clara looked for the pitcher and poured him some water and gently held the cup to his mouth. He used his tongue—which Clara speculated might have been the only part of his body that wasn't injured—to lap some water into his mouth.

"Thanks. As you know, I've been trying to locate the convict who beat me up."

"Yes, I know."

"Not sure how *he* knew."

Clara waited for him to go on.

"He sent a friend to the courthouse at the trial. Told me he could lead me to him."

Clara said, "Rest for a minute. Let me repeat what you said. You were at the trial and someone approached you who said he was a friend of the convict, and he would take you to him."

"Sort of. He wanted money to tell me where."

Clara wrote and nodded. "Was he a friend of the convict who stole your car?"

Gene's eyes stayed closed. Although anxious to hear his story, Clara was not about to wake him. She got up and started to leave.

"I'm awake, Clara. You need to get this story so we have exclusive."

"Of course." She sat down. "Take your time."

"Where was I? Friend of convict who stole car."

"Can you describe him? Did he give you his name?"

"He was dressed in a suit. It was mussed and his shirt was stained and his hair uncombed, but you know how we reporters can be. So, I thought he was all right. Mistake."

"Yes, one of the Court guards saw you leave with him and thought he was a reporter."

"We went to my car. He pulled a gun."

Clara waited while Gene closed his eyes again. She watched him breathe one careful breath after another. She saw flashes of him in the car, reminding her that there was more to life than becoming an author. And chiding her for pursuing the "saga of the statue."

"I'm still here. He made me drive. I should have jumped out right away. I wanted to see where we were going."

"I understand. Did you give him any money before you got into the car?"

"Yes, but I didn't have much. I told him I had to go to the bank."

"Did you go to the bank?"

"No. He didn't seem to want money then."

"Strange. What did he want?"

"Mystery. He had me drive—no talking—to Dobberson place up in mountains. Old man said go away. Didn't understand. No convict there."

"What happened next?"

"Pushed me out of car. I pushed him back and ran. He started shooting. Not a good shot. He missed. I zig-zagged. Pretty smart, huh?" He made as if to smile but his lips were so swollen that it only looked like a grimace.

"Did he chase you?"

"Yes, and he kept shooting. Must have run out of ammo. He got close. I'm no fast runner. He pushed me off cliff. I rolled much. Came to. Couldn't move. Didn't see anyone until dog licking my face."

"So, you lay in the forest for how many days?"

"I guess three? You were slow to rescue me. Rain tastes good when you're thirsty."

"Sorry. I didn't get the address until I was almost drowned looking for another one of those statues. The guy who rescued us recognized it and told us about the blacksmith, whose name is Dobberson. Then, when I was going through your notes for the third or fourth time, I recognized the same address."

"You went there?"

"Yes. And only the old man was there. But the townspeople know him and told us he's got mean nephews. I also discovered that he sold most of the statues to a local Japanese farmer." She filled him in about the barn, leaving out the part about how she forced her way, but letting him know she bought all the statues he had. "And I'm going to try to track down the Japanese farmer and give him back his statues. They really made the barn a happy place."

"Happy. Japanese farmer not happy."

"No, that's one of the reasons I want to give them to him."

"You want to get a story. You won't be able to see him."

"Yes, and you'll help me do it."

A nurse entered and said, "I think it's time for Mr. Walker to get some rest."

Clara asked, "Is he being guarded?"

The nurse shook her head. "I don't believe so."

She turned to Gene. "Just one more question, then you need to sleep. Did this friend of the convict ever give you a reason for kidnapping you?"

"No. Did you find my car?"

"We found your borrowed car. It was at Dobberson's. That's how we knew to search for you."

"Stu will be relieved. It's his car."

"Get some rest. I'm going to fill in some of this story by talking to the police. I'll see you later today or tomorrow."

She left his room and searched for a phone which she found in one of the offices on the first floor. She called Fred at the Santa Rosa police station. Fortunately, he was there. "Listen, can you get some protection for Gene Walker at the hospital? He was kidnapped by someone claiming to be a friend of the first escaped convict, for no reason. And it was deliberate. The guy tried to kill him. I'm afraid he'll try again. And we don't know why."

"Mebbe 'cuz he can identify the one that beat him up."

"But don't you have photos of him?'

"Not good ones. I'll check with my detective and see what we can do. Sure am glad they found him all right."

"Me, too."

Clara hung up and searched the area for anyone looking suspicious on Gene's floor and then in the lobby. She notified the somewhat-elderly guard on duty who said he'd keep an eye on Gene.

She sat in the lobby and drafted a follow-up to her story and went back to the phone and called the typist. She read her story to the woman, but said she might have an add-on, so asked her to hold it until after she spoke to the police. "If Stu wants to run it as is, that's all right. It's accurate. But I want to fill in some details about the Dobbersons."

She hung up and then called Herb, her friendly clerk/owner at the hotel in Herferdton. Again, she was fortunate that he answered the phone. After identifying herself, she asked, "Can you tell me more about the Dobberson family? Who else is there besides the old man and the two nephews?"

"Let me think."

"What about the nephews' parents?"

"Nope, they're long dead. I can't think of no other family, but those boys used ta hang out with a bunch of fellas that weren't too welcome. Always gettin' into trouble."

"Did anyone stand out who might today have a job where he'd wear a suit?'

"Yeah, now that you mention it. One of them's made good at selling Japanese properties. What was his name? They called him "Stick Bones." Give me a second—got it— Avery Jacobson."

"Thanks. You've been a big help."

"How's your friend doing? I understand he was lying out there for quite some time."

"He's really banged up. The doctor says he'll make it but it's going to be a while."

"Sure would like to meet him. Mebbe you can bring him here to stay some time when he's feelin' better. It would be my privilege to give him a night free of charge."

"I'll let him know. That will give him something to look forward to."

She hung up and immediately gave the operator Fred's number. "Hi, it's Clara again. Listen, I just learned that the two convicts used to hang around with a guy named Avery Jacobson, who's now selling Japanese properties. He wears a suit and fits the description of the guy who kidnapped Gene."

"I'll get on it. Where is this?"

Clara gave him the name of the town and also Herb's name and number. Then she went back to Gene's room, and sat outside his door until a policeman arrived. By then it was dark, and she had to ride her bike home. It was only a few miles, but again the dimout made it tricky to see

She found her bicycle where she'd left it just outside the main entrance to the hospital. She started toward home moving at a slow pace so she could spot the ground. She chose a route that had some light, but finally decided it would be safer to walk her bike. She would ride again when she came to an area with light.

She didn't get home until almost nine o'clock. Her parents were listening to the radio—the Glen Miller Orchestra. And Clara was delighted to see that they were dancing. She stowed her bicycle in the entryway and gave them each a kiss. Her mother asked, "How's Gene?"

"Oh, he looks so bad. Every part of his body is bruised or bleeding. I don't know how he survived. I called the police to guard his room. He was kidnapped, you know, almost killed. And I got to worrying that the kidnapper might try again so I asked the police to send someone and then waited for them to show up. That's why I'm later than usual. Sorry."

"Thank you. There's apple pie and some vegetables for a salad."

They went back to dancing and waved at Clara—both smiling.

Clara was pleased to see them—to see anyone, but especially her parents—so happy.

But I need to continue the search for my story. I need to find Mr. Osaka. The search isn't over until I hear his story. It's time to complete the search.

Chapter 26

The next morning, Clara biked to the hospital after letting Stu know she would report to work after talking to Gene. She filled him in on the possible kidnapper and let him know that the police were tracking down the name. It was a long shot, but worth investigating.

She was disappointed to discover that there was no policeman in front of Gene's door. She knocked on it and was relieved when she heard Gene say, "Come in." He still had no roommate, so they could talk freely.

"Hi, Gene." When she got no response, she said, "It's Clara. Are you awake?"

"I am now."

"How are you feeling?"

He moved a little revealing his face. Clara tried not to gasp. It looked worse today than the previous evening. "Oh, you don't look so good."

"I don't feel too good, either. Can you bring me my notes and papers the next time you visit?"

"Of course. Hey, I might have a lead to your kidnapper. I talked to the hotel clerk last night—great source. He knows everything that goes on in that town. Anyway, he told me that the two cousin convicts used to hang around with a guy who currently helps sell Japanese land. It's the type of a job that requires him to wear a suit. I let the police know, and they're checking him out. He might be the one who picked you up."

"Good work. You're—good reporter."

Clara had difficulty hearing him, because he spoke so softly. "Thanks, Gene."

"What are you working on now?"

"What am I working on? I'm still working on your story."

"You know what I mean. What's next? Tell me."

"I don't want to worry you. Actually, I was hoping you'd be well enough to join me."

"Tell me."

"I want to visit Tule Lake relocation camp and give Mr. Osaka his statues so he can have some happy things around him."

"Of course, you do. You think his barn decorations will make him happy?"

"Yes. They're really fun when you put them all together. And it would make such a good story."

"They'll never let you visit, and it's a long drive. You'd need lots of gas coupons and a car with new tires."

"But maybe they'll at least give him the farm animal statues. I don't have to see him."

"Well, if you're intent on doing this, check with Stu." He stopped to catch his breath. Clara waited without interrupting him. "He has contacts in the Army who control the camps. He's been in touch with Japanese friends."

Clara smiled. Gene had been eager to give her that piece of information, but he had to make her realize that it would be difficult, so he could solve the problem.

"I didn't know that. Thanks for sharing. And before doing anything I'll wait for you to get better."

"What's happening with the Santa Rosa Dobberson family and Lowry? Have they found stolen loot?"

"No, and they slammed the door in my face the last time I visited, and Lowry pleaded with me to stop investigating."

"Story there somewhere."

"I need to find a reason to visit them again."

"Well, spring on its way. Maybe they'll give another garden party."

"Marjorie might have some ideas."

"You might let them know you tracked down the other animals and know who owned them."

"Good idea. But they never claimed that the cow statue was theirs. Why would they care that I found the owner?"

No answer. He was asleep.

Clara was relieved that she was able to carry on a conversation with him without crying at the sight of his battered body. She also suddenly realized that she cared more for him than she knew. She was eager for him to get back to work, so that they could be together. She missed him.

In the meantime, she needed a plan. Gene was right. She'd forgotten about the Dobbersons and their strange reaction to items stolen from their house—twice. And why did Lowry change his approach and ask her to stop investigating? Did they threaten him? She decided to call Marjorie, who was friends with them, and ask what she'd recommend. For now, she needed to get back to the newspaper office to see what stories she needed to work on.

But where was the police guard to watch over Gene? Just as she was walking out the door, a uniformed police officer appeared. "Sorry I'm late. How's he doin'?"

Clara shook her head. "Not so good, although well enough to talk back to me."

He laughed. "That's good. It's amazin' he's alive."

"Yes. Thanks for doing this. I may be over-reacting but I'm uneasy that the kidnapper might try it again, although I'm not sure why."

"He didn't know either?"

"He may know, but he's not thinking too clearly. I have to get back to the newspaper. I'll come back this evening to check on him."

She left and retrieved her bicycle and pedaled to the office, thinking about how she could approach the Dobberson family and also how to ask Stu to see if he could get her in to see Mr. Osaka. Asking a favor from her boss was probably not going to get her a promotion. In fact, just the opposite. But if Gene recommended that she contact him, she would do it.

What started to excite her was that she was beginning to see her novel's theme shaping up. And it had to do with barn animals and happiness even in "bad" times, like the Depression. She wouldn't restrict it to wartime. It would have to do with any bad times and how we see our way through them, whether a death in the family, a loss of something special, or just plain having a bad day.

Next she had to talk to Mr. Osaka, and that would take some doing. She set her bag down on her desk and checked the pile of notices there to see if she needed to draft or research anything in a hurry. Nothing looked too time-critical so she decided to ask Stu for help getting into Tule Lake while she had the nerve. She could always back out and say she was just checking in.

However, she needn't have worried. He wasn't in his office.

She returned to her desk, and picked out a news item involving the projected requirements for labor during harvest season. Always a critical time for farmers, harvest this year was going to be especially difficult with so many men off at war. She pulled together a story based on the necessities and timing for harvesters. She checked her almanac and other sources for timing, and called the library for other statistics. She called several of the local farming

178

associations and if their projections were even close to accurate, harvest time would be more difficult than anticipated. Last year the schools closed so teenagers could help and stores closed to enable clerks to pick cherries. Even she had helped pick apples. But this year would be even more demanding.

She finished typing her story on the run-down typewriter Stu had provided, and decided to try again to see if he was available. Handing him a story might serve as an unofficial bargaining chip to get information on how to visit someone at Tule Lake War Relocation Center.

She was in luck. "Hi, Stu. Here's an article looking ahead at the harvest needs this year—they're going to be even more dire than last year."

"Yeah, I thought you might pick up that story. This looks good. I see you even quoted the projected wine-grape association president. You're becoming quite the reporter."

Timing was good.

"Stu, I was wondering—well, Gene said you might be able to help."

He looked up although he had already turned his attention to another article in front of him.

"Would you be able to get me in to see a Japanese at the Tule Lake Relocation Center?"

"What? Why would you want to see someone there?"

"Well, I have something that belongs to an inmate there—"

"Error. Not an inmate."

"Prisoner?"

He shook his head.

"Guest?"

"Don't be flip. Try 'detainee.' Do you know this person's name?"

"Yes, and he owned a farm near the small town of Herferdton close to where they found Gene. I have several statues that belonged to him that I think he might want. They were part of his barn."

Stu shook his head and smiled in a way that discouraged Clara. "Do you think these so-called statues helped him to farm?"

Clara shrugged. "Well, probably. They were throughout his barn, and he was successful."

"He was probably successful due to his knowledge of irrigation systems. I hear the detainees at Tule Lake have developed an extensive agricultural program. They even sell some of their vegetables to the locals. You might be able to present these statues to your—what was his name?"

"Mr. Osaka."

"Let me see if I can get you in to see him. How do you plan to get up there? It's a bit of a drive."

"I know. I'd go on a long weekend, assuming you could give me off a day or two as well."

"I'll let you know." He looked at her story. "Good bribe."

"I didn't mean to—"

He laughed. "That's all right. Gene's teaching you well."

"Thank you. I'll bring write-ups on the remaining stories. They might need a little more information, but most of them should stand on their own."

Clara decided she should leave while she was ahead, assuming she was.

He waved and started reading.

She finished within a few hours, and decided to see Gene before heading home. She also wanted to talk to Marjorie about how to approach the Dobberson family. She wondered if the wealthy Santa Rosa Dobbersons were related to the criminal Dobberson blacksmith. At least that would give her

180

an opening to approach them. And saying that he was a criminal would require them to answer. Mrs. Dobberson would not allow it to be suspected that they were related to criminals—or to a blacksmith.

She pedaled to the hospital and found Gene sitting up. "Well, hello again. Two visits in one day."

"I'm on my way home and thought I'd see how you're doing. And, also, to thank you for letting me know that Stu might be able to help me get into Tule Lake."

"Good luck with that."

"Oh, and I thought of a good way to solicit information from the Dobberson family. I'm going to ask them if they're related to the Dobberson blacksmith and if they are cousins to the convict nephews."

Gene laughed. "That will get their attention. Ouch, that laugh hurt."

"I'm glad to see you're doing better."

"Yes, but I still hurt. No word yet though on when I can go home."

"I can stop by there as well, if you need me. Marjorie might be able to help, too. I'm off to get home early tonight. By the way, I'm saving money to see if I can get my own room somewhere. If you hear of anything, let me know."

She left Gene much cheered. She'd call Marjorie from home to see if she'd go with her to the Dobberson mansion and also to see if she could help her get an appointment there. What she really wanted to know was more about the stolen items, and if they'd actually found them somewhere.

It felt good to have a direction to follow in the search. And if Stu were able to get her into Tule Lake, wow! What a book she would write. The story was creeping along.

Chapter 27

Clara and Marjorie stood outside the Dobberson mansion waiting for someone to respond to their knocking. Marjorie had intervened and requested a visit from Clara and her to ask some questions about the Dobberson name. She didn't exactly mention the Dobberson blacksmith, but she did explain that it concerned someone who lived in a nearby small town. At first, Mrs. Dobberson had refused, but Marjorie begged her as a favor. She figured it would probably be the last favor the matriarch would give her, once she found out that the "relative" was a blacksmith with two convicted nephews.

Finally, the door opened to Hiram and Mrs. Dobberson, who said, "Marjorie, this is ridiculous. I don't understand why you're insisting on my talking to this woman."

Clara had been called worse, but she did offer her name. "That's Clara Wilson."

"Well, come in then, and let's get it over with. You did say you're looking for information about someone name Dobberson near a small town in the northern part of the county, is that correct? Well, I don't know anyone of that name who's related to us."

Hiram asked, "Where exactly did you meet this person?"

Clara had to guess that they hadn't read the article about Gene's kidnapping, as she knew the blacksmith Dobberson's name was mentioned. She'd been holding her breath that they'd seen that article and not want to speak with her.

"As you'll recall, I've been trying to track down the Dobberson whose name was etched into a statue that I found.

Well, we got a lead on the Dobberson who actually produced that statue and many more like them. He sold them to a local Japanese farmer whose land has been subsequently sold.

"Anyway, I guess he has two nephews who are the escaped convicts we've been reading about, and I thought maybe the items that were stolen from you might have been taken by them."

"Outrageous!"

Clara feared that the blood vessel in Mrs. Dobberson's neck would burst; her face was so red.

"What rubbish! That you would think that there would be convicts in our family! Get out of here at once!" She started to move to open the door.

Hiram interrupted and held her back. "Just a minute. I'm as outraged as you, Mother, but maybe you could tell us more about these statues, Clara."

She was surprised at Hiram's reasonable response. She did not expect that either of them would be interested in the statues. She merely used that as a ploy to understand the mystery behind the stolen items.

"Well, first have you recovered any of the stolen items?"

Hiram responded, "No. More to the point, they're no longer missing."

"Have you even looked for them?"

"No. Again, they're no longer missing."

"What about your former gardener, Mr. Lowry? Have you hired him back?"

"No, we're quite content with his nephew. Now, about the statues."

"But I thought you'd also fired the nephew. I'd like to talk to him or his uncle. Can you tell me where he is?"

Hiram shook his head. "No, but his nephew probably can. I believe you have his phone number."

"Yes, I do." Clara couldn't think of any more questions. "Now about the statues. I'm surprised that you're interested in them, but they do have the Dobberson name etched on them. They're all farm animals—at least all the ones I've tracked down. They were purchased by a Japanese farmer named Osaka. He collected them for his barn. I hope to return them to him at Lake Tule."

"What?" Mrs. Dobberson asked. "Why would you do that?"

Clara assumed the woman figured that a Japanese prisoner didn't deserve any respect for his property.

"Well, I bought them from the current owner of the farm, and Mr. Osaka had them arranged throughout his barn in such a way that it made his barn happy."

"So?" Hiram asked.

"Well, I understand that Tule Lake has become an agricultural center, and I thought the statues might contribute to the growth of crops there." It sounded weak even to Clara, but she had to find a reason for wanting to return the statues in order to respond to anyone who would accuse her of pandering to the enemy.

Hiram said, "If you're interested in the items stolen from our home, please drop your inquiry. We don't care about them, and they were reported by mistake by a temporary maid we hired to help with spring cleaning. Now, I believe that we have been more than patient with you, and ask that you please stop bothering us about these trivial goods."

Clara said, "Thank you for seeing us today. I'll check with Mr. Lowry and if his story agrees with yours, I'll drop it. Oh, by the way, how's Hedda? She seems to also have taken a dislike to me."

Hiram smiled. "She's fine. She, however, was appalled at your nasty persistence at harassing us. And, Marjorie, I expected better of you than this."

Marjorie said, "Oh," but didn't seem to know what else to say.

He opened the door. Clara gathered her bag and followed Marjorie out, with the door slamming behind them. They got into Marjorie's car saying nothing until both car doors were closed and Marjorie started the engine and pulled away from the Dobberson house.

Marjorie said, "I don't get it. Sure, maybe those objects weren't hugely expensive, but they weren't worthless. Why do they not care about getting them returned?"

"I don't know. Their statements are confusing. Hiram even said they'd been found. And that's the second time Hiram has expressed interested in the statues. Why?"

"Probably because the Dobberson name is on them. But in his defense, he responded to Ed's inquiry during the murder trial and did seem to want to help."

Marjorie turned and looked directly at Clara. "Are you really going to go to Tule Lake?"

"Yes, if my editor can get me in, and I can find transportation. I plan to return the statues to Mr. Osaka in the hopes of learning about them and why he adorned his barn with them."

"Aren't you afraid of what people will think? They might accuse you of spying."

"Yes, they might. I'm not sure why I feel it's so important, but I need to take the statues to him and get their story. I need to complete the search. And hang the consequences."

"You could get arrested, even."

"Maybe, but I doubt it. Probably just be ostracized and even my best friends will desert me." She winked at Marjorie. "But not you, of course."

"How are you getting to Tule Lake? I can't drive that far."

"I don't know. I'm waiting for Gene to get better. Then maybe he'll drive Stu's car. Or maybe I'll take a bus. Or maybe my father will loan me his car—probably the least likely since he has to get to work every day."

"I didn't know you could drive."

"Well, I can. I passed the test last year and even have a license, but I don't have the chance to use it too often."

"By the way, I got a letter from Ed yesterday."

"Oh, that's wonderful. How is he?"

"Putting on a good front, but I can tell he's lonely. I wish I knew where he was located."

"It's probably not a good thing to know. You'd worry even more every time there's a news story from there."

Marjorie sighed. "You're probably right."

Clara smiled and then patted her friend's arm. Although she occasionally would remember and regret that Ed was training to face a battle somewhere, Marjorie was living with it every minute of every day. She'd improved and seemed to have adapted, but she'd lost weight, her eyes were usually puffy, and she could seldom stay seated more than a few minutes. She only worked a few days a week for a few hours in her volunteer job so she had few diversions.

Clara got out of the car when they reached her parents' house. She couldn't think of anything else to say so she just said, "Good-bye. I'll see you."

Her mind went back to the Dobbersons. Why the refusal to report the stolen goods? And why the interest in her statues—almost like they wanted her to stop trying to identify them?

Chapter 28

Gene went home from the hospital a week after he was rescued. Clara helped him get settled and assured he had plenty of easy-to-access food. He refused to let her help him get undressed or dressed, so the hospital arranged a nurse for bedtime and mornings. Marjorie also helped when she was available.

Clara avoided bringing up anything to him about the statues and her plans to return them to Mr. Osaka at Tule Lake, designated a maximum security segregation center where the most problematic immigrants were sent. It looked like it was the largest center with tens of thousands of detainees. The Army called them dissidents. Clara wasn't sure exactly how the Army defined dissident, so she called Herb at the hotel in Herferdton.

"Hi, sorry to bother you again, but I was wondering if you knew exactly what Mr. Osaka did to be called a dissident?"

Herb was quiet, then said, "You'd probably have to ask them."

"But don't you know?"

"It's dangerous around here to talk positive about a Japanese."

"I'm only trying to uncover the definition. I'm not accusing him or the Army of anything."

"All right. He tried to fight the sale of his farm. It was done fast and he barely got a quarter of what it was worth. Then he refused to sign a loyalty clause."

"I see. And I also forgot to ask you, did his family go with him?"

"Oh, yes—his wife, daughter, and sons."

"But that doesn't sound like a crime that deserves punishment in a camp."

Silence.

"Thanks for trusting me with the information. I won't divulge you to anyone."

They hung up.

She really wished she could discuss her plans with Gene to go to Tule Lake. Their editor, Stu, had been working on getting her permission, but so far the Army had not responded to his inquiries. But Gene would help her understand the pros and cons of seeking out Mr. Osaka. And he would also help her understand why she was worried about whether to continue her search.

He'd also offer continued insight into why the wealthy Dobberson family refused to report their stolen objects.

Law enforcement had still not caught the convict who had caused Gene's perilous drop down the side of the steep hill. And the blacksmith Dobberson was not talking, according to the last conversation Clara had with the police.

She arrived at Gene's with a burger and French fries from their favorite haunt, Victory Lunch. She knocked on the door and waited while he shuffled his way to unlock it. They were trying to get another key from the landlord, but so far had not been successful.

"Hi, Clara. Are those my hamburgers?"

"Yes, sir. Hope you're hungry. How are you today?"

"Doing a little better. Every day seems better, but it's slow going."

She saw him stop and reach for support. She grabbed his arm and steered him to his chair. "Take it easy."

"Thanks."

She pulled out their hamburgers and found two plates for them. "Water?"

"There might be some cider. Stu brought it. Home made."

She found a bottle of cider in the ice box and poured him a glass. She got some water and joined him in the small sitting room. He'd already started on his burger. She wasn't quite as eager.

She asked, "Is it all right?"

"It's great. Aren't you going to eat?"

"Oh, yes." She took a bite. "It's delicious."

"Yep. No one makes hamburgers like the Victory Lunch. Oh, by the way, Stu called and asked me to tell you that Mr. Lowry called you. I wrote down the number. He said Lowry sounded like it was urgent that you reach him. Is that the gardener at the Dobberson mansion?"

"I believe that's the nephew of the original gardener, but, yes, he's the one they have now. I've been trying to reach him."

"Still trying to track down those stolen objects?"

"Yes and no. I'm still trying to understand why the Dobberson family doesn't seem to care about them. And I don't get why not. I'll finish my hamburger, then can I call him from here?"

"Sure. I'll charge it to the paper. What else have you been working on? I never did find out exactly what you discovered from old man Dobberson."

Clara took a bite before answering. Gene would detect her plans if she told him everything, but he would also realize if she held anything back. "Well, I told you already, you might not remember, that Dobberson was the one who made the statues."

"So, there was more than the cow?"

"Yes, different farm animals."

189

Gene looked at Clara, shook his head, and said, "You might as well tell me. Stu let me know that he's trying to get you into Tule Lake to see a Japanese farmer."

"I should have known I couldn't keep this from you, but I know what you'll say, and I wanted to keep things friendly between us until you're well."

Gene laughed. "When were things ever friendly between us?"

"Whenever you get beat up, which you seem to do a lot."

"Stop stalling. Tell me what's up. I promise I'll be patient and understanding."

"I can tell by your expression that you don't mean that. All right. I found out from old man Dobberson, as you so politely called him, that all of the statues of farm animals he made were bought by a Japanese farmer. I made a friend at the hotel where we stayed waiting for them to find you.

"Anyway, he told me that his son went to school with one of the farmer's sons, that they were forced to sell the farm, and then he was sent off and ended up at Tule Lake. He explained that the farmer, Mr. Osaka, displayed the farm animals throughout the barn to make it a happy place." She stopped.

"Go on."

"I went to the farm and was greeted by a nasty man at the house, but I ignored him and went to scout out the barn."

"Of course, you did. Were you alone?"

"No, Marjorie was with me. She kept the car running so we could escape fast. But it turned out all right. Yes, he caught me but I bought all the statues—I think he's a little greedy. Gene, I wish you could have seen them. They did make the place feel happy. So, I want to return them to Mr. Osaka, and maybe get the story of why those animals create such a pleasant atmosphere."

"I see. And how do you plan to get to Tule Lake even if Stu can get you permission to visit?"

"Well, I'm not sure. Marjorie can't drive that far; she doesn't think her car would make it. But there's a great story there, and even one that could be published in our newspaper."

"Don't be absurd. Writing anything positive about a Japanese person would only bring trouble to the paper. You might get away with it in a novel, but not in a newspaper. You better go call Lowry."

She found the number, gave it to the operator, and waited for a response. He picked up after the fourth ring. She identified herself and waited for him to explain why he'd called.

"Listen, you've got to stop bothering the Dobbersons about the stuff that's missing. They think I put you up to it."

"But I don't understand. When we first spoke, you wanted me to look into it because your uncle was being blamed."

"I know. I'm sorry about that, but you need to stop now. People will get hurt if you keep it up. Besides, we found my uncle. He's visiting other relatives back East."

"What? You found your uncle?! People will get hurt? Who will get hurt? The thieves?"

"No, you just don't understand. You're getting into more than you know. Just stop. Please." And he hung up.

Clara turned to Gene. "This just keeps getting more curious. Lowry doesn't want me to investigate the robberies because, are you ready, 'people will get hurt' and I'm 'getting into more than I know.' And, you won't believe this, his uncle isn't missing. He's back East. What is going on?"

"I don't know, but there's definitely a story there."

"What should I do?"

"Did you ever check the police report that they gave?"

"Not really. Lowry sent me a list. That's a good idea. I'll do it. And while I'm there I'll check to see if there's any news on the escaped convicts or the guy I saw rob The White House department store."

"Yeah. With all that's happened, I forgot about that."

Clara smiled. "Me, too, except the same guy was the one who destroyed my bike, and made me afraid to visit The Victory Lunch. And, I haven't told anyone this, but I think I saw Hiram Dobberson talking to The White House burglar at the Army parade."

"What? That's—I'm not sure what that is, maybe hard to believe. Are you sure?"

"Yes, well, sort of. I couldn't get a close look due to the parade, and then they disappeared." She stood and gathered the plates and trash from their hamburgers and took them to the kitchen. "Do you need anything else before I leave?"

"No. I'm fine. I might be able to drive to work next week. The sheriff that rescued me returned Stu's car so I have a car available. Surprising that it's in good condition. I'm looking forward to getting out of here. But I'm not sure you can leave with that last piece of news about Hiram Dobberson."

"I know. I've been too timid to bring it up to him. But I'm sure it was Dobberson."

"He'll deny it, of course. But it sure adds a new wrinkle to all that's been happening."

Clara was pleased that Gene believed her. But she grew concerned about his state of mind. She looked around at the small room with its two easy chairs. She understood how it might feel claustrophobic. She finished cleaning up and picked up her bag and started for the door.

"Hey!" Gene said. "I thought it had become customary for you to give me a kiss before you left."

"Oh, no. We're not going to make a habit of that. You'll do just fine dreaming about that first one." Laughing, she opened the door, then turned back and waved.

Chapter 29

Clara was surprised when she heard from Stu a few days later that he had information about a possible visit to Tule Lake. None of the information was final, but at least he had a contact for her. She now had to focus on how she'd get there if she were allowed to see Mr. Osaka.

Meanwhile, she was inundated with articles to write for the newspaper and had little time to explore leads for the convicts or her assailant. Marjorie had continued her volunteer job working with a group of artists dedicated to helping the war effort through their art. Clara was pleased, because it kept Marjorie busy and feeling like she was doing something to help.

And Gene was still recuperating—which meant she had to cover for him and arrange her own transportation, which left little time for anything else.

However, she had to cover a crime story at the police station so she took advantage of the time there to ask a few questions of the clerk on duty.

"Have you heard anything more about those two convicts who escaped? I'm interested because my fellow reporter was beat up pretty bad by both of them and then kidnapped."

"Let me check. I think we got an update just yesterday. Hold on." He searched through a pile of papers. "Yep. The Folsom escapee was spotted up north along the coast, but they didn't catch him. Looks like they gave chase though. He was with some Japanese lady they think mebbe escaped from Tule Lake, but they're not sure, accordin' to this here report 'cuz no one was reported missin' from there."

"Really?! I didn't know it was possible to escape from there. I thought it was the most secure camp in California."

"Yep. So it's supposed to be. But somehow—accordin' to this here report—he had a Japanese woman. That could be treason, ya know. Don't know what they're up to."

"I wonder what he was doing with her?"

"Probably got paid a bunch of bucks to help her. Maybe from a rich farmer family."

"What about the guys that did the robbery at The White House department store? Any leads? I brought you the name of one of them a while ago, but I never heard back."

"Nope. Nothin' about that."

"All right. Thanks for the information about the Folsom convict. It's most likely not enough to print an update, but I'll add it to my notes. Oh, and one more thing. Can you fill me in on a report that was eventually withdrawn by the Dobberson family? Apparently they had two burglaries, which someone on their staff reported, and they decided they didn't want to follow up on them."

"When?"

"It was around the same time that the family gave a garden party—a couple months ago. Hold on, let me check my notes." She pulled out her notebook and flipped back to a possible date, and finding it then gave it to him.

He went to his file cabinet and checked through several files. "Yep, here 'tis. What I can tell ya is that it was filed and then they said never mind."

"Do you have the name of the person who reported it?"

"Nope. Don't know why not. I'll look more later to see if I can track it down."

"Well, thanks anyway."

"Any time."

Clara left feeling like she gained significant leads, but she wasn't sure where they'd lead her. The Folsom convict was seen on the coast with a Japanese woman who might have been from Tule Lake, and she confirmed that the second batch of items missing from the Dobberson mansion were reported stolen. She was eager to get to Gene to tell him, so she peddled to his place as fast as she could. He might find the information more significant than she did.

Before she was even in the room, she started telling him what she'd found out. She was delighted that he was interested.

She said, "I just realized that this gives me two reasons to visit Tule Lake—to meet Mr. Osaka and to learn about a missing woman who might lead us to your Folsom convict."

Gene laughed. "Oh, it does, does it? Yes, actually I believe it does. Did the police report say exactly where the convict was spotted?"

"Yes, near Klamath."

"Interesting. Why would he be taking a Japanese woman to Klamath?"

"I don't know, but it's intriguing, isn't it? And I could go there to see if I could find him after going to Tule Lake."

"It's a fair distance between the two. I'm not sure if you could handle that all on your own."

Clara hesitated before responding. "I know this trip is way out of line and that I'm *only* a poor woman. But I want to do this so much that I know I will do it one way or the other, and it will make a difference to me and maybe others."

Gene smiled. "Yes, I believe you will. You've become quite the reporter and I'm certain you will become quite an author—if you live long enough! However, the drive to Tule Lake is a long one, and requires a car and scarce petro."

"Don't make fun of me."

"I wasn't. But this could also be dangerous, what you're doing."

"I know. I've got you to show me how dangerous."

"And if this," he pointed to his injuries, "could happen to me, imagine how much worse it could be for you."

"Maybe you should come along." Clara had wanted to ask him for days. She waited for his response, focused on his face for his reaction.

"We can't both go. Stu needs a reporter here."

"I know. He just hired someone—another woman. She's from Los Angeles and just moved here with her husband. She's experienced and eager to get to work. We can leave over a weekend and only take off a few days. And we might end up with one heck of a story for him."

Clara was pleased. He didn't respond "Hell, no." which was encouraging. But he hadn't agreed either. And he'd want to help train a new person and want to get to know her.

Gene said, "I'm starting back tomorrow and will do a week of half days. Let me see how that goes. When is the new reporter starting?"

"I believe tomorrow."

Over the next few days, Clara waited for more commitment from Gene. She felt that urging him more than she already had would be useless. Now it was up to him to decide.

And, she needed to inform her parents. They'd been treating her as an adult, rather than as their daughter, but she knew that announcing she was taking a trip with a single man to a relocation camp might cause alarm.

But her plan was becoming more real every day. She and Gene had proposed their idea to Stu. He agreed, pending he had enough reporters to cover stories for at least a week. Gene was working with the new reporter, who turned out to be very experienced. Stu had received tentative approval for them to visit Mr. Osaka and even said they'd allow Clara to bring the statues—after they were thoroughly examined. And Stu also agreed to let Gene borrow his car, and threw in an extra tire and gas coupons for the trip.

What remained was for Clara to inform her parents. She'd already hinted that she was planning a trip for the newspaper, but hadn't filled in the details. She chose dinner as the best time to let them know that she and Gene would be driving to Tule Lake to visit Mr. Osaka and give him his farm animal statues, and that it was arranged by her editor, Stu, in the hopes that it would result in a special article for the newspaper.

"You know that it's important for me to complete my search for them by hearing their story from Mr. Osaka."

At first her parents were quiet, then they looked at each, smiled and said, "Of course, we understand."

Her father asked, "I understand Tule Lake but why are you going to Klamath?"

"We're not planning to do too much there. Gene wants to check in with the local law and see where the escaped convict was spotted. And we'll also check in with the local newspaper and maybe investigate a few bars. But we don't intend to go hunting for him. If he's traveling with a Japanese woman, she'll be conspicuous so maybe someone saw her."

Mr. Wilson studied his daughter and then looked at his wife. "We appreciate your drive. You've always had it from the time you pushed the judge in Ventura to let you teach the young boy in prison to learn to read, through becoming a reporter. But remember how you almost got killed that time in Ventura so promise us that you won't take any chances. We know you're an adult, but you'll always be our daughter."

"I promise. No unnecessary chances."

"Now how about some apple pie? And, Dad, don't say anything about my baking skills. I've gotten much better since I was five and burned my first sugar pie."

Chapter 30

Clara and Gene sat in Stu's office the Friday before they were to leave for the Tule Lake Relocation Center. The American Automobile Association had mailed him maps, which he was reviewing with them, along with likely spots for purchasing gas. "Do you have enough coupons?"

Clara responded, "My dad gathered some from guys at his work. And Marjorie got some from her friends. And my mother from some of the other teachers."

Gene said, "And I have yours, Stu, and some from two friends. We should have enough."

Stu said, "Be careful with the tires. Rubber is at a premium. I was hoping to maybe get some of those new synthetic rubber tires, but couldn't get any yet. I had the car oiled up and checked over so it should run well. And there is a new spare tire."

He pulled out the maps. "Here's the route the triple A recommended. It's highlighted. Basically, you first go east toward Sacramento to pick up Highway 99. I'd go the first day as far as Redding and stop there overnight. Most of the second part of the trip is going to be backroads after you leave 299, which you'll pick up in Redding. They're well-marked on the maps. What time are you leaving?"

"I'm picking up Clara at her house at seven."

"All I can say is good luck and have a safe trip. I hope you learn something about the relocation camps. I was never a fan. Otherwise, I probably wouldn't have worked so hard to get you in to see Mr. Osaka. But he was a friend of a friend who, when he heard what I was doing, pleaded with me to help. However, I didn't tell you that. Regardless, bring back a prize-winning story."

Stu stood and offered his hand to Gene who shook it. "Well, that's all, kids. Best of luck to you." When he withdrew his hand and didn't offer it to Clara, she held out hers to shake. He laughed and shook her hand. "You're absolutely right."

As they were leaving his office, Clara turned to Gene and whispered "I didn't know that about his friend, did you?"

"No, but I was wondering why he's been so very helpful at the risk of his own career."

They left the office and decided to go to Clara's home to review everything to make sure they were prepared. Clara had filled some empty milk bottles with water so they'd have plenty to drink. Her mother was preparing sandwiches, and Marjorie had baked some cookies. Mr. Wilson gathered some apples and cherries.

Gene showed the maps to Mr. Wilson who nodded that the route looked good. Then he gave Mrs. Wilson a copy of the hotels where they were staying that showed two rooms at each location in Redding and Klamath. They weren't sure where they were staying in the town of Tulelake. (Both reporters noticed that the town spelled their name without a space between the Tule and Lake, but the relocation center did.) The town was small, and they hoped there was a hotel, or they might travel overnight to Klamath.

They promised they'd call.

Gene left Clara with her anxious parents who hugged her before going to bed. She was sure she wouldn't be able to sleep but nodded off shortly after retiring, and it seemed like only minutes before her alarm went off. She lay in bed for a few minutes experiencing the anticipation of what she considered to be the biggest adventure of her life. She felt encouraged by Stu's and Gene's support and relieved that her parents understood.

She dressed and went downstairs to carry the food items to the porch. Both parents helped, but said nothing. She was surprised when Marjorie showed up, but pleased. She and her parents could talk together after they left.

Gene arrived right at seven and her father loaded the car, which he inspected: first the tires, then he looked at the engine, and then he asked Gene to turn on the windshield wipers. "Everything seems fine. But keep an eye on the oil as well as the gas. Do you have enough coupons?"

Gene smiled. "Yes, sir. I believe we do."

Marjorie ran up. "Oh, I got you another one from a friend who had some extras." She handed him another gas coupon.

Mrs. Wilson called, "Breakfast is ready!"

Clara walked back into the house and stopped to study the scene. She wanted to remember it exactly as it was. This was the beginning of a momentous day in her life to end the search for her inspiration for her first novel. She saw the table with its empty plates, a bowlful of scrambled eggs, toast, juice, and some leftover apple pie. Her father had a cup of coffee in his hand, and Marjorie was putting utensils on the table. Gene stood next to her smiling with his arm on hers. He steered her to the table.

Clara said, "Thanks. This looks like the breakfast of an adventure."

Her parents were less enthusiastic, but co-operative. They said nothing. Marjorie busied herself passing the food. Clara ate more than usual. Gene seemed amused to watch her. Marjorie kept her head down. Both parents kept looking at Clara and then at each other.

Marjorie said, "Look, it isn't like they're going off to war. I mean, come on."

Mrs. Wilson said, "Oh, Marjorie, you're so right. We've been insensitive to your situation with Ed. So sorry." She turned to Clara. "She's right. Are you ready to go?"

Clara smiled. "One last stop at the bathroom."

Then they led the way to the car with Marjorie and her parents following. Gene started the engine and gave Clara one more chance to wave to her parents and Marjorie, and then they pulled away.

The adventure had begun.

Chapter 31

Clara checked the map again as they approached Redding looking for the Temple Hotel on Main Street. They'd traveled most of the day stopping only for lunch and gas. They were both ready to check into the hotel that Stu had reserved for them and get some dinner.

"Oh, wow! Look at the mountain—the map says it's Mount Shasta!" Clara was impressed. It was covered with snow. Clara spotted the hotel first and guided Gene to the front door. He found a parking place on the busy main street that wasn't too far from the hotel.

He grabbed the luggage—only a small bag for each— and Clara picked up what food remained. They walked to the entrance and arrived just as a group of young men dressed in work clothes—blue shirt, suspenders, and khaki pants—left the hotel.

Gene watched them leave. "I didn't realize how busy this town is."

They approached the desk where a young woman was sitting with a magazine. She stood when she saw them. "May I help you?"

Gene gave her their information and she nodded. "You need two rooms?"

"That's correct."

"You couldn't share by any chance?""

Clara said, "No. We're here on business. We're not connected otherwise."

"Oh, are you somehow working on the dam?"

Gene shook his head. "No. That's right. They're building the Shasta Dam. That might be interesting to go see."

The clerk said, "Don't know about that. But if you're not here for that, then what?"

Stu had suggested to both of them that they not tell people where they were going or why. Tule Lake and the Japanese were not popular, and disclosing their destination could get them in trouble. But Gene didn't see how they could avoid answering a direct question.

The smiling clerk said, "I need to put down a reason for your visit."

Gene responded, "We're just passing through on our way to Tule Lake."

"What? Why would you be going there?"

"We have some business with the workers—maybe getting them to sell some of their farm goods. The Army's aware of us coming."

The clerk stared at Gene and Clara with tight lips and no smile. She slammed the two keys onto the counter and told them their room numbers. "Sorry I couldn't get you closer together."

Clara asked, "Can you recommend someplace for dinner?"

"Sure. There's a café right across the street. Don't know how you missed it."

"Is it good?"

"Sure." She turned away and went back to her magazine.

Gene and Clara hauled their luggage up the stairs to the third floor and found the two rooms. They decided to meet in a half hour in the lobby to go for dinner. Clara arrived first and stood by the front door doing her best to keep out of the way of the comings and goings of groups of men in work clothes. She was relieved when Gene arrived.

They left the hotel and crossed the busy street only to find that there was a line to get into the café. Gene asked a boy in line, "Is it always this busy?"

"Yes, sir. Did na used to be. Buildin' the dam brung all these here people to town."

Clara pulled out of line to determine if she could tell how long a wait it would be. She walked toward the front and noticed a man dressed in an ill-fitting suit—far too small for the broad-shouldered, six-foot-tall man. But he looked familiar. He noticed her and turned back away from her. She figured it would be at least a half hour before they'd be eating and returned to Gene to tell him.

"It's a long wait. How hungry are we?"

"How long?"

"At least a half hour."

The boy nodded. "Yep, that sounds about right."

Although her back was turned to the front of the line, she saw movement as someone left the line and headed away from them. The boy saw the man and said, "Well, that'll help. One less."

Clara pointed out the departing man to Gene. "Do we know that guy?"

Gene watched the retreating man, but shook his head. "I don't think so. It's not likely we'd know anyone here."

"Why did we come on this trip? Wasn't one of the reasons that someone spotted your convict?"

"Yes, but that was in Klamath."

"Is it really that far between here and Klamath? We're going there day after tomorrow, right? I never saw your convict in person, but I did see a photo of him. And that could be him."

By now, the big man was too far away for either of them to see anything but his profile. The line moved closer to the door.

Clara couldn't tell if the man walking away was the convict, but why else would he leave after seeing her or Gene?

Gene said, "I'm hungry and we're almost there. Even if it was my convict, we can't do much to catch him now."

Clara turned to the boy and asked, "Did you see that big man leaving?"

"You betcha. That got us up closer."

"Do you know him?"

"Nope. Never see'd him before. He come out of the hotel, though, like you did. I see'd him."

Gene nodded. "Maybe he'll be at breakfast, and we can clear up if he's my convict guy or not."

The boy was looking for some excitement. "Ya think ya know'd him and he's a convict?"

Gene rolled his eyes at Clara. "See what you've done?" He turned to the boy. "No, he just looks like someone maybe we knew a while ago."

The boy licked his lips and said, "The sheriff will get a posse and round 'im up. You just go tell 'im."

The man in front of the boy turned around. "Johnny, are ya botherin' these nice people?"

"They saw a man that's a convict, Pa."

The man looked at Gene who shook his head. "He misunderstood a conversation we were having. We saw someone who resembles someone I knew a while ago."

"Was he a convict?"

"Well, maybe, but it wasn't him."

207

The boy's father studied Gene. "You're a stranger here, so let me tell ya. We don't tolerate no criminals here. So if'n ya seen one, ya need to tell the sheriff."

"Yes, we will but we didn't. We thought he looked like someone from back in Santa Rosa down near San Francisco. Not likely the same person."

The man nodded and turned back as he heard his name called. His son waved and said, "Ya are next. Hope yar hungry."

Gene nodded and smiled. Clara waited until they were out of hearing range, then said, "Are you sure that wasn't—"

"No, I'm not. But I only caught a glimpse of him. Why would he be here?"

"Why would he be in Klamath?"

They heard the call for next in line and stopped talking about the possible sighting of the escaped convict. Instead, once they were seated they focused on the menu posted on a chalkboard overhead and then discussed the local sights. "The mountain is so stunning from here," and "The Sacramento River is bigger than I thought."

When they finished eating they walked up and down the main street to check out stores and businesses, mostly for exercise after being cooped up in the car all day. The lights of the town were dimmed just as they reached their hotel. The lobby was empty compared to earlier.

"People must retire early here," Clara suggested.

"Probably early work day."

"But isn't tomorrow Sunday?"

"Yes, but remember we're at war. They probably work seven days a week. The dam is an important project."

"We should check with the hotel clerk in the morning about the roads through the mountains—hope they're clear."

"Yep. Good idea."

They retired to their respective rooms. Clara was tired but uneasy. If the man she noticed was the escaped convict, he definitely saw them and given his quick departure, he did recognize them. She made sure her door was locked. Then she pulled out the maps and studied their route for tomorrow.

If all went well, they'd be at the Tule Lake camp in time to meet Mr. Osaka mid-day. She would finally learn the story behind her cow statue.

Chapter 32

Clara unfolded the map covering the latest route they were following. The roads had been rough and challenging after they turned off Route 299 to go north. Fortunately, they'd been clear of any snow even at the highest points. However, few cars passed them, and the deserted area concerned Clara. She held onto the dashboard with white knuckles most of the time, which is probably why Gene, who seemed less concerned, asked her to check the map.

Clara said, "We didn't pass any turnoffs so we must still be on the correct road. I'm glad you filled up in Redding."

"This country is sure beautiful." He was looking over the side of the road at the forests below them and a stream—idyllic mountain scenery.

Clara was surprised he wasn't unnerved by the scene, given his fall over a similar hillside. "Are you all right with this?"

"I admit at first I felt a little shaky, but now I'm more impressed—than concerned— with its beauty."

"Oh."

Gene laughed. "You, not so much, huh?"

"No. I've always had a fear of falling. I get the floppiness in my stomach."

"Floppiness, eh?"

"Please focus on your driving."

"Will do. Are you getting excited about talking to Mr. Osaka?"

"Yes, actually I am. I can't believe that it's going to happen. The end of my search."

Despite her eager anticipation of uncovering the possibility of the story of the stature, Clara was feeling uneasy. The vastness of the mountains with no buildings or people in sight triggered a floating sensation—like she was dreaming. They hadn't seen another car for the past hour which added to her sense of forlornness.

Suddenly she heard what sounded like another car. She looked back and saw a black coupe coming up fast behind them. "Gene, watch out for that guy. He's coming fast."

"Yes, he is. He's also using all of the road. I hope no one's coming from the other direction."

"You don't have much room to maneuver. I think he's trying to pass you."

Gene said nothing. Clara could see that he was holding on to the steering wheel tightly. He checked his rearview mirror frequently. "Here he comes."

Clara looked back and saw the coupe move into the oncoming traffic lane, barely missing their car. Then suddenly, he moved toward them causing Gene to brake to avoid being side-swiped. But the coupe also braked allowing him to stay beside them. Clara screamed as she saw the driver turn his wheel toward them but Gene somehow managed to hold onto the car without causing it to crash over the edge.

Just then, they heard the sound of a horn. A car had pulled up behind them and was blowing his horn at the coupe, whose driver pulled ahead at high speed and proceeded down the road. Gene pulled over on the narrow shoulder and stopped the car. Clara noticed he was pale and shaking. She suspected she looked the same. The car behind also pulled over and the driver got out of the car and ran to Gene's door.

"Are you folks all right?"

The man was dressed in a uniform which suggested he was from a sheriff's department.

Gene looked up. "Yes, thank you. I believe you might have saved our lives."

"I got his license plate number, and I better write it down before I forget." He pulled out a small pad and wrote down the number. "I'm a deputy sheriff for the County of Siskiyou. Where are you headed?"

Gene answered. "Tule Lake Relocation Center."

"Are you feelin' all right? You look a little peaked."

"Yes, I'll be all right."

Clara said, "Gene, I can drive if you'd like."

"Not on these roads. I'll be all right. Besides I'll feel safer if I drive than if you do." He gave her a weak smile.

Clara frowned at him.

The deputy said, "I'm going to follow you. I'm headed in that direction. That bump that guy gave you was deliberate, so I want to give you some protection. Did you recognize the driver?"

Gene shook his head. Clara said, "Well, maybe, but we're not sure. We thought we saw an escaped convict back in Redding. He beat Gene up when he was trying to interview his wife in Santa Rosa a while ago. He was recently spotted in Klamath, but we couldn't be sure it was the same man. We only saw him for a second or two. And I was focused on the edge of the cliff, so didn't pay attention to the driver."

"Escaped convict? I'll check it out. For now, we need to get going on this road. You've got at least another thirty miles before you can pull over. Do you have arrangements at Tule Lake for meeting there?"

"Yes, it's been arranged with the Army."

"Can you drive now, sir? And before you leave, could I please see your license?"

Gene pulled out his wallet and showed his license.

"I'm gonna follow you. Let's go."

He returned to his car and Gene, with shaking hands, restarted their car and pulled out slowly. The deputy did likewise. Clara reached over and patted Gene's arm. She wasn't sure what to say. Finally, she said, "That was him, wasn't it?"

"I think so, although I can't be sure."

"But assuming it was, why would he be on this road? Do you think he's going to Tule Lake, also?"

"Why?"

"I don't know. But he was seen with a Japanese woman. Maybe he has a reason."

Clara withdrew her hand and asked, "Would you like some water?"

"No, thanks. I'm sure glad that deputy's with us."

The deputy followed them until they reached the next turnoff for Tule Lake. He signaled for them to pull over at the crossroads. He got out and approached Gene's door.

"You look a little better now. Feeling better?"

"Yes, thanks."

"There's a roadside stop up ahead. You might want to pull over there, get your bearings. I plan to have my lunch there so why don't you follow me. See you at Jenny's Road Stop."

They waited for the deputy to pull in front and followed him. Clara was relieved to see more evidence of people—goats and sheep grazing, shacks and even a country store. They arrived at Jenny's and were thankful not to see the coupe that had attacked them. Also, when they got out of the car, they were greeted with the smell of barbeque which Clara noted with, "Wow!"

The deputy nodded. "Yes, ma'am. I think you'll enjoy this place. And I noticed there's no black coupe here."

Clara said, "Thank you for your kindness. We really appreciate it."

"Well, mebbe you'll repay me by telling me why you're goin' to Tule Lake."

Clara nodded. "Of course. We'll start by saying I'm a writer and we're both reporters."

They entered Jenny's and while chomping down on the best barbecued ribs she'd ever had, Clara explained to Deputy Marlin Jenks, who explained that he was a ten-year veteran of the sheriff's department, the real reason they were going to Tule Lake. When she'd finished, he shook his head. "Well, I sure hope you get your story. And I'd like to be on the list to buy your book. Anyone that'd go to all this trouble to track down a story, well, it's gonna be good."

Clara smiled. "I hope so."

"I gotta leave now. I hope your convict don't show up again. I'll report it to the State Police as a possible sighting. Now, don't you two go trying to track him down."

Gene said, "No, but we are going over to Klamath after we finish at Tule Lake to check-in with the sheriff there. But only to poke around where he stayed and visited."

"I wish you wouldn't, but I can't stop you. You shouldn't have any trouble now getting into Tule Lake. You'll have to check in with the Army first. Your friend shoulda let them know you were comin'. 'Bye now."

Clara held out her hand and to her pleasure he shook it. "Thank you for everything."

Gene said, "Yes, we can't thank you enough."

They watched him leave. And when the waitress asked them if they'd like to pack up any of their leftover barbecue, they ordered two more helpings to take with them. The waitress added some molasses cookies, and they left filled with good cooking and good will.

When they were settled in the car, Clara said, "Deputy Marlin Jenks and this restaurant certainly restored my positive feelings about the world."

Gene smiled and nodded. "By the way, where are we staying tonight? I've forgotten."

"In the town of Tulelake, but we don't have reservations. We weren't sure we'd get in to see Mr. Osaka today. But let's try."

Gene nodded and followed the mountain road to their destination. They were quiet for most of the drive. Clara was reviewing what she wanted to say to Mr. Osaka. She also was uneasy that the Army might not let them see him. She wondered what life was like at Camp Tule Lake.

"Oh my god!"

She stared at the tall fences topped off with barbed wire that stretched for what seemed like miles, separated frequently by guard towers with men and guns. Beyond the fence she glimpsed a road, and buildings—more like long, squat shacks—that seemed to be clustered in blocks, like tiny villages. As they drove toward what they hoped was the entrance, the vastness of the camp was overwhelming.

Gene said, "This isn't a camp—it's a prison."

"How many people are here?"

"We can ask our Army representative. I think we've finally reached the entrance."

Clara noted the sign that said 'Camp Tule Lake.' "But where's the building to check in?"

Gene drove the car up to a gate. Within moments an armed soldier appeared, opened the gate, and held up his hand for them to stop. He marched to Gene's side of the car and asked, "Identification, please."

Clara handed Gene the papers Stu had prepared for them. He gave them to the soldier who read through them and nodded. "Drive straight through and follow the road to the left until you come to the headquarters building. Ask for the Officer of the Day. Give him these papers and he'll arrange your visit. He'll want to examine anything that you plan to take with you to speak with the dissident." He pronounced the last word with emphasis and glared at them with distaste. He then threw their documents back at Gene.

"Whew. I guess we're not exactly welcome here." Clara gathered the strewn documents and put them back in their envelope.

Gene drove through the gate and followed the directions. Clara heard the gate close behind them. She also noticed the guard towers on either side of the entrance had guards with rifles. She'd heard that the Army guarded the Japanese from being harmed by anyone coming in to kill them. "It looks more to me like they're guarding against anyone escaping from the camp."

"Yes, but this is not the place to be making any smart comments. Promise me you'll hold your tongue."

"You don't have to ask me twice."

They arrived at the headquarters and got out of the car. Clara picked up the documents, and Gene carried her two bags of statues to be checked out. She really did want to give them to Mr. Osaka and hoped it would be allowed.

They knocked on the door and heard someone shout, "Enter!"

Gene went first, and held the door for Clara. The room smelled of stale cigarette and cigar smoke. She first saw a man dressed in shirt sleeves with suspenders holding up his Army pants seated at a small desk similar to hers at the newspaper. He looked up and said, "Papers?"

She handed him the documents and said, "I'm Clara Wilson. And this is Gene Walker. We're here to see Mr. Osaka."

"I hope you've got a full name for him. Osaka is a common name." The soldier held up his hand and shook his head, then started reading the documents Clara had given him. "Ah, here it is: Hiroko Osaka. You have something you want to give him?"

"Yes, these are statues from his barn. He was a successful farmer, you know, and used these to help settle barn animals and enhance crops."

"Sounds like some kind of magic they'd use. Let me see."

He opened the bags and examined each animal statue, one leg at a time. He pounded each of them on his desk then against each other.

"These are all right, although I can't imagine why he'd want them. Do you both want to see him?"

Gene nodded. "Yes, sir."

The soldier picked up his phone and asked that Mr. Hiroka Osaka, Block 17, Hut 3, be brought to the recreation hall by the headquarters building. "It will take a while to round him up. One of my men will lead you to the recreation hall and stay with you. We never know when they might turn violent. Do you know this one?"

"No, we've never met him."

"Well, if he's here, he's probably not a friendly. Mebbe I better have two guards. Hold on." He picked up his phone again and asked for Sergeant Bolin and Private Packer to join him at HQ.

The two soldiers arrived within five minutes, each armed with pistol and rifle. Clara rolled her eyes at Gene, who shook his head slightly. The clerk instructed the soldiers to escort Gene and Clara to the recreation hall. "Stay with them. They plan to meet with Mr. Osaka and give him these statues." He handed them the two bags. "I checked them; they're all right. Not worth anything but to Osaka. I'm not sure who's bringing him to the rec hall, but you stay no matter what. I don't want no incident on my watch."

Clara interrupted. "I'll want to talk to him. How long can we meet?"

The clerk shrugged. "They need to be ready for dinner at five. So, you got about two hours."

"Can you tell me how many people are imprisoned here?"

"Lots. Thousands. Maybe fifteen or twenty thousand. Why'd you wanna know?"

"Oh, just curious. The place seems so huge. I wasn't expecting it to be so big."

"Yeah, well it is."

Clara was relieved that the two soldiers were carrying the bags. The metal statues were quite heavy. They followed the soldiers who marched in unison, which seemed a bit ludicrous to Clara. She tried to talk to them. "Have you been here long?"

Neither soldier responded and both continued to lead in unison. Gene took Clara's arm and guided her to follow the soldiers. She was sure that if she tried to say anything else, he would squeeze her arm until she stopped.

They reached the double doors to a large, unfinished barn-like building that served as the recreation hall. The private unlocked the door and they entered a large room with rudimentary wooden tables and straight-backed chairs. The ceiling was unfinished—the wood beams were exposed. And the only lighting fixtures were bare lightbulbs hanging from the ceiling.

The sergeant said, "I guess he's not here yet. But he should come soon."

They had driven directly from Jenny's Stop earlier, and Clara was feeling the need for a bathroom. "Excuse me. But is there someplace where I could, er, freshen up?"

The Sergeant responded, "The ladies' latrine is a ways down the road. Mebbe you want to wait until after you've had your talk with the dissident."

"I beg your pardon? Oh, you mean Mr. Osaka. I believe he's an American citizen."

"Oh, yeah?"

At that moment the door opened. Clara was surprised to see a stern-looking Japanese man who appeared angry, and not subservient. Although his clothes were worn and too large for him, they were clean. His gray hair was brushed and full, and he was clean-shaven.

His escort joined the other guards, who pulled away from Clara, Gene, and Mr. Osaka to a table not too far away, but far enough that they could carry on their own conversation.

"Who are you? Why are you here?" Mr. Osaka asked, holding both hands in fists as he approached them.

Clara spoke quickly. "Let me reassure you that we're here only to talk to you and learn about some statues you had in your barn. I've brought them to you. I spoke with Mr. Herbert Jones of the hotel in Herferdton near your farm. He said to say hello and he remembered these statues being in your barn and making it a happy place. So, I thought that you might like to have them here to make your new home happy."

"What? You came all this way to bring me my barn statues?"

"Yes. And it's been cleared that you can have them." She and Gene pulled them from the bags and placed them on the table top.

"My name, by the way, is Clara Wilson. And this is Gene Walker. We've come from Santa Rosa to see you. We're reporters. That's what we do for a living."

Mr. Osaka looked around to see if the sergeant and private were listening. They were busy lighting cigarettes and talking with the third guard. He asked in a whisper, "What about my daughter?"

"I'm sorry? Your daughter? I don't understand." Clara also whispered.

"You're not here to tell me about my daughter? She wasn't with us when they rounded us up."

"No. I thought your entire family was here with you."

He studied both of them. "You're really here to give me these statues that the old man, Mr. Dobberson, made for me."

"Yes. Well, I have a favor to ask about them. You see, I found the cow first in a forest near Glen Ellen—where Jack London's home is. And it sort of, well, spoke to me. You see, I want to be a writer, and finding that statue challenged me to search for its story. Oh, it does sound silly, I know. But it became an obsession."

Clara thought she saw the beginning of a smile on his face. Then he laughed. "Unbelievable. You're serious, aren't you?"

Gene responded, "Oh, yes. She's serious."

Mr. Osaka laughed again. "And she convinced you to be part of this? You must be acquainted with my daughter. She would do the same. You have made me happy. I can hardly wait to read your book."

Clara wasn't sure if she should laugh or not, but he seemed genuinely joyous, so she joined in. Gene simply rolled his eyes and motioned at the guards with his head.

"All right, young lady. I will tell you the story of my farm animal statues. First, my son—the one who was a friend to

Mr. Jones's son—actually created them when he was recovering from an injury he suffered while helping me clear a field. He broke both his legs, and he was quite depressed. He wanted to be part of the football team at his high school, and the doctor told him that he would never be able to play any kind of sport. I found it unlikely that he would have been allowed to play anyway, given his Japanese ancestry, but he was hopeful." He paused and took a few steps, then turned back.

"He spent several weeks moping. His mother was the one who suggested he might want to design artwork for the barn to 'bring back the happy spirits', she said. He had always been good at art.

"At first, he did not respond. He wouldn't eat, and he hardly would speak to us. But she brought him paper and charcoal. And one day when we entered his bedroom, we found that he had drawn several farm animals with charcoal. He then created molds of them out of clay. I suggested we ask old Mr. Dobberson, the blacksmith, to turn them into metal. He charged us a fortune for them, but we didn't mind because our son did become happy again."

Clara nodded. "That energy must be what I felt. It's inspired and driven me. Is your son here with you?"

"No. He's chosen to join the Japanese regiment to fight for our country—America. He continues to believe in it."

"And your daughter?"

Osaka glanced again at the two guards, who were still talking to each other and didn't appear to be paying attention. He whispered, "I don't know where she is. She wasn't with us the day they picked us up. Someone slipped me a note about her, but I'm worried."

"A note?"

"Yes, it said they knew where she was but it would cost me money to get her to me."

"What? That's awful."

Gene asked, "When did you get this note?"

"Why, just today. That's why I thought you might be the person who knew about her."

Gene looked at Clara. "You don't suppose it's our convict friend?"

"It would explain why he was up here. And if he heard we were coming here, he would want to stop us. But how did he get hold of Mr. Osaka's daughter?"

The sergeant broke free from his conversation with the private and said, "All right. No whispering. We want to hear what you're saying. It's required."

Clara said, "Oh, we're sorry. We didn't want to disturb you."

The sergeant glared, but did not respond.

Gene said, "We may know something that will help. We'll check it out."

Clara asked, "Is there anything else we can get for you and your family?"

Osaka shook his head. "Only our freedom. But we'll manage here as best we can. And thank you for the happy farm animals. My wife will appreciate them, especially."

Clara wanted to hug him, but wasn't sure that he or the guards would allow it. However, she did reach out and touch his shoulder. He withdrew and bowed. She and Gene both bowed back.

"Are you allowed to get mail?"

"Yes, but it's censored."

"Well, I'll get word to you somehow about the book I'm writing—and, er, the heroine in it."

He seemed to get the message that they would help try to find his daughter. But Clara felt uneasy about leaving him.

Osaka looked at the sergeant and private and motioned to the two bags. "May I take these, please?"

The sergeant answered. "Yes, the lady here got them cleared. You can take them, although I don't know why you'd want them."

Clara managed to wink at him, and he smiled back. His guard made no offer to help him carry the bags with the statues.

Osaka started to follow the guard, then turned to Clara and said, "Thank you. You restored my faith in people."

"We'll do what we can."

Clara watched him leave and turned to Gene. "I don't know—"

"I know. We'll talk about it later." He turned to the guards. "We'd like to go now."

The sergeant asked, "Does the young lady need to use the latrines?"

"No. I think I'm all right for now. We're going to a hotel in Tulelake. We'll stop there."

"All right. We'll escort you to the exit."

They followed him, but both took turns surveying the camp. Clara wasn't sure if she would ever forget the restrictiveness she felt there. Only the strength she saw in Mr. Osaka would enable her to overcome her horror of the prison camp. She saw children playing in the distance, and men and women walking from building to building. She spotted what she assumed was the women's latrine.

They reached the gate and the guard asked for it to be opened. They drove out—without the statues. After several months of carrying one around, Clara now was without her inspiration. She felt as if her burden was much heavier now. Her story would not be an entirely happy one.

Gene pulled over and stopped a few minutes outside the camp. They sat in the car, quiet. Finally, Gene started the engine, and they pulled out of the area and headed into the town of Tulelake—Clara hoping that she'd never have to return to the Camp Tule Lake Relocation Center.

Chapter 33

Clara finally spoke as they approached the town of Tulelake in an effort to help find the Sportsman Hotel & Club, touted as the "Hunters Paradise." The town was small—fewer than a thousand people. Although unable to get them a reservation, Stu had tracked down the name of the Sportsman Hotel & Club as a possibility.

They found the hotel, still barely speaking. Gene parked on the street. They pulled out their small suitcases. Clara missed not having her bag with the statue. The lack of it only reminded her of the day's interview with Mr. Osaka.

Gene led the way into the hotel and the clerk at the desk. They were in luck and were able to check in. He gave him their names and signed in. The clerk handed Gene a single key.

Clara asked, "But where's my key? We each have room."

"No ma'am. Only one room's available. Ain't got no others."

"But we can't sleep in the same room."

"Well, it's that or the street."

"Could you call another hotel and see if they have any rooms?"

"Lady, this is it. The best I can do is wheel in an extra bed."

Gene interrupted. "That will be fine. We'll manage."

"Bathroom's down the hall."

Gene asked, "Is there someplace we can get something to eat?"

"Diner down the road. But she closes soon, so you better hurry."

They rushed up the stairs to their room. Both were in need, so they hurried to the bathroom, one at a time. Then they rushed down the stairs and out the door toward the direction the clerk had pointed. They arrived just in time to keep the waitress from hanging out the "closed" sign.

Gene said, "Please. We've been traveling all day. Do you have anything you could still serve us?"

"Sure. How about a cheese sandwich and mebbe some salad."

Gene looked at Clara, who nodded. "That sounds great. Thanks."

She asked, "Lemonade to drink?"

Both of them nodded. Then they sat down. Clara said, "I wasn't expecting that."

"The camp?"

"Right."

"I'm more concerned right now about our convict friend. This is a small town. He could be anywhere."

"Yes. Do you really think he has Mr. Osaka's daughter?"

They were both speaking as quietly as they could.

Gene nodded. "I know it sounds unbelievable and highly coincidental, but why else would he be here? And it's reasonably close to where he was sighted with a Japanese woman."

"But how could he have gotten her? I mean, where was she and why didn't she go home when the order went out? She surely would have heard about it. I'm surprised she didn't want to help her parents pack as much as they could take with them or else sell what she could."

"What's interesting is that whoever wrote that note to Mr. Osaka assumes he has money to ransom his daughter."

"He may assume that Mr. Osaka hid it somewhere. You said that his friend at your hotel in Herferdton—what was his name— Herb Jones? near Mr. Osaka's farm was friends with him. Maybe he has his money."

"Then why wouldn't the person who wrote the note go to him?"

"He might not know who he is, but rumor has it that the wealthy Japanese managed to hide their funds somewhere."

Clara asked, "But how did he get hold of her? And it's been almost two years since the order was issued. Where has she been all this time?"

Gene shook his head. "I don't know. But I'm more worried about our convict friend. He's dangerous and you only have to look at me and what he did to me to know that. If we run into him, we're in trouble."

The waitress set their sandwiches on their table and smiled. "Would you mind paying right now so I can close up the register?"

Gene reached for his wallet, checked the bill she'd placed on the table, and gave her five dollars. "No change. Thanks for the special service."

She smiled. "My pleasure. Thanks."

For the next few minutes, they focused on eating. Clara said, "I didn't realize how hungry I was."

"Me, too," Gene mumbled with a full mouth.

They were alone with the waitress, who was busy cleaning up.

Clara asked the waitress, "Are you open for breakfast?"

"Yes, ma'am. We open at seven. But we're kinda crowded for breakfast so get here early."

"Thanks."

They gathered the remainder of their sandwiches and left. It was dark, and the lights were already dimmed, so they walked slowly and took care. Clara noticed that Gene kept turning and looking around. She assumed he was checking for any signs of the convict. However, they arrived back at the hotel with no trouble and got to their room.

The clerk was as good as his word. A second bed had been added to the room. Clara had already decided she would sleep in her clothes. So she used the bathroom down the hall, and then collapsed into bed. Gene did likewise. She wasn't sure if she fell asleep first or if Gene did, but she woke up only once during the night hearing some kind of noise she couldn't identify. She realized they hadn't planned what time to get up and get started, but she was too tired to care.

The next time she woke up it was light outside and Gene was gone. She assumed he was using the bathroom, so she stayed put, enjoying the extra time to relax. She pulled out the maps for the trip to Klamath and was reviewing them when Gene knocked lightly and then entered. He found her sitting up in bed with maps spread out around her.

Gene said, "Good morning. We didn't review our route last night to get to Klamath. It's not an easy trip over the mountains."

"I noticed. Stu recommended going up through Oregon through Grants Pass, and then south."

"Yep. That's what the desk clerk suggested. I filled up already and got us some water for the trip. You were sleeping so I figured I'd let you sleep. By the way, the clerk told me that Grants Pass has a new movie theater that's supposed to be spectacular called Rogue's Theater. He also recommended a hotel. If we decide to stay there overnight, we might want to take in a movie."

"If we go nonstop to Klamath, it looks like a seven-hour trip."

"We might have earned a little entertainment. Can we keep an open mind about stopping at Grants Pass overnight?"

Clara smiled. "Of course. I do feel better this morning, but still feel kind of miserable about Mr. Osaka."

He touched her shoulder. "Me, too."

"I wish we could do more to help."

Gene sighed. "I think the only thing that will help him and all Japanese Americans is for the war to end."

"You're probably right. But it doesn't seem fair."

Gene nodded and finished packing. "I know. But for now, would you like to go for breakfast?"

"Yes. Give me a moment to freshen up."

"No hurry. Especially if we decide to stay over at the city of Grants Pass."

Clara got out of bed and headed for the bathroom. She returned to find Gene reviewing the maps. He handed her one. "This one will get us to Grants Pass. We can pull out the next one from Grants Pass to Klamath later. Let's pack up and leave from the restaurant."

"I'm ready." She closed her suitcase. "It still feels strange not to be carrying the statue with me everywhere."

"But you've got quite a story to tell."

"Yes, but I'm not sure how I'll tell it."

They carried their two small suitcases down the stairs. Gene left their key on the desk. After putting the suitcases in the car and locking it, they walked to the restaurant where a line of two outside the door had already formed.

Clara watched Gene look into the restaurant. "Are the tables all full?"

"Yes, but one group is leaving. She's cleaning their table. And it looks like two other tables are finished. So, the wait shouldn't be too long."

Gene turned to look into the door again. This time, however, he turned around quickly and said, "Let's go."

"What?"

"He's here."

"Our convict?"

"Yes. We need to find the sheriff."

"Did he see you?"

"I don't know."

The people in front of them in line were let into the restaurant, so they had to find someone else to ask for the sheriff's office.

Gene said, "I'll run back to the hotel. You stay here, but stay out of sight. Keep an eye out for him. He's wearing a blue striped shirt, suspenders, and I think brown corduroy pants. Don't let him see you."

Clara nodded and watched him running back to the hotel. She peered into the restaurant again, and saw that she would be next to be called. She turned to the people behind her and said, "Please, go ahead. I need to wait for my friend."

She watched as the next people in line took her place, and did her best to stay hidden behind them. She couldn't see Gene any more so figured he must be in the hotel. She moved to see inside, but she couldn't make out the man that Gene had described. She worried that, given Gene's history with the convict that he might have imagined it—or worse, that he really did see the convict—who had also spotted Gene and was planning his next move.

She looked back and saw Gene approach. Just at that moment, a big man wearing a stiped blue shirt and brown cords came barreling out the door. He stopped suddenly and stared at Gene, who didn't see him in time to duck. Clara continued to hide behind the people in line, but wasn't sure if he'd spotted her.

The convict darted toward a side street and disappeared. She was alarmed when she saw Gene following him, but she couldn't stop him. A car marked "Sheriff of Siskiyou County" pulled up, and she flagged it down. She pointed to the side street where she saw Gene and the convict run.

The people in the line called, "What's happening? Who was that?"

She said, "We think he's an escaped convict. He's been following us and almost ran us off the road. He beat up my friend back in Santa Rosa. We think he's afraid we'll identify him."

One of the women in the group said, "You stay here with us. Let the sheriff handle it."

"Yes, thank you. I hope my friend doesn't catch up to him. He's dangerous. He's a murderer."

"The sheriff'll get him," her companion said. "You come in with us. We'll make sure he don't get ya."

"Thank you. I'm not sure—I'm worried about my friend. Shouldn't I stay here and watch for him?"

The woman took her arm. "No, you come with us. He'll know where ya are."

Clara allowed herself to be steered into the restaurant, and found it surprising that she was hungry. The frying bacon smelled enticing. She sat down with her new friends and ordered bacon and eggs and toast. However, she couldn't stop looking out the window.

The waitress was serving her breakfast when the driver of the sheriff's vehicle walked in with Gene who looked sweaty but all right. He went over to Clara and shook his head. "He got away."

"But he was right ahead of you."

231

The officer said, "He musta had a car nearby, and we couldn't tell which way he went. I'll get the word out. How was he dressed?"

"Blue striped shirt, suspenders, brown corduroy pants."

Clara's new woman friend said, "And his hair was dark."

Her husband said, "And he was wearing Oxfords—you know, Allie, shoes like Charlie has."

"That's right, Hun. He was. And he's a big fella. Tall and husky."

The officer stopped the waitress and asked. "Has that guy been in here before—the one with the blue striped shirt?"

"Last night for dinner and just today. Never seen him before that."

"Thanks."

He turned back to Gene. "I think I got everything I need. Where are you folks heading now?"

"Up to Grants Pass to go to Klamath. That's where he was last seen, and we want to check out the spots where he might have stayed to see—"

"I don't want you goin' after this convict. He's dangerous. You leave it to the law."

"Of course, we're only going to check out places he might have stayed to see if we can understand what he's about."

The officer shook his head. "You'd best be gettin' back ta Santa Rosa."

"We promise we'll be careful."

The officer again shook his head and left. Clara started eating her bacon and eggs. Gene ordered the same. The couple at their table talked about the dangerous convict they'd almost caught.

Clara felt surreal, as if she were watching herself from afar. She took bite after bite of her food, interspersed with flashes of the escaped convict, her statue in the woods, Mr.

Osaka, the hotel clerk in Herferdton, Mr. Dobberson, the blacksmith, the Dobberson family, the robbery at The White House department store, Gene being attacked, her parents, and her typewriter.

And something was happening between Gene and her that was confusing. She was eager to be with him, enjoyed their conversations and confidences, and appreciated his humor—more than as colleagues. More disturbing, she kept studying him with a longing to feel his arms around her.

And now she was sitting in a restaurant in Tulelake, California, eating bacon and eggs and talking about an escaped convict as if it were just another ordinary day.

Chapter 34

They pulled into Grants Pass later that afternoon with no additional run-ins with the convict, traffic, or car trouble. They hadn't planned on staying overnight, which meant they didn't have a hotel reservation. But both were tired, and the town was inviting, especially the elegant Rogue movie theater with its visible tall vertical marquee.

Gene drove up and down the main streets until they spotted the hotel the clerk in the town of Tulelake had recommended, which turned out to be close to the theater. He went inside while Clara stayed to guard the luggage. She was eager to explore the town. She was thrilled to see "*Casablanca*" was playing. Stu had mentioned that it was a terrific movie and recommended it highly. He was a huge Humphrey Bogart fan, and the descriptions she'd heard were enticing.

Gene opened her car door. "We've got two rooms for the night." He held out two keys.

"That's great. Did you see that they're playing *Casablanca*?"

"Stu's current favorite film. I guess we'll have to see it. We should call in from here, and let the hotel in Klamath know our plans. The clerk said we could use their phone and he'll put it on our bill. But first let's get our luggage to our rooms."

They carried their bags upstairs. After freshening up and lying down for a few minutes of relaxation, Clara knocked on Gene's door and they went downstairs to the lobby where Gene asked to use the phone to call Stu long distance. He asked for time and charges to be supplied at the end of the call.

Clara heard his side of the conversation as he described their interview with Mr. Osaka, the confrontations with the convict, and the help from local law enforcement. He reassured Stu they would be careful, but planned to go to Klamath. Then he listened without responding for a few minutes. "All right. That's interesting. Have you heard anything else?" After a few more minutes, he hung up.

Clara saw that he was upset. "What? What's happened?"

"Your friend, Mr. Lowry?"

"What about him?"

"They found him alongside the road outside Santa Rosa. He'd been beaten to death."

"Oh, no!"

"Of course, the police are investigating, but Stu said they had no witnesses or leads so far."

"They need to talk to the Dobbersons."

"Apparently, they already have. And both Mrs. Dobberson and her son said they hadn't seen him in weeks. He seemed to have disappeared."

"I don't believe it."

"Me neither."

"Is Stu covering the story?"

"No. The new reporter."

Clara shook her head. "I'm more confused than ever. He literally ordered me to back off. Lowry said his uncle was all right. And that the Dobbersons really didn't care about what was stolen."

"I know." Gene shook his head and started to walk to the door. "Let's take a walk and see when the next showing of the movie is. I assume they'll have a newsreel. We can get caught up."

"But I don't get it. You said he was beaten up, so it wasn't a car accident."

"C'mon. Let's go. A movie will take our minds off it."

"I just hope your convict isn't going to the same movie."

They walked to the theater, and saw that the next showing was in an hour and a half, which gave them time for dinner. The ticket seller suggested a restaurant around the corner, and recommended the beef stew. However, he said to get back early in order to get good seats.

Clara remained silent during most of dinner, other than to praise the stew. But her mind was on Lowry. She recalled talking with him at the Dobbersons' garden party and then his urgent plea for her to stop investigating the robberies. Did she cause his murder? Did the Dobbersons murder him?

It was difficult to imagine Mrs. Dobberson beating someone up—but Hiram might.

"Hey! Come back." Gene gazed at her and when she was focused, he asked. "What are you thinking about?"

"Whether Hiram Dobberson could have beaten up Lowry."

"It could have been a robbery that has no connection whatsoever with the Dobberson family."

"I suppose. But I don't think he was rich. Not sure what they might have stolen."

"Are you finished?"

"I'd kind of like a piece of that cherry pie. Do we have time?"

Gene flagged down the waitress and asked for pie for two. Clara focused on her dessert and they got to the theater with twenty minutes to spare. The movie pulled her away from thinking about Mr. Osaka, Lowry, and convicts and into the romance and heroism of Humphrey Bogart and Ingrid Bergman. By the end, she was crying, and feeling emotionally drained but relieved. And she couldn't stop saying to Gene, "'This is the beginning of a beautiful friendship.' I really liked it. Thanks for agreeing to go."

"I liked it, too. It was a great interlude, even if it was about the war."

They walked back to the hotel, and it wasn't until they reached the entrance that Clara realized they'd been holding hands. She pulled her hand away and pushed ahead of Gene, stomping to her room.

Before she could unlock her door, Gene said, "I'll meet you in the lobby at eight tomorrow, and it should only take us three to four hours to get to Klamath. They provide a 'light breakfast' here—I don't know what that means. But if isn't enough, we can search for a breakfast place."

"Sounds good." She unlocked her door, entered, and closed, and locked it.

What was she thinking? Gene was a colleague. She was in no way attracted to him, despite what she considered his rugged handsomeness and their recent shared deep experiences.

Besides, she doubted that she was his type, given her straight figure and plain looks. Why did she let him hold her hand? They'd had no issue up to now. They even slept in the same room and nothing happened, nor had she wanted anything to happen. She couldn't afford a complication in her life. Her goal was to become an author. There was no time for anything else.

Chapter 35

The hotel's "light" breakfast was more than adequate—juice, toast, eggs, and bacon. And, it was a quiet one. Clara barely said "good morning," and Gene seemed to sense that he should follow her lead.

However, once they were in the car and on their way to Klamath, he said, "All right. Let's talk about it."

"About what?"

"You know what."

"I thought you didn't want to talk about Lowry's murder."

"Clara, holding hands doesn't mean we're engaged or even going together. We've had an eventful trip, had just heard some bad news, and viewed an emotional movie. We simply reached out to each other for comfort. What's so wrong with that?"

"Nothing. Why should there be anything wrong? I didn't even notice." She hoped that she didn't show that he was correct.

"All right. Let's talk about what we plan to do in Klamath. I'd like to check in with the law there to learn exactly who saw the convict and where. Then maybe we could check out the place or places where he was spotted and find out if he's returned."

Clara hesitated, then said, "If he's back in Klamath, we could be in danger. He doesn't seem to like us."

"I know. We'll have to be careful. That's the reason for a plan. I think it might be wise if only one of us checks out places and the other stays behind. That way if something happens, the one staying behind will know the other's location and can report it to the law. How does that sound?"

"So, if you go to the sheriff's office and don't return by a certain time, I would report you missing to the sheriff's office?"

"Yes. Don't be sarcastic—it's not funny. Because most likely I'll have been attacked after leaving there. More than anyone else alive on Earth, I know what this guy's capable of. And we should work out our routes, so the sheriff would know where to search."

"Sounds reasonable. I hope our hotel is comfortable and that there's a nice lobby to wait in."

Gene glanced at her and then back to the road. "Are you getting anxious to get home?"

"Not exactly. I'm anxious about Mr. Osaka and his daughter. Do you think we could help find her when we get back to Santa Rosa?"

Gene shook his head. "If the Army can't find her—and I'm sure they're looking—I'm not sure we could."

"What if the Army doesn't know about her?"

"Unlikely, but possible. However, if we find her, we'd have to turn her in."

"Only if she's in danger. We could somehow get word to Mr. Osaka that she's all right."

Gene shook his head again. "You like to try to fix things, don't you?"

"Yes, when I think I can. Sometimes I can't. But I found out about the statue, didn't I?"

"You certainly did. And I bet you're already working on your plot."

"Oh, yes, I am."

"Well? What is it?"

"I never tell my plots or let anyone see my work before it's finished—a rule from my short story days. You'll just have to wait."

Gene smiled. "I'm really looking forward to it."

"Sure you are."

"Yes, I really am. I mean it."

They reached Klamath mid-afternoon after a drive through redwood forests. They were pleasantly surprised when they arrived at their hotel. After checking in, they went to the elegant dining room for dinner where they could view both the Klamath River, known for its salmon fishing, and the Pacific Ocean. The tables were covered with white table cloths and fine china and silver cutlery, and decorated with bouquets of purple wild flowers.

"Wow! This place takes my breath away. I think I could live here." Clara kept staring out the windows.

"It doesn't look like a place where a convict would hang out."

Clara asked, "Do you think they even have a sheriff's station here?"

A waiter, probably in his fifties and dressed in a suit, approached with a hand-written menu. "Welcome to our hotel. Here are the selections for today."

Clara asked, "Is there a sheriff in town?"

"Oh, yes. But it's just him and his part-time deputy. Not much call around here for him. Just sometimes on a Saturday night when some of the boys drink a little too much down at the bar."

Gene asked, "How many people live here?"

"Six or seven hundred. Are you here to fish?"

"No, we're here on our way home to Santa Rosa down near San Francisco." Clara was relieved Gene didn't tell him their real reason for stopping. They needed guidance from the sheriff first. If there was only one sheriff and a deputy, no wonder the convict had stayed there. But where?

Gene asked, "Is there a camping area nearby?"

"Yep. Well, not exactly. Small cabins or rather, shacks. Mostly for the fishermen, though. Down by the river. There's some more back among the redwoods."

One of the other customers yelled, "Hey! How about some service over here?"

Gene said, "Oh, I'm sorry. We didn't mean to be taking up all your time. We'll look at the menu and let you know what we want. We do like to eat." He grinned. The waiter scurried away.

Clara said, "I can understand why our convict would stay here with just a sheriff and a deputy and a gorgeous setting. He could even fish for his own food. But how did the sheriff spot him? He must be fairly sharp to have noticed him."

"As you'll recall, he was seen with a Japanese woman. They probably noticed her rather than him."

"Gene. That's it! That's got to be Mr. Osaka's daughter. He must have kidnapped her, or maybe she got lost and asked for his help and he figured out her father was wealthy."

Gene frowned. "That's quite a jump—to connect our convict to Mr. Osaka and the statues."

"But it explains the note to Mr. Osaka and why we kept seeing the convict on our route. If he's still here, maybe so is she."

"And those fishing cabins by the river indicate where they might be. But he wouldn't be able to leave her alone while he traveled."

"Someone must be with him. Maybe his cousin."

Gene nodded. "Do we know where old man Dobberson is?"

"I thought he was in jail for his part in the attack on you."

Gene shook his head. "I don't know. I'll call Stu and ask. Regardless, you might be right. They have Mr. Osaka's daughter and they're extorting him thinking he's got money hidden somewhere. I'll run that theory by Stu."

"But I don't think he should run the story. We hardly have enough to go on, and it could be dangerous for Mr. Osaka's daughter. Also, I'm re-thinking our plan to check out the area. I think we should both go to the sheriff's station to introduce ourselves. Then we can break out how to visit, one at a time."

Gene nodded. "Good thinking. Want to take a walk after dinner to get our bearings so we'll be ready tomorrow? It's a beautiful evening for a walk."

"As long as it isn't too dark. We're so close to the ocean that I bet they turn off all the lights that might attract Japanese submarine bombings."

When the waiter returned, they ordered salmon (given that it was fresh from the river). And they weren't disappointed. They both lapped it up and then asked for dessert—home-made ice cream with fresh cherries.

It was too dark to take a walk so they decided to retire. Gene got directions to the sheriff's station and also asked how to get to the cabins. The waiter let them know the cabins were quite rustic. "The lady would certainly not want to visited them. But the fishermen don't seem to mind. By the way, breakfast here is from seven to nine. You won't want to miss it."

They decided to eat at seven to get an early start. They planned to walk to the sheriff's office following breakfast and take their time checking out the small town.

Clara went to bed less despondent than earlier. If the convict did indeed kidnap Mr. Osaka's daughter, they might be able to uncover the plot and save her. But maybe it was unrealistic to believe there was a connection between her and the convict. Nonetheless, they'd encountered him enough times to make Clara uneasy about running into him again. He was a murderer, and he'd almost killed Gene and tried to run them off the road. They had to be careful.

Chapter 36

Clara and Gene walked into the stark, one-room sheriff's office, which had two small desks and a telephone. A robust, red-faced balding man, who Clara could tell was accustomed to being in charge, took his time to look at them. "Yes?" he said from the desk closest to the door. When he stood to greet them, they realized that he was at least six feet five inches tall and muscular. Gene took the lead and introduced himself and Clara. The sheriff shook hands with Gene and nodded at Clara.

"You two together?"

Clara started to respond but noticed a softness to Gene's expression before he said, "Yes. We're colleagues. We're here to learn more about the spotting of the escaped convict that you filed. The Santa Rosa police might have contacted you that we were coming. We want to reassure you that we're not here to try to track him down or catch him. That's for the law to do. We just want some details about what you saw and why you recognized him."

The sheriff sat again. "Sorry we don't have any chairs here. This is a small office as you can see. You two married?"

This time Clara definitely noticed a gleam in Gene's eyes, but it was more mischievous than anything. Before he could respond, she said, "No, we're just colleagues."

She looked around and seeing no door to a jail cell asked, "Where do you lock up your prisoners?"

"We send 'em up to Crescent City. It's the county seat of Del Norte County. We don't have much call for lockin' up

244

prisoners here. We do have one patrol car—my deputy uses it to transport 'em when we do have one."

Gene asked, "But about the convict—"

"Well, yes. What happened was my deputy here saw him crossin' the bridge by the fishin' shacks. One of them fisherman had reported seein' someone with a Japanese girl, which is unusual around here and cause for investigatin'."

He stopped and wrinkled his face as if trying to think of something else.

Gene asked, "And was he the convict?"

"Well, my deputy didn't recognize him then. He seemed like jest another fisherman. It wasn't until later when he saw the bulletin that we realized he was the convict. We get bulletins here just like any law enforcement office, ya know. Anyway, we went down and searched all them fishing shacks, but didn't turn up nothin.' We found some food scraps and a couple cans of beans and some apples. Now it's possible that was left there by a fisherman, but they usually don't keep that much. Mostly, if they stay overnight, they just have snacks like cookies or crackers."

"Did anyone else see them?"

"We got a small food store in town. The clerk there thinks he come in a couple of times. But he was the only one. He mighta been here three or four days."

Clara said, "It's possible he kidnapped the girl and was trying to extort money from her family at Camp Tule Lake."

"What makes you think that?"

Gene described the note to Mr. Osaka and the encounters with the convict. "He might have come back here."

The sheriff picked up the phone and gave the operator a number. "Charlie, it's possible that that escaped convict mighta come back here. Be on the lookout but don't approach.

He's a killer. Call me if you see him. And watch for the Japanese girl. She might be a kidnap victim."

He turned back to Gene and Clara. "We'll keep all of this in mind. Now, what are you two plannin' to do? And can I ask what you were doin' visitin' a Japanese at Tule Lake?"

Gene turned to Clara, who hesitated and then said, "It's a long story, but it has to do with my wanting to be a writer. I found a statue that turned out to be one of several that Mr. Osaka's son had designed and had made by a blacksmith— who turns out to be a relative of the convict. Anyway, I brought him the statues with permission from the Army."

The sheriff stared at her. "If I didn't have a daughter of my own, I'd think you're crazy. But she wants to be an artist, and she does the damnedest things to create the perfect painting." He turned and looked at Gene. "What do you think about this?"

Gene smiled. "I'm just along for the ride. Well, that's not quite true. This convict beat me almost to death, so I kinda want to see him caught."

"And why did he beat you?"

"I'm a reporter and was interviewing his family for the story of his escape. He attacked me and stole my car."

"All right. Both of you. If he's returned, you better be careful. But I guess you already know that. If anything happens, call me here—and if I don't answer ask the operator to reach me at home or wherever. She'll know how to reach me. Where are you stayin'?"

They gave him the name of the hotel, and thanked him for his time. They decided to walk along the river to check out the fishing cabins. Although they both thought it was unlikely they would find anything, Clara wanted to see for herself the kind of place where the convict might have been hiding as well as if there was any trace of Mr. Osaka's daughter.

Also, they wanted to view the picturesque Klamath River up close, which they were told was the second largest river in California.

"Wow! The river with the giant redwoods as a backdrop—absolutely incredible!" Clara gushed. "At least our convict appreciated outstanding scenery!" She enjoyed the walk after being cooped up in the car, and she welcomed the scenery and fresh air.

They reached the first cabins, which appeared to be occupied. When Gene found an empty one and opened the door, he muttered, "'Rustic' overstates their appeal. The term 'cabin' is an overstatement as well. They definitely qualify for 'shack' status."

Clara laughed. "But what a beautiful setting."

The one-room structures had no windows and only a dirty cot and a single chair. The smell was a mixture of fish and dank, wet clothes. The door had no lock and barely latched when closed. Clara asked, "Why would a fisherman want to stay here?"

"In case of rain or just to rest for a little while. Get away from the bugs. Clean their fish."

They continued to walk along the river and came across more cabins further back among the redwoods.

Gene said, "If I were a convict, I'd want to get as deep into the woods as possible—less risk of being seen. Let's keep going."

They opened the door of the last cabin. The smell was worse here than the others, largely due to rotting food on the floor. Clara covered her nose and mouth and said, "You explore this one. I'll meet you outside."

Gene nodded and held his nose. He used a twig he found to push the garbage around and stopped suddenly when he found a pendant with Japanese characters on it. He picked it up, went outside, and dangled it in front of Clara.

"Uh my gosh! She was here."

"Yes, but we know that the convict traveled at least as far as Tule Lake where we saw him. But he was alone. Did she stay here by herself?"

"Maybe his cousin guarded her."

"Then where are they now?"

Gene said, "They're not here. Nothing in that cabin is newer than a week ago. Let's head back to the hotel and check places where they might be hiding. We'll be careful."

"All right. But if you want to hurry ahead to get the car, that'll give me time to take in more of this scenery. I'll meet you at the road leading to the trail down here."

"Sounds good. Don't get lost."

"I'll just follow the river. If either of us gets lost, we'll meet at the bridge—that one with the two bear statues."

He nodded, waved and left her peering at the redwoods and the river. She waved to some fishermen in a canoe and started to follow the same path Gene had just taken—only she walked slowly, breathing in the fresh scent of the redwoods and the river. She was about to wave at a man coming toward her when she stopped quickly and looked around for a place to hide. She was sure he was the convict. He hadn't seen her yet. He, too, was looking at the fishermen. She ducked into the nearest cabin, doing her best to hold her nose, and left the door open a crack to watch. She waited a few minutes and finally glimpsed him ambling toward the end of the row of cabins, but then he turned and headed back from the direction he'd just come from.

She waited until he was a safe distance away and opened the door slowly. He was far enough ahead that she felt safe following him. She knew she couldn't stay with him too far, or she would indeed be putting herself in danger. But she thought she could follow him for a while in hopes of discovering where he was staying.

She did not try to keep up with him. He walked much faster than she did, and only once turned to look behind him. At that moment, a fisherman carrying rods and gear walked between them screening her from the convict's sight. She smiled at the fisherman who nodded.

As soon as the fisherman passed her, she looked for the convict and saw him heading toward the bridge. If he decided to cross the bridge, she'd have to wait until he reached the other side so he wouldn't see her. With a little luck, Gene would have gotten back to the car and might be nearing the bridge to meet her there. Then they could both follow the convict.

But she was not that fortunate. She waited until the convict was far enough ahead and started after him. Echoes of her promise to Gene and the sheriff that she would be careful made her hesitate. But she figured she wouldn't get close enough. She'd stay a safe distance behind. She wasn't going to confront him.

He kept walking and Clara crossed the street to remain out of view. She was focused on the convict, who wasn't slowing. She was glad she was in good physical shape and accustomed to walking now that her ankle had healed. They'd gone at least a mile so far, she guessed

But he kept going, increasing his pace. Fewer people were around, and she feared by now the convict must have noticed her tracking him. She pretended to study the redwoods as a tourist might, almost losing sight of him. But she found him again sitting on a log, smoking a cigarette. She ducked behind some trees and hoped he didn't notice her.

She waited a few minutes and then peered around the trees. He was grinding out his cigarette with his foot, and moving on. She gave him a head start and then followed again. She was beginning to tire. They must have gone another mile. She felt more conspicuous given that now she was the only other person on the road which had narrowed to little more than a dirt path. She found fewer places to hide.

Clara needed to rest, but feared if she stopped she'd lose him. He continued his fast pace. She tried to rationalize stopping to rest because the road seemed to go in only one direction. She could catch up to him later. But common sense told her he could disappear into any number of places that she would be unable to search. So she labored on hoping he would soon stop.

But then she paused. What was she going to do when he ended his journey? How could she get back to Gene or the sheriff? She'd need to at least find a phone, but certainly there would be no phone in a forest. She'd have to wait to see where he went, hoping he'd reach his final destination and remain there until she could get help.

She trudged on—dodging behind trees with the hope he didn't see her. He did not slow down or appear to have noticed her. She felt like they'd walked at least another mile.

And then he stopped—and disappeared. Where did he go? As she got closer, she saw a hill leading down to a farmhouse below.

Suddenly the convict appeared in front of her and grabbed her arms. She screamed.

"Shut up, bitch! Who do ya think's gonna hear ya out here?"

"Let go!"

"You're one of them reporters. I shoulda got rid of ya on the road up to Tule Lake."

"You tried to kill us!"

"Yep. Sorry I missed. I'll make up for it now. Get goin'"

Clara was confused. "Go where?"

"See that empty farmhouse down there? We're gonna go there and then mebbe we'll see how ya can help me get to Osaka."

"You have his daughter, don't you?"

He pushed her down the hill, and Clara felt herself tumbling, then skidding on her stomach. She tried to stop, but he kicked her from behind and she rapidly slid the rest of the way down. She felt her arm hit a rock and then both her legs were tangled in the brush. Her face smacked the dirt path. Finally, she stopped but only because a pair of boots attached to legs and a full body holding a rifle stood between her and the rest of the hill.

But the rifle was pointed at the convict. The man in boots said, "That wasn't so nice pushing this young lady down here. Who are you?"

Clara tried to talk, but her mouth was full of dirt. She couldn't get her arm to move. She felt dizzy. She heard the convict say something, but couldn't decipher it. The man in boots didn't move.

She thought she heard the convict say something about the farmhouse. "I'm sorry. I didn't realize someone lived there. I didn't mean to push the young lady. I was trying to help her down. We was just gonna explore. We're tourists from Santa Rosa. Mebbe if you gotta phone we could call fer help."

The boots spoke. "I don't think so."

Why couldn't she speak? Maybe that wasn't dirt in her mouth. It was blood. She must have hit her mouth. She needed to tell the boots that the man who pushed her was an escaped convict. He musn't let him go.

251

The convict said, "I tell ya what. If'n ya don't believe me, call the sheriff."

"They're on their way."

"Well, then ya don't need me anymore."

Clara felt something hit the boots and his rifle fired in the air and she screamed when she was rolled over onto her injured arm. She saw flashes of the convict heading back up the hill, and boots trying to free himself from her. Then things went dark for a while. The next she knew, she was on a stretcher being carried back up the hill.

She thought she heard Gene, but that wasn't possible. Where was the convict? And what happened to her rescuer, the boots?

When they reached the top of the hill, she saw Gene. He was staring at her—his eyes wide and his mouth opened—but then looked away. After a moment, he managed to ask, "Clara, are you all right? What were you doing here? What happened?" His voice was husky and shaking.

"I followed the convict." She couldn't manage much more.

"Of course, you did. You're going to be all right. I'll yell at you later. Right now we're taking you to a clinic in Crescent City."

"Tell Boots thank you."

"Boots?"

"He rescued me." But that was all she could manage. She'd tell him about Mr. Osaka's daughter later.

Chapter 37

Clara was sitting up in a bed at a small clinic in Crescent City waiting for Gene to pick her up reviewing in her mind how Gene happened to be present when she was rescued from her confrontation with the convict. He'd been on the bridge waiting for her as they'd agreed when the sheriff pulled up behind him and yelled to follow him—that she'd been attacked. He'd received a phone call from the people who lived in the farm house. He pointed to the ambulance parked on the opposite end of the bridge. When they reached the end of the path, they encountered two men carrying Clara up the hill on the stretcher. And that's when she regained consciousness and saw him.

She was anxious to hear updates about the convict. Gene, the sheriff, and the FBI were now searching the area for him, but so far he slipped away again.

There was no word about Mr. Osaka's daughter or any Japanese woman.

Clara's arm was in a plaster cast and held in a sling. She'd needed a few stitches in her lips, which were still swollen along with her bruised cheeks and blackened eyes. Her legs had somehow escaped serious injury although they were scraped and now scabbed over.

Gene entered with another man and introduced him as an FBI agent. "Clara, he needs to talk to us privately."

Clara noticed that neither man could look at her and tended to talk to some place above her head. She'd not looked in a mirror but suspected she must look, well, damaged.

She said, "All right. What do you need to tell us? Have you caught the convict yet? He seems to want both Gene and me dead."

The agent answered, "No, but we're definitely trying. However, I need a pledge from both of you about the farmhouse you saw."

Clara looked puzzled. "Farmhouse? I barely saw it."

"But you both know where it is. You must not under any circumstances discuss it with anyone."

Gene said, "It's a radar station, isn't it? To track down Japanese subs. I heard about them, but never saw one."

"Yes. And the security of America depends on keeping it a secret."

Clara said, "Of course. There's no doubt that I'll keep it a secret. But what about the convict?"

"We're intensifying our search for him. We also understand that he's been seen with a Japanese woman. If he realizes that the farmhouse is a radar station, rather than a farm, he could reveal that to the enemy."

Clara said, "But if the Japanese woman is who we think she is you don't need to worry about her. She's from an American Japanese family and was brought up as an American, and her brother is a soldier fighting for our side. I don't believe she would ever betray her country."

"Maybe yes, maybe no. We can't take the chance."

Gene stood between Clara and the agent. "Neither of us will reveal the location or the nature of the farmhouse. However, we can't promise that we'll stop looking for the Japanese woman. Or that we won't visit Mr. Osaka again."

Clara was surprised at Gene's belligerence.

The FBI agent said, "We'd rather you didn't. You could be exposing your country to great harm."

Clara shook her head. "No, Mr. Osaka is loyal. Like I said, his son is even fighting in the war." She looked at the agent and added, "—on *our* side."

Gene turned away and shook his head at Clara, then said, "Even if we do speak with him again, we'll never reveal or discuss in any way the deserted farmhouse. That I can pledge."

"Me, too."

The agent shook hands with Gene and nodded at Clara. "We actually owe you our thanks. If you hadn't tumbled from the path, we might not have seen your assailant. He might have snuck down and got a glimpse inside the building. That could have been a serious breach of security. We've increased our guard duty to cover all approaches to the farm from increased distances."

Clara resisted saying, "Tumbled? You're welcome," especially since Gene was glaring at her. She really wanted to go home. "Can we leave now?"

The agent nodded. "Thanks. And take care."

Gene helped Clara stand, and she started to walk out of the room. Although she felt unsteady and weak, she did not slow down. She thought she managed to leave the room with some dignity. Gene and the agent followed. Gene held onto her good arm. Her doctor came out of one of the other rooms and said, "Where's your wheelchair? You shouldn't be walking. You need to rest for a day or two before making the trip to Santa Rosa."

Clara did not slow down. She waved off any help and found her way to the exit. Gene helped open the door as the doctor said, "Make sure you have yourself checked out when you get home."

Gene ran ahead and opened the car door for her. The agent hovered over her and then winked at Gene. "You've got your hands full with that one, don't you?"

Gene smiled. "You have no idea!"

He waved to the agent and got in the car and faced Clara. "All right. We're staying at the hotel at least one more night—for two reasons. First, the car needs some attention. It's been stalling." Proving his point, the car wouldn't start. He choked it more and gently tapped the gas pedal and the engine finally turned over. "Second, it's a five-to-seven-hour trip back to Santa Rosa, so let's see how you're feeling tomorrow. And no faking it. Understand?"

"Have you talked to Stu?"

"Yes. He's up to date. However, we're going to have to pull together a story that doesn't mention the farmhouse."

"I can't believe the sheriff and the FBI couldn't find the convict. I found him, and I wasn't even looking!"

He ignored her comment. "Also, I talked to your parents."

"Oh, you probably shouldn't have done that. They'll be worried now."

"They've been worried the entire time we've been gone. I thought it was better to let them know ahead of time rather than to see you as you are without forewarning. Have you looked in a mirror?"

"No. I've avoided it. Not so good, huh?"

"The FBI agent had to look away, and I bet he's seen some pretty gruesome things before."

"Is the car going to make it to Klamath?"

"As long as I don't stop."

"Well, here's hoping you don't have to stop before we reach the hotel."

"It's less than an hour to Klamath—about twenty-five miles. I met a friendly Klamath mechanic who plans to work on the car tomorrow. He's a fun guy. He can't wait to meet you. He isn't sure that young ladies should be chasing convicts."

"Well, somebody has to."

"Oh, my! Aren't we feeling superior!? And who rescued you, by the way?"

Clara wanted to retort with something, but she felt very tired and her head was heavy so she leaned back in the seat to rest. She'd spent the past few days seeing flashes of herself falling down the steep hill. She kept hoping these flashbacks would stop, but so far she was still seeing them.

"Are you all right?" Gene asked. "Should I stop?"

"No. Keep going. I don't want to get stranded if you can't start again. I'm just tired. Drive and get us to our hotel so I can lie down."

Clara must have fallen asleep because when she woke up they were at the hotel, and Gene was gently prodding her. Gene and their waiter from the previous day helped her get out of the car. However, not without Clara noticing the waiter's expression and quick avoidance at looking at her. Gene held her steady with his arm around her waist. They walked her over to the steps then made a seat for her with their arms. She sat, feeling somewhat awkward and then unsteady as they hoisted her up the steps one at a time, slowly.

When they reached the top, Gene took over. "I've got her now. And thank the management again for giving us downstairs rooms."

He kept his arm around her waist and walked her into a new guest room which was more spacious and had a view of the river.

Clara said, "This is nice, Gene. Thanks. I don't feel so well."

"Let's get you in bed. Can you take off your clothes?"

She managed to glare at him. "If I need to, I can, but I don't need to. I'll just lie down for a while. Then I'll feel better and maybe we can have dinner."

"All right. And I promised your folks you'd call them. Will you be up to it?"

"I'll make myself be up to it." But she felt her eyes closing and knew she was about to fall asleep. "Please wake me up in an hour." She fell asleep wondering how she would explain chasing a convict to her parents—and also wishing that she'd caught him.

Chapter 38

Clara missed dinner, but felt much better the next morning and was eager for breakfast. She was up and feeling stronger and well-rested when Gene knocked on her door.

"Hi. I'm starved."

"That's not a surprise. If I've learned nothing else on this trip, it's that you've got a voracious appetite."

He smiled and offered her his arm which she normally would have ignored and led the way. However, this morning she took his arm and let him lead her to their table. The friendly waiter saw them coming and poured coffee and apple juice.

Gene said, "I've already taken the car to the mechanic, and walked back."

She couldn't resist. "During your walk back here, did you happen to see the convict?"

"No, I didn't. But the sheriff might have. He's stopping by in a half hour to talk with us. Since we have no car, we're spending the day here."

She looked around at the elegant dining room with its view of both the Pacific Ocean and the Klamath River. "Well, if we have to stay somewhere, we couldn't have chosen a better place."

Gene nodded. "I know what you mean. I'm not sure Stu is going to appreciate our expenses."

"By the way, I've never prodded, but do you know how Stu got us in to see Mr. Osaka? That couldn't have been easy."

"I don't know if it was easy, but Stu has connections with our newest governor. I'm sure he contacted him. But then how he got the U.S. Army to let you in, that's a mystery"

"Have you heard anything more about Lowry's murder?"

"No, nothing."

After the waiter served their meal, Clara told him, "Thank you for helping me yesterday. I'm feeling a little stronger today."

The waiter once again averted his eyes so he was not looking at her. "That's all right. You must be more careful. Don't you go searching for bad guys."

The sheriff approached their table. The waiter asked him if he'd like coffee. He nodded. "Thank you. I can't stay long enough for breakfast."

Gene said, "You said you had some news for us?"

"I do. It's not really news, but I've talked to a couple of local people who remember seeing the Japanese lady, and I assume also your convict. However, the description of the man with the Japanese lady doesn't exactly match the convict who attacked you. And each person gave the same description without the other present."

Clara, surprised that the sheriff didn't look away when speaking to her, said, "Maybe his cousin was with him. Gene, can you describe him for the sheriff?"

"Sure. He was short, stocky and recognizable with a short scar on the right side of his face."

"No. This fella was tall—at least six feet—slender, not muscular, dark hair, dressed in a suit, and had a new car. Neither witness could say what kind of car, just that it was new. And he was dressed in clothes they claimed cost money. Don't know what that means. I'm guessing not work clothes. And the Japanese lady seemed to know him. They talked to each other like close friends, although she hid her face from anyone seein' her."

Gene shook his head. "That doesn't sound like either of the convicts, especially the well-dressed part. And our convict is somewhat heavy and muscular."

Clara joined in. "Well, maybe it does. I recall that one of them had a friend with a job selling Japanese real estate, and he might have worn a suit. He would have been the one who picked you up at the courthouse."

"No, that guy was short and stocky—or maybe overweight. And I don't care what kind of clothes you put on either of the convicts, both were scruffy looking. This gets more curious every day."

Clara took a bite of pancake, a special treat from the waiter. She tried to get his attention to thank him, but he still refused to look at her. She guessed the sheriff was more accustomed to someone with her appearance. He didn't hesitate to look at her when he spoke or when she responded. She thought maybe that was one of his interrogation techniques.

Gene asked, "When did these two townspeople see this new guy?"

"Recently, like maybe last week."

"Where?"

"Down by the fishing shacks."

It pleased Clara that he called them "shacks," rather than "cabins." That was more accurate.

He continued, "The lady appeared somewhat weak. She was leaning on the gentleman."

Gene said, "If we'd gotten here sooner, we might have intercepted them."

The sheriff turned to Clara. "Did you happen to hear why the convict went to the location where he assaulted you?"

"Yes. He was looking for an empty building, and he'd seen that farmhouse before. He walked right to it. He needed a place to hide, I think. But he was alone. And, if he'd kidnapped the woman—and I'm sure he did—he couldn't have left her alone. So, this other person must have been his partner."

The sheriff said, "I'm not convinced. The description doesn't match the normal criminal type. Also, earlier witnesses from more than two weeks ago described the man as short and stocky. So we may have two men involved, after all. Well, I have to get back to the office. No tellin' what's been goin' on since I've been gone. Charlie should have your car fixed in good time. There's no one better than him at fixin' cars. When do ya plan to start home?"

Gene looked at Clara. "It depends on when she's up to it."

Clara nodded. "I do feel better than yesterday. It might be due to this great food."

The sheriff nodded. "If I hear anything else, I'll let you know. And I'd appreciate the same from you."

Gene said, "Of course. And thank you for your help."

They watched him leave, and then both returned to finishing their breakfast. After Gene had eaten the last morsel, he said, "You need to call your parents. I let them know last night that you're all right but had fallen asleep before you had a chance to call them."

"Yes, I know. But they'll be at work."

"It's Sunday, Clara. They should be home."

"Oh, is it really Sunday. You're right. They should be home."

"Yep. Let's go. The manager said we can use his office."

"Gene, you're not paying for all this, you know. I will give back every cent you've spent on me."

"We can talk about that later. Let's go."

He helped her out of her chair and led her into the office. The manager showed her the phone. Using her good arm, she held the receiver and gave the operator her parents' phone number, asking for time and charges at the end of the call.

Her father answered. "Hi, Dad. It's Clara." She heard him tell her mother she was on the line. "I had a little run-in with the convict up here but I'm doing much better now. We're at this beautiful hotel with a great view of the ocean. It's gorgeous! You and Mom have got to come here."

"It's good to hear your voice. Tell me quickly before you talk to your mother, how bad is it?"

"I guess the worst is a broken arm, and I'm bruised all over. But I'm feeling better, and we should be home as soon as we get the car fixed."

"All right, here's your mother."

"Clara? You promised not to do anything dangerous!"

"I know. I didn't think I was doing anything dangerous. I was just following him. Unfortunately, he saw me and threw me down a hill. But I'm doing all right, Mom. I'll be better in no time. But I look pretty bad right now."

"Oh, no! All right. Did you get accomplished what you needed to do?"

"Yes. Oh, yes, yes, yes. I can't wait to tell you! I know I'm going to become a good author. I'm feeling things, Mom."

"All right, Clara. Thank you for calling. We don't want to run up the phone bill. We'll see you when you get home, and you can tell us all about it."

They hung up. Clara looked at Gene. "She asked me if I got what I needed. I really did, Gene. I *feel* it."

"What you *feel* are bumps and bruises."

She almost laughed.

Gene said, "None of this with the Japanese woman makes sense."

"Unless this third person is a partner with the convicts who's just better positioned to reach out to Mr. Osaka to get his money."

"Maybe, but why would he take the daughter away before the convict returned from visiting Tule Lake?"

"Good question. I'll mull it over during this afternoon's nap."

Chapter 39

Clara and Gene spent the next two days relaxing and enjoying the views. Charlie returned the car after Clara went to bed the next night. So Gene suggested over coffee in the morning that they take a drive along the river and then through the redwoods.

"It will give us a chance to see how easy it is for you to ride in the car."

Clara was annoyed that Gene hadn't informed her that the car was ready, but secretly was relieved that they didn't have to drive back so soon.

"I do feel better, but I'm a little stiff and sore. I'm glad we have Stu's car rather than my dad's. This one has more legroom."

They pulled onto the highway and drove north. The car ran fine and Clara felt comfortable. Gene found the lookout the waiter had recommended, and they sat in silence watching the relentless waves of the Pacific Ocean hit the shore.

Clara broke the calm. "Did you talk to Stu today?"

"Yes. They still haven't tracked down Lowry's killer. And he really needs us back at work. He's been doing double shifts himself to cover everything."

"I think I can make it. If I get tired I can sleep in the back seat."

"You still don't look too good."

"Thanks. I don't recall critiquing your appearance after either of your bouts with the convicts."

Gene ignored her. "I wish we could have found out more about Mr. Osaka's daughter. They must be worried about her."

"Me, too. I hope the statutes bring him some peace."

"Kind of hard to be at peace locked up—"

"Don't. There's nothing we can do."

"I wonder."

"Let's go back. I'm ready to go home, but I'd like to rest tonight."

Their sightseeing jaunt was short, just two hours. Gene drove back to their hotel, Clara insisted on walking to the steps to show how strong she was. Gene obliged her, but held her arm until they were inside the lobby, where the waiter ran up to them.

"Call the sheriff. He thinks they spotted your convict."

Clara said, "Go call him. I can make it."

The waiter said, "I'll take her."

She asked to sit in one of the easy chairs outside the dining room. "Tell Gene where I am. I'm anxious to hear what the sheriff wanted."

She didn't have to wait long. He hurried over to her. "He thinks they've caught your convict."

"Really? Where, how? Was the Japanese woman with him?"

"No. He denies ever having a Japanese woman with him. Claims someone made a mistake. But the deputy in Humboldt County caught him trying to rob a gas station and food store. He knocked out the attendant, but the deputy was nearby and caught him trying to flee. Apparently the convict tried to attack the deputy, so he shot the guy."

"Is he dead?"

"No. Just wounded. They treated him at the jail. They said we could come see him if we want."

"Do you think he'd answer any of our questions?"

"Don't know. But it's in Eureka which is the way home. So, we could stop. Ask questions as reporters, and give Stu a story."

"We owe him something."

"I'll let them know we'll stop by tomorrow on our way." He turned and went back to the manager's office.

Clara felt tired. She would have preferred to go straight home, which surprised her. Her typical response would have been the urge to interview the convict and the deputy who caught him. She would normally be excited about the opportunity. Her lack of enthusiasm, she realized, was most likely due to her injuries, but she regretted her sense of fatigue. She wanted to bounce back quickly.

Gene returned after calling the sheriff again. "All right. It's arranged. I explained that we're working on a story for the paper. They said we earned it—or at least you did."

Clara smiled. "It'll be interesting to hear what he has to say."

"I'm not sure it matters. We've got a story with the deputy who caught him; and we can add that he assaulted you, if you want. But we obviously can't say where. That's one of the reasons that they're granting the interview. We won't explain where it happened."

"But will the guy talk?"

"He might, but they'll keep him away from doing any other interviews. Also, all he knows is that it was a deserted farmhouse. He doesn't know those were federal agents who saw him."

"Is it time for dinner? I can't believe how hungry I am!"

Gene smiled. "I can. It's that voracious appetite again." He stood, ignoring her glare. "It's early, but let me see if they'll seat us now. It probably depends on if the food's ready."

"If not, I can wait here. I'm comfortable. Hey, Gene, where'd he get the car?"

"The convict? Probably stole it."

"But where's your Studebaker? The one he stole when he beat you up."

"Maybe with his cousin. The car he had wasn't mine. I asked."

"Oh, sorry."

Gene returned in a few minutes, saying, "They'll serve us now. I explained that we planned to get an early start tomorrow and want to retire early. They understand. I didn't tell them you're starved!"

Clara couldn't get up from her seat. Gene started toward her to help, but she shook her head. The second time she tried, she stood, and they headed slowly for the dining room.

"I hope there's time for breakfast here in the morning. I've enjoyed our meals here."

Gene nodded, and grinned.

Clara ignored him.

Chapter 40

They pulled up to what both decided was the most ornate county courthouse either had ever seen. The central spire of the Humboldt County Courthouse in Eureka with its clock tower overlooked a rectangular space surrounded by columns that stood atop a three-story building. It looked like there were at least a dozen statues on the roof. In fact, Victorian architecture dominated buildings and homes throughout Eureka.

The drive from Klamath to Eureka had taken about an hour and a half. Although Clara was feeling some pain, she was awed by the quaint town. "This will be a great city to write about as a backdrop to a captured convict."

Gene nodded. "Do you want to wait here until I find out the location of our convict?"

Clara glanced at the steps leading to the front door and said, "Yes. Thanks."

While Gene was gone, she tried to look around at the interesting buildings. A trolley car passed by amid the cars on the road. She would have enjoyed getting out and walking, but knew she wouldn't last too long.

Gene descended the steps. He opened her door, and said, "He's here for interrogation. The gunshot wound wasn't too serious. They said we can interview him and the deputy now."

"This town is incredible! I'd like to return when I can explore."

"Agreed."

"He didn't have your car?"

"Apparently not. Nor was the Japanese woman with him."

Gene helped Clara up the stairs. For a change, she didn't resist and instead took his arm without hesitation. She was eager to interview the person who'd caused her so much pain. And she would write as brutal a story about him as she could.

A deputy met them at the door and led them past several rooms where other deputies and clerks were doing County business. He didn't slow down for Clara, but Gene didn't speed up, so the deputy had to wait. Clara shuffled as fast as she could, with Gene holding her steady.

They reached the door of a room where a deputy stood outside. He'd obviously been briefed and opened the door for them. Another deputy inside the room pointed to two chairs in front of a table. "Hold on a minute. We'll bring him in. Did he do that to you?" He pointed to Clara.

"Yes."

"I'm glad I shot him."

Gene asked, "You're the deputy who apprehended him? We'd really like to talk to you. Your superior, I believe, gave permission for an interview."

"You bet. But you gotta talk to the bastard son-of-a-bitch first. We need to get him back in his cell."

"All right."

They waited for almost five minutes before they heard clanking chains. The door opened and the manacled convict entered the room with a deputy on either side of him. They steered him to a chair across the table from Clara and Gene. He was wearing the same clothes Clara had seen him in, except now one sleeve was stained with blood. He took a look at Clara's face.

"Jeez. I guess I got you good, huh?" he laughed.

Gene clenched his fists and Clara noticed that the deputy closest to him took a step toward him, but then backed off.

Clara responded, "Not as good as they got you. You're going back to prison—probably for life."

The convict laughed. "Smart-aleck broad. You weren't so smart rolling down that hill."

"And you won't be so smart behind bars for years on end. But we're here to interview you for an article in the Santa Rosa paper."

Gene interrupted. "What do you have to say?"

"I'm innocent, of course." And he laughed.

"What were you doing in Klamath?"

"Nice place to visit."

Clara had pulled out her notebook and was doing her best to get his quotes. Fortunately, it was her left arm that was in the cast, and she was right-handed, but she had difficulty holding her notepad steady while she wrote.

Gene asked, "Why did you leave?"

"You're really gonna put this in the paper about me?"

"Maybe. If you tell us anything worth printing."

He grinned. "Like do you wanna know how I broke outa that jail?" He turned to the deputy. "You better listen. This jail you got here ain't nothin'."

The deputy glared and said, "I got no problem finishing the job. Next bullet's going much closer to your heart, if you have one."

"Ha. All right, reporters. What do you want to know?"

Clara said, "Tell us about the Japanese woman."

"There's that Japanese woman again. I don't know nothin' about no Japanese woman."

"Several people in Klamath saw you with one."

"Not me."

"So, you deny ever being with anyone in Klamath?"

"Sure. Why not?"

Gene said, "Because you were seen with someone, that's why."

"Not me. I was alone."

Clara asked, "Where'd you hide?"

"Well, now if I tell ya that I can't hide there the next time I 'scape."

"I followed you from the fishing cabins by the river, so I'm going to assume that's where you were hiding with your cousin and the Japanese woman."

He leered at her. "'Sume all you want. But I don't see no reason to tell you where I was in Klamath. Me and Cuz were both there. Good place to hide after this little lady here got us alerted to them deputies in Klamath. We couldn't stay no more—'less we found us a new place to hide."

"One more time for the record: You deny having a Japanese woman with you."

"Yeah."

"And you never left Klamath until a couple days ago."

"Yep."

Clara asked, "And what about a well-dressed man—over six feet tall? Is he another one of your helpers?"

The convict lost his smug look. "What are ya talkin' about?"

"Someone saw the Japanese woman with a tall man dressed in a suit and driving a new car. Friend of yours?"

"Lots of people in Klamath seemed to be seein' Japanese women."

"Who was he?"

"Lady, fallin' down that hill musta smashed your brains. Don't know no Japanese lady. No tall feller, neither"

Gene interrupted, "One more time for the record: You deny having a Japanese woman with you."

"Ya got that right."

"And you never left Klamath until a couple days ago."

"Yep."

"Is there anything you want to tell the public?"

"I'm innocent. I never did nothing wrong. Ya got it out fer me. That officer I shot was gonna shoot me. But we'll get even."

The deputy shook his head, and grabbed the convict by his arm and yanked him up. He yelled, but a second deputy got on the other side of the manacled prisoner and dragged him out of the room. Clara and Gene were alone in the small office.

Clara spoke first. "What a piece of trash."

"I couldn't have said it better myself. But we didn't learn anything. I wonder why he denies having the Japanese woman. He can't ransom her now."

"No, but maybe the tall man in the suit who was seen with her—maybe he can. It's strange that the description of the person with her didn't match the cousin. He's got to be the one who has her."

Gene nodded. "It would seem so. But the witnesses' descriptions can't both be wrong. And they were similar."

"I guess."

"Want to stay here overnight? We could write our story and phone it in. That would give you a chance to rest."

"Yes. Good idea. And this is certainly a pleasant town. Maybe we could drive around and see some more of the Victorian houses."

"Let me ask the deputy for a good place to stay and somewhere to eat. Wait here."

Clara was happy to remain seated. Light-headed, she yearned for a bed. She hoped for a nap before checking out the town. Also, she couldn't think how to write the story about the escaped convict. She hoped Gene could do it without too much of her input.

Clara watched Gene leave the room, feeling uneasy for the first time about discussing hotel arrangements with him. Although staying in the same hotel for the entire trip had not bothered her before, given her new feelings about Gene, she'd begun to feel on edge about it the past few days, since Klamath. And, now, here again she felt a little weird about spending the night with him in the same hotel. Maybe her queasiness was due to having spent the past week in his company. She'd feel more like herself once she was home and back to her routine.

Gene returned to the interview room with a note. "I got a great hotel listing—nice but not expensive—and the deputy called and got us a reservation. We can check in now. That will give you time to rest. Then we can explore the town and have dinner. While you're resting, I'll write our article and you can review it and add comments after your nap."

Clara stared at Gene. All she could say was, "Perfect plan."

He smiled and nodded, then offered his arm to help her stand.

While walking to the car, she said, "At least we don't have to worry about running into one of the convicts."

"At least not the one we just interviewed."

She got into the car, relieved to be sitting again. Gene joined her and asked, "Can you read the directions to me—be my guide?"

She looked at the note he handed her. It all felt so natural, like they'd been together forever, and he could anticipate her. She stared at the directions. Although the words at first appeared blurry, she blinked and said, "Go straight for several blocks until you come to a café with a tree in front of it, turn there."

Chapter 41

They pulled into Santa Rosa the next afternoon and headed for Clara's house first. Their time in Eureka had been pleasant, and Clara was even alert enough to make suggestions for their article about the convict. The restaurant where they'd eaten dinner offered a limited but satisfactory meal, and the tour of Eureka was rewarding.

However, Clara was relieved to be home and already felt some of the pressure from her feelings about her travel partner lifting.

Gene said, "I'll drop you off and then go the office. Is anyone home at your place?"

"No, but I'll be all right. I'll probably just fall asleep on the sofa. My bedroom is upstairs, and I don't feel like making the climb."

"Do you have enough material to write your novel?"

"It wasn't 'material' that I wanted. I still don't know exactly what I needed, maybe an idea. Or maybe this was just the right time to go searching. And I believe that I can't stop looking for *it*."

"I think maybe you went too far looking for *it* this time. Here we are. I'll help you inside."

"It's a huge relief to be home."

"Are you still planning to find a place of your own?"

"Yes. It's time. I just need to be able to afford it. I've saved some money, but it might be a few months before I can rent a place."

He helped her up the few steps to the porch. She pulled a key from her bag and handed it to him, then took his arm to walk into the house and collapsed on the sofa. "Thanks, Gene. Please tell Stu I'll come back to work as soon as I can."

"Will do. Can I get you anything before I go?"

Clara smiled. "We're reversed. I used to ask you that when you were hurt."

"I know. And I hope you appreciate it as much as I did."

"Water would be nice."

Gene poured some water into a glass and handed it to her. "I've got to go now. I promised Stu. He sounded really desperate."

"Can you find out if there's anything new about Lowry's murder?"

"Will do. By the way, I think Marjorie's coming over as soon as she's finished at the artists place, which should be soon. Should I leave the door unlocked for her?"

"Sure. Good idea. That way I won't have to get up."

She watched him leave, but instead of a lifting of the pressure about her feelings for him, she suddenly felt like something was missing. She rationalized that it was because she'd spent the past week with Gene and now he was gone. That's all it was. But then why did she feel the need to talk to him? And she still yearned for more. She closed her eyes and drifted off.

The next thing she heard was Marjorie saying, "Oh my gosh. What happened to you?"

"Oh, hi, Marjorie. Guess I fell asleep. Sorry, I know I look awful, but I'm actually feeling much better. Didn't Gene warn you?"

"He did. But he couldn't possibly have described how terrible you look. I hope they got the guy who did this to you."

"They did. He blamed it on me. Not a nice guy. I really want to get back to normal. I don't like being an invalid."

"I believe it. Do you need anything?"

"I don't think so, but I'm not sure. Gene got me water before he left."

"How was it traveling with him? Did you two get closer or are you still mostly ignoring each other?"

Clara hesitated, unsure of what to say. "No, it was all right. We worked together. He's getting more tolerant and less picky."

"I talked with your mom. She's teaching a late class, but I told her I'd be here. One of her colleagues is bringing her home."

"Thanks." Then Clara timidly asked, "Have you heard from Ed?"

Marjorie shook her head. "Not in the past week. But I've been keeping busy."

"Anything new with the Dobberson family?"

"You heard that someone murdered Mr. Lowry, their new gardener?"

"Yes. Is there any update?"

"No. They don't seem to have any clues about him."

Clara hesitated, then said, "I'm thinking of going to his home and talking to his family. He said he lived in San Jose with his parents."

Marjorie studied Clara for a few moments, then said, "I don't think you should do that."

"Why not? I want to do an interview with them. My guess is that Stu hasn't had time to do any background interviews, and I want to know who killed Lowry."

"Maybe when you look a little more presentable."

"Yeah, in a day or two."

"Or three or four or five."

Clara asked, "Anyway, what about the Dobberson family? Have they done anything to help find his killer?"

"Not that I know of. But I'm not exactly welcome there anymore, either."

"You think they'd welcome you since you're alone and your husband's at war."

"Maybe that's the issue. Remember, they lost a son there, and Hiram hasn't joined yet."

"Can't say I blame him. But he's bound to get drafted."

"Yep."

The door opened and Clara's mother rushed into the room. Her expression when she saw Clara said it all, then Marjorie told her, "You get used to it after a few minutes."

But Mrs. Wilson did not appear to believe that she would get used to seeing her daughter's injured face, broken arm and body covered with scabs and bruises. Clara said, "The bruises have darkened over the past few days, but I'm healing fine."

"Right. I'll make an appointment with our doctor. Marjorie, can you drive us?"

"Of course."

Mrs. Wilson went to the phone, gave the number of her doctor, and asked for an appointment. She explained that her daughter had been beaten up and needed immediate attention. Clara tried to protest, but failed.

"We can go right now. Can you stand?"

"Of course. Marjorie, can I borrow your arm?"

The trip to the doctor served little purpose except to calm Clara's mother. He gave the patient some salve for the scrapes and told her to rest for a few more days. It was too soon to remove the cast, but he could do that when it was time. They returned home just as Mr. Wilson arrived. His expression upon seeing his daughter was similar to that of his wife's, but he was quickly reassured that the doctor had said she'd be fine in a few weeks.

As they entered the house, the phone rang. Mrs. Wilson picked it up and then turned it over to Clara. "It's Gene, for you."

"Hi, Gene. What's up?"

"They think they may have caught the guy who killed Lowry. They think it was the cousin of your convict. And, you won't believe this, he had a friend the same name as the one the stranger, the Mexican man, gave you at the restaurant. Can you believe that they were all together? The convicts and the guy you saw rob the store?

"What? The one I saw burgle The White House department store?"

"Yep. Apparently, there's some connection between him and the two convicts. They went to the same school, I believe, but I need to corroborate that. I haven't got all the details yet. How are you doing?"

"I'm fine. We've just got back from seeing the family doctor. What else did you find out? And why did they kill Lowry?"

"What did the doctor say? Anything new?"

"Not really. Same prognosis. Should be a lot better in a week or so. What do you know about the two who murdered Lowry?"

"They're still being questioned. I'm going to see if I can get an interview. Want to come?"

Clara looked at her parents and Marjorie who were staring at her with grave expressions. "No, I think I better stay here. Fill me in after you talk to him? How did they catch them? And who caught them?"

"Not sure of the details. The Santa Rosa deputies found them trying to break into—are you ready for this?—the Dobberson home. Mrs. Dobberson called the police and they got there in time to catch the guys."

"What?!"

"Yep."

She turned to Marjorie. "They caught the guys who they believe killed Lowry trying to break into the Dobberson house. And one of them was the same one who I saw robbing The White House!"

"Really?!"

Gene said, "Heck of a coincidence, isn't it? Even more of a strange coincidence they found the body outside the Victory Lunch diner, which I didn't know until today. Apparently he'd been dead for a while. Sometimes criminals don't need a reason for killing. Anyway, I gotta go if I'm gonna interview them—hope they'll let me. It will be interesting to compare what the convict says with what his cousin said in Eureka."

"Yes, it will. I wish I could go with you. Anything more on the six-foot man and the Japanese woman, whom we're assuming is Mr. Osaka's daughter?"

"No. Rest up so you can come back full force. We really need you here. More and more men are being drafted. Fewer and fewer qualified reporters are available."

"Thanks for updating me. Let me know if I can help with the story from here."

Clara spent the rest of the evening talking with her parents and catching up on their work and Santa Rosa news. Her mother fixed a pot roast and Marjorie joined them for dinner. When it came time for bed, Clara said she'd sleep on the sofa. "Stairs are hard for me right now. I just need a blanket—no need for sheets."

By the time she fell asleep, her parents and Marjorie had grown accustomed to her appearance and talked freely with her, although she noticed that occasionally one of them would look away. She was happy to be home and looked forward to delving into her work at the newspaper and starting to plot her novel.

She'd sort out her feelings about Gene later.

Chapter 42

The next day, Clara was pleased to see that Gene gave her a by-line next to his on their article about their experience in Klamath and catching one of the convicts. Stu hadn't edited it much. It read almost exactly as they'd written it.

However, when she read the short article about the murderers caught breaking into a local home, she was surprised to see that the name and address of the home was not mentioned. Evidently, the Dobbersons had asked for their name not to be divulged and the request was granted.

But why would the criminals try breaking into a home? Surely it would be easier to steal from a business where cash might be available. And this was the third time the house had been burgled even if the Dobbersons didn't want it on the record that they'd lost a variety of items in two previous robberies. Plus, if you counted the time she and her mother had been attacked in front of their house, that would be four times. What was it about their house that attracted crooks? And if the assailants didn't take anything of much value, the risk didn't seem worth it.

Clara was getting restless. She hoped that was a sign of healing. She was eager to start tracking down the story about Lowry's murderer. The published article barely covered his background. Maybe the Dobbersons had kept quiet the information that he worked for them. But the article didn't even mention who survived him.

The phone interrupted her reverie. She was glad for the interruption, especially when it turned out to be Gene. She missed talking with him, discussing what was on her mind.

Gene asked, "How're you doing?"

"I'm okay. How about you?

"Well, I was wondering if you felt well enough to go to San Jose to interview Lowry's parents."

"Yes. I'm ready. There's more to the story there. I can feel it."

"I agree. But we can't do it today—it's at least a two-hour drive each way. But I'll clear it with Stu for tomorrow and call to make us an appointment. I'll confirm with them. Can you make it until tomorrow?"

She laughed. "I guess. By the way, as I recall, the mother doesn't work and stays at home, so someone should be there. But you'll find out when you check with them. After visiting the Lowry family, I want to make one more pass at talking to the Dobbersons."

"I agree with you that there's more to Lowry's death than what's been printed. Stu didn't have anyone to cover it during our absence. All he had to go on was the police report."

"What time will you pick me up?"

"How about ten, depending on what time they're available? That will give me time to check with Stu to see if anything else needs to be covered."

"I'll be ready."

"How do you look? Are you still going to scare whoever we talk to?"

"I'm afraid so. Maybe I could wear a mask?"

"No, that would be threatening. Try to not face whomever you talk to."

"Sure. That'll be easy."

The next morning Clara was able to get up and dressed, although she was still sleeping in the living room. Her mother greeted her with a question, "What are you planning to do today?"

"Gene and I are going to San Jose to talk to Mr. Lowry's family. You remember. He was the gardener at the Dobberson home who was recently murdered. Both Gene and I believe there's more to the story than a robbery attempt."

Her father walked in as she was finished speaking. "Are you well enough to be working?"

"I feel good, Dad. And I'll be in the car most of the time. Gene is setting up an appointment. This certainly shouldn't be dangerous. We just can't figure out why anyone would kill him. He wasn't wealthy, so we don't believe it was attempted robbery."

He looked at her. "You might want to wear a mask."

She laughed. "Yeah, I suggested that to Gene. He told me not to face anyone. I'll be all right as long as I don't have to run or go up steps."

"Or move in any direction." He gave her a peck on the cheek. "Just be careful. Don't over-do it."

While waiting for Gene, she kept repeating her father's words, "Don't over-do it." She and Gene both anticipated that it would not be a dangerous visit, but interviewing the mother of a murdered son would not be easy. However, they'd been surprised before: she and her mother getting attacked; driving on a highway when the convict tried to force them off the road; and above all, the beatings she and Gene had both received at the hands of escaped convicts.

Lowry's mother had confirmed with Gene that she'd be available about lunch time, although she wasn't sure she could tell them much. Her nephew would be home from school for lunch. Otherwise, she would be available. Her husband and sister were both at work. Her sister and nephew lived in a small cottage on the property.

Gene said, "I was careful not to pressure her. She's still grieving for her son. But I think she wants to talk to us. I also

284

asked her to let us talk to her sister, but I don't think she plans to mention it to her."

They were in the car on their way to San Jose. The directions Gene had gotten from Mrs. Lowry said it would take at least two hours to reach their farm, outside of the main city. "I found out that they have apricot and cherry trees, and also grow vegetables. How are you feeling?"

"I'm glad I brought a pillow. It's helping my back. Mom suggested it."

Gene smiled. "By the way, my landlord is looking for renters at one of his other buildings. Should I tell him you're interested?"

"Yes, I think so. Does he have many rooms?"

"I'll give you his number and you can call."

"All right. Back to the Lowrys—what are we going to ask them?"

"I think we should be straight with them. Ask if they have any idea who might have attacked him."

"Upfront questions."

"Yes. On the phone she seemed sincere, although she also seemed afraid to talk to us."

"Maybe she thinks the person who killed her son would come after her and the rest of the family."

"But that would only be a threat if there's a reason. That's what we have to discover. Why was her son killed? What does she suspect? And what ever happened to his uncle—would that be her brother?"

"We can ask her."

But when they arrived at the farmhouse, no one answered the door. Gene even knocked on the door of the small cabin on the property, but no one responded there either.

He shook his head. "I don't get it. If she didn't want us to come, why didn't she just say so."

"Maybe she's not in charge of the family."

"I gave her my number. She could've called."

"Let's go back to that little grocery store we passed a while back. Maybe they'll know something. If not, we can check again."

"All right. But this is strange." He turned the car around and they headed back the way they'd come. The grocery store also had a gas pump, so Gene decided to have the attendant fill up. He told Clara to stay in the car. "You'll scare everyone away."

She stayed put while Gene went inside the store to pay for the gas and also inquire about the Lowrys. He came out looking perplexed.

He got into the driver's seat and said, "This gets curiouser and curiouser."

"What?"

"He said the parents were picked up today by a guy who he heard the mother call, 'Hiram.'"

"What? You don't suppose it was Hiram Dobberson?"

"I think we need to visit the Dobbersons."

"But will they see us? I've been told never to return to their house. And what about the rest of the Lowry family?"

"The clerk thinks they moved to their own house up near Santa Rosa. He wasn't sure of the name of the town. I gave him a couple names, and he thought Petaluma sounded right."

"Wow. Did he know anything about the missing uncle?"

"No. He said the family wouldn't talk about him, but the guy's been missing for months. How well does Marjorie know the Dobbersons?"

"Quite well. She went to school with Hiram, I believe. But I got her into trouble last time we were there, and they told her to never come back."

"We need to lay out all the pieces to this puzzle, even if we don't think they connect—even the convicts and the robbery at The White House department store."

"You're right," Clara said. "If nothing else, it will help us eliminate what positively doesn't fit."

Gene pulled over and stopped the car. He looked at Clara and then asked, "How tall would you say Hiram is?"

Clara's eyes opened wide. "No, don't be silly. Yes, he's over six feet tall and typically wears a suit, but what would he be doing with a Japanese woman?"

"I bet he drives a nice car."

They spent the rest of the trip listing all that had happened over the past few months—with the Dobbersons, both the uncle and the nephew Lowry, the convicts, the Dobberson blacksmith, Mr. Osaka and his missing daughter (whom, they thought, was probably the one seen in Klamath with the convict), and the burglaries at the Dobbersons including the assault involving Clara and her mother after the garden party. Despite her casted arm, Clara managed to write everything in her notebook so they could review it again, but all the occurrences still appeared jumbled.

She reviewed the list. "Do you know if the convict or the thief from The White House who tried to break into the Dobbersons confessed to anything?"

"I don't know."

"Let's go to the Santa Rosa police office now and see if they have any updates. However, I'm surprised they didn't call me to identify him as the thief."

"That's because I asked them not to. But they do want you to identify him when you're up to it. Maybe. Or they may have gotten him on some other crime by now. But he might know something about the escaped convicts and the Japanese girl It's worth a try." Then he added, "Are you feeling up to it?"

Clara nodded. "Yes. But, I'm not looking forward to walking up those steps."

"I'll help. We're almost there."

Gene let Clara out in front of the steps leading up to the front door of the Santa Rosa City Police Station. She started to go up with the help of the railing, but was relieved when Gene joined her and put his arm around her waist to support her. They made it to the top in a reasonable amount of time, but Gene joked, "What speed, oh speedy one!"

She was smiling when they entered the building, but noticed that the clerk's eyes got big when he saw her. Gene spoke first. "She met up with one of the escaped convicts."

"And it's not as bad as it looks," Clara added.

The clerk shook his head. "It looks bad."

Gene said, "We have follow-up questions about some of the criminal activity we've encountered."

Clara's turn. "Were you able to connect the criminal who broke into the Dobberson home with the one who burgled The White House department store? We gave you a name for him. Also, we think he's connected with one of the escaped convicts—was there one from San Quentin and one from Folsom?"

"Yep. And you're correct. We did capture The White House burglar. He hasn't talked too much, but we got another witness besides you—one of the other burglars rolled over. We planned to reach you to identify him, but your friend here asked us to wait. And I can now see why. Mebbe you could come in tomorrow and identify him. We're in no hurry."

Gene looked at Clara and smiled. "She'd love to. What time?"

"Any time in the mornin'."

Gene continued, "Good. We can manage that. Now what have you found out about Lowry's murderer?"

"Funny you should mention him. We think there's a connection between your White House burglar and him. But we can't get him to talk."

Clara asked, "Why do you think there's a connection?"

"Well, didn't you say that your convict was seen with a Japanese woman?"

Gene answered, "Yes, up in Klamath."

"It's not real firm, but we have a witness who says he saw the burglar fella with your convict push a Japanese woman into a car being driven by Lowry right here in Santa Rosa."

Gene said, "What?!. But how did they get in Klamath and then down here? Was this a reliable witness?"

"Not so great, but reliable enough that we're takin' serious what she said. It's possible that one of 'em killed Lowry and they took the Japanese woman back up to Klamath and then tried to get money from Osaka." He turned to Gene. "Thanks for keepin' us filled in about the Japanese woman, by the way. We'd have never knowed about her 'cept for you."

"But she was seen in Klamath with a well-dressed, tall guy after Lowry was killed."

Clara said, "So they probably killed Lowry and then kidnapped the Japanese woman and took her to Klamath. But then another man took her back."

The clerk asked, "When? What other man?"

Gene described the man about whom the sheriff had informed them in Klamath. "Sorry, I forgot to update you on that. He was tall, dark hair, wore a suit."

Clara stared at Gene.

"What? Do I have something on my face?" He brushed his cheek and jaw but could not feel anything.

Clara said, "I think you were correct. I don't understand why, but Hiram Dobberson fits the description."

Gene nodded.

The police clerk shook his head. "No, he wouldn't be messin' with no Japanese girl. No convict, neither."

Clara continued staring at Gene. "Yes, it fits. I don't know why but the Japanese girl and the robberies and the convict and the burglar—they're all connected somehow."

The clerk continued shaking his head. "No. But you let me know if you find anything that links 'em, and we'll investigate."

Clara and Gene looked at each other and thanked the officer. As they left the building, Clara almost forgot she needed help getting down the stairs until Gene grabbed her around the waist.

She said, "I know the Dobbersons are somehow involved in all this. I just know it! They've behaved so strangely not wanting those robberies reported and treating Marjorie and me like we'd done something really wrong. And I'm sure I saw Hiram with the burglar at the Army Parade."

"I agree. Let's go surprise them with a visit."

"Do you think we should ask Marjorie to come along?"

"No, but I think we should alert Stu where we're going. Let's stop by the office on our way, and we can fill him in."

When they arrived at the newspaper, Clara waited in the car. Gene ran into the building and returned within ten minutes. "He's on board. He agrees with us but he's nervous about the danger. I convinced him by pointing out that both convicts are incarcerated, and we believe Lowry's murderer is in jail, and I don't really believe the Dobbersons are criminals. But I explained that's why we were telling him where we're going. If he doesn't hear from us within an hour, he'll call the Santa Rosa Police station and report where we are."

Clara nodded. "Good plan."

It was getting dark when they arrived at the Dobberson mansion. Clara realized that she should have left a note or called her parents, but it was too late by then. Although unlikely, maybe the Dobbersons would let her call. Gene helped her up the steps to their porch and pushed the bell.

It seemed forever to Clara before Hiram opened the door. He first stared at Clara, mouth open. "My god! What happened to you?"

Gene said, "Your convict beat her up."

"My convict? What are you talking about?"

Clara feigned weakness, and asked, "May we come in, please, at least until I feel better?"

"Of course." Gene took hold of Clara's good arm, and Hiram supported her on the other side. They steered her to an overstuffed easy chair.

Hiram asked, "Can I get you something?'

Clara responded as softly as she could, "Water would be nice."

A female voice from behind a closed door nearby asked, "Who is it, Hiram?"

"It's Clara Wilson and her reporter friend Gene Walker."

"Oh."

"I can handle it, Mother. Don't worry."

Clara asked, "Handle it?"

"I'll get your water. Stay put."

Clara wondered where the servants were. Whenever they'd previously visited, a servant had opened the door. But this time Hiram himself did so, and Mrs. Dobberson seemed to be the only other person in the house. Gene must have been wondering the same thing because he shrugged.

Hiram returned with a cup of water which Clara gulped. She was only partially faking. She really did feel a little shaky, and the water did help.

Hiram spoke first. "So, what is this visit about? Why are you here?"

Gene responded, "What do you know about the murder of Mr. Lowry?"

Without hesitating, Hiram said, "Only what the police have told me."

Clara decided to push more. "What about the Japanese girl?"

Hiram could not hide his surprise, but he answered quickly, "What Japanese girl? What are you talking about?"

Clara said, "Lowry was seen with the man I saw robbing The White House department store, and with the escaped convict who assaulted Gene, and a Japanese girl. She was later seen in Klamath with the escaped convict with her, and we believe he sent a ransom note to a Mr. Osaka at Tule Lake for her. And I'm sure that I saw you with one of the convicts at the Army parade here in town. More to the point, the Japanese woman was seen with a well-dressed man over six feet tall." She stared at him. "Someone about your height."

But Hiram ignored the last comment. "And this is the same convict who assaulted you both?"

"Yes."

Hiram walked to a side door and opened it. "Mother, you need to come down here now please."

Clara started to speak but Hiram shook his head. "This has gone on long enough. Two people have died and you, almost."

Gene asked, "What's been going on?"

Mrs. Dobberson entered the room. "It's all my fault." She spotted Clara. "Oh my goodness, my dear! What happened to you?"

Hiram said, "Our friend the convict beat her up."

"Oh, my. You're right. We must tell them, but then what, Hiram? I can't part with him."

Gene helped Mrs. Dobberson sit and said, "Can you trust us to do whatever we can to help you?"

She shook her head. "I don't think you can help. Hiram has done so much. He could get into such trouble."

Clara felt sorry for the woman. What had caused such grief?

"You know that our other son was killed a while ago. I believe you covered the story. It was hard for him to go to war against the Japanese even after Pearl Harbor. He knew he had to do his duty, and was relieved when he got orders to go to Europe. You see, before he left he got married secretly to—"

"Mr. Osaka's daughter," Clara said.

Gene said, "What?!"

Mrs. Dobberson nodded. "She's a wonderful girl. We love her."

Clara continued, "And you've been hiding her. That's where all the stolen furniture items went. You gave them to her so she'd be comfortable. Did she live with the Lowrys? And how did they get married? Where?"

"Yes. It wasn't easy getting them married, but my late husband and I had an old friend who's a priest. He managed to get a marriage certificate by misspelling our daughter-in-law's name so it wouldn't appear to be Japanese. But that isn't the whole story." Mrs. Dobberson looked at Hiram.

He nodded. "Go ahead, Mother. Tell them the whole story. They might be able to help us."

"You see, she had a baby, my grandson." She stopped speaking for a moment, then caught her breath and continued. "The Lowrys were hiding my daughter-in-law and taking care of the baby. They managed to get the baby here to me, but when Mr. Lowry was moving my daughter-in-law, they kidnapped her and killed poor Mr. Lowry. We hired that other one—your burglar from The White House department store—to protect us. Instead, he joined them. I'm sorry. At the time, we didn't know he was a criminal. He protected us at first, but then the convict told him he could get lots more money if they blackmailed poor Mr. Osaka."

Mrs. Dobberson bit her lip. "And I'm so sorry about him robbing you and your mother. We needed to get the statue back. Please forgive me."

Clara could think of nothing to say. She just stared at the woman. "Why did you need to get the statute back?"

Hiram answered. "Actually, my sister-in-law's brother, whose name was Niko, had given it to my brother. Apparently he designed it when he was ill, and it was special to him. He thought it would help them figure out their future. The area where you found it was one of the places where they could meet and not be seen. But my brother was so despondent about going off to war and maybe having to kill Japanese that he threw it down and stormed away. I was afraid you'd link it to Mr. Osaka, which, of course, you eventually did."

Gene asked, "Where are your grandson and your daughter-in-law now?"

"Upstairs. We converted the attic and Hiram did his best to sound-proof it so no one can hear the baby. There's a bathroom and everything up there. But the Lowrys have paid with their son's life to protect them, and now you've been injured." She started to sob.

Clara asked, "But how did you get your daughter-in-law back? And where are the Lowrys now? And why did Lowry ask me to investigate the stolen items if he knew about your daughter-in-law and your grandson?"

Mrs. Doberson responded, "Oh, he didn't know at first. He really believed we accused his uncle unfairly and fired him. His mother finally let him know."

Hiram said, "The convict said if I came to Klamath and paid them, I could have her back. I was able to raise the money and drive up there, I believe, while you were at Tule Lake. She was torn between joining her father and taking her son to Tule Lake or staying here with us. As you can imagine, Mother would have been distraught had she gone to Tule Lake. I convinced her to come here before making a final decision. As for the Lowrys we moved them to Petaluma. They have relatives there. But now that the convicts have been captured, they might come back to their farm."

Gene looked at Hiram. "As far as we're concerned, we won't tell anyone, but I'm not sure how long you'll be able to keep your secret. They've caught the burglar who was trying to get into your house. I guess he wanted more money. He was the same one Clara saw trying to rob The White House department store and apparently the same one who stole Clara's mother's purse outside your home. As you suggested, he hooked up with the two convicts to extort money from you and Mr. Osaka. Does he know you're keeping the baby and his mother here?"

Mrs. Dobberson nodded.

Hiram said, "We need to find a new hiding place or turn the baby and his mother over to the authorities and hope they'll send her to Tule Lake with her father."

Mrs. Dobberson screamed. "No. No, you can't, Hiram. You promised. This is your brother's son, and his wife."

Clara looked at Mrs. Dobberson, then at Hiram, and finally at Gene. No one spoke.

Mrs. Dobberson put her hand on Hiram's. "We must find another hiding place."

Gene said, "I think that could be treason—hiding a Japanese."

Hiram said, "She's an American and the wife of a fallen soldier. Can you give us twenty-four hours before reporting us?"

Clara said, "Of course. But—"

Hiram put his hand out to stop her. "Gene's right. It's treason if you help us. All we ask is that you keep it quiet for the next day. I have an idea, but I'm not going to tell you what it is. I just need some time."

Clara looked at Gene. "Please, Gene."

He started to speak, but Hiram interrupted. "Please don't ask any questions." Then he looked at Clara. "I hope you write your novel and tell this story. It's breaking our hearts."

Clara said, "Please tell your sister-in-law that I gave the statue back to her father along with all the others that were still in the barn."

Mrs. Dobberson said, "How kind of you. Thank you." She was still crying.

Gene said, "Good luck. You need to move fast. The burglar may have already divulged information to the sheriff."

Hiram shook his head. "Maybe not. They want to blackmail us and Mr. Osaka. If they tell the police anything they won't get a penny."

Mrs. Dobberson stood and reached out to Clara. "Thank you."

Clara nodded and did her best to give a one-armed hug to the grandmother. Then she and Gene left the house. They were silent as they drove back to the newspaper. Clara had asked to go with Gene to talk to Stu but needed to call her parents before they talked to him. She made a quick call from the office letting them know she was all right and would be home soon.

They went to Stu's office and told him the entire story. Gene finished, "We promised we'd give them twenty-four hours, but we'll need to report them to the authorities or we'll both go to jail for treason."

"Well, you can write about the capture of the two convicts and The White House burglar without divulging the Osaka link. Let's get that story in tomorrow's edition. Then when you believe it's safe, what will you tell the authorities about the Dobbersons?"

Clara looked at Gene, who said, "I don't know. I just don't know."

Stu pursed his lips. "I have a suggestion."

They both asked together at the same time, "Really? What?"

"The husband and father of the baby was an American soldier killed in action. Right?"

Clara and Gene nodded.

"That should entitle them to a soldier's widow's rights. Let me get in touch with my governor friend and see what I can arrange. That way, you'll be fulfilling your obligation to report them, and we might be able to oblige the Dobberson family."

Clara started to weep. "Oh, I can't believe I'm crying! After all we've been through, and now I cry."

However, when she looked at Gene, she noticed that his eyes were wet, also.

He said, "If you could arrange that, maybe something good will come out of all this."

Chapter 43

The next day Clara sat by the phone at home waiting to hear if Stu had managed to pull off a miracle, letting the Dobbersons and their son's widow and the baby remain together. The reporters had not informed the family of their efforts in case they failed, given that they'd promised not to talk to the authorities for twenty-four hours. Gene was at the office covering other stories, but Clara was sure he was near a phone.

She allowed her mind to wonder. So much had happened in the past few months when she'd been driven to search for a secret about a statue at a time of war. She encountered serious restrictions in her country especially the rights of Japanese Americans. She'd become a full-fledged reporter and found the inspiration for her first novel.

And there was Gene. She wasn't sure about their future, but she would never forget what they'd shared. He'd definitely helped her embrace the search she undertaken. Besides, she'd gotten used to having him around. He was fun to be with. And he helped her understand where she was heading. She comprehended that, he, too, might have to go to war, and wondered what would become of them.

And what about Stu? An incredible editor of a local newspaper who shared his heart by enabling so much to happen.

Nor did she forget her parents. They'd allowed her to grow no matter how painful the push was.

The phone rang interrupting her reverie. She took a breath and picked up the receiver. "Hello?"

Gene responded. "It's done. They're safe and with the Dobbersons. For their safety, we're not being told where. But they'll be together. It's being worked out."

Clara didn't trust herself to speak, but still tried, "That's good. Thanks for calling. I'll be ready to return to work tomorrow. Can you let Stu know?"

She hung up the receiver full of emotion that something positive had come out of their search beyond the story concept for her novel.

She wondered if the time to search was over. Or was it just beginning? Perhaps the statue of a cow inspired more than just the idea for a book.

I'll never stop searching.

About the Author: Joyce T. Strand

Photo of author by Erin Kate Photography

Http://www.erinkatephoto.com

Joyce T. Strand writes contemporary and historical who-done-it mysteries that typically involve a murder or two, often a touch of romance, and always a few red herrings.

Jillian Hillcrest, a public relations executive at a Silicon Valley biotechnology company; Brynn Bancroft, chief financial executive turned winemaker in the Sonoma Valley; and Emily Lazzaro, manager of a B&B in the southern California town of Ramona—solve her contemporary mysteries, They are the protagonist in three standalone mysteries each.

Her novel, *The Judge's Story*, is her first historical mystery. Set in the small California town of Ventura in 1939, the story features a California Superior Court Judge. Her second historical mystery, *The Reporter's Story*, is set in 1912 San Francisco and features a female reporter who pushes to become an investigative reporter in a male-dominated field.

Although fiction, the Jillian Hillcrest, Brynn Bancroft, and Emily Lazzaro mysteries are inspired by real California cases. The character of the judge in *The Judge's Story*, also fiction, is based on the memoir of a California Superior Court Judge (1941). The reporter in *The Reporter's Story* was inspired by a front-page reporter of the time.

Strand headed corporate communications at several biotech and high-tech companies in California's Silicon Valley for more than 25 years. She currently lives with her two cats, Holmes and Watson, and her collection of cow statuary in Santa Rosa, Calif

Printed in Great Britain
by Amazon

21679496R00180